THE FINGER OF DESTINY

AND OTHER STORIES

The DANCING TUATARA PRESS
Books from RAMBLE HOUSE

CLASSICS OF HORROR

1. Beast or Man! — Sean M'Guire
2. The Whistling Ancestors — Richard E. Goddard
3. The Shadow on the House — Mark Hansom
4. Sorcerer's Chessmen — Mark Hansom
5. The Wizard of Berner's Abbey — Mark Hansom
6. The Border Line — Walter S. Masterman
7. The Trail of the Cloven Hoof — Arlton Eadie
8. The Curse of Cantire — Mark Hansom
9. Reunion in Hell and Other Stories — The Selected Stories of John H. Knox Vol. I
10. The Ghost of Gaston Revere — Mark Hansom
11. The Tongueless Horror And Other Stories — The Selected Weird Tales of Wyatt Blassingame Vol. I
12. Master of Souls — Mark Hansom
13. Man Out of Hell and Other Stories — The Selected Stories of John H. Knox Vol. II
14. Lady of the Yellow Death and Other Stories — Selected Weird Tales of Wyatt Blassingame Vol. II
15. Satan's Sin House and Other Stories — The Weird Tales of Wayne Rogers Vol. I
16. Hostesses in Hell and Other Stories — The Weird Tales of Russell Gray Vol. I
17. Hands Out of Hell and Other Stories — The Selected Stories of John H. Knox Vol. III
18. Summer Camp for Corpses and Other Stories — Weird Tales of Arthur L. Zagat Vol. I
19. One Dreadful Night — by Ronald S.L. Harding
20. The Library of Death — by Ronald S.L. Harding
21. The Beautiful Dead and Other Stories — The Weird Tales of Donald Dale
22. Death Rocks the Cradle and Other Stories — Weird Tales of Wayne Rogers Vol. II
23. The Devil's Night Club and Other Stories — Nat Schachner
24. Mark of the Laughing Death and Other Stories — Francis James
25. The Strange Thirteen and Other Stories — Richard B. Gamon
26. The Unholy Goddess and Other Stories — The Selected Weird Tales of Wyatt Blassingame Vol. III
27. House of the Restless Dead and Other Stories — Hugh B. Cave
28. Tales of Terror & Torment Vol. 1 — Edited by John Pelan
29. The Corpse Factory and Other Stories — Arthur Leo Zagat
30. The Great Orme Terror and Other Stories — Garnett Radcliffe
31. Freak Museum — R. R. Ryan
32. The Subjugated Beast — R. R. Ryan
33. Towers & Tortures — Dexter Dayle
34. The Antlered Man — Edwy Searles Brooks
35. When the Batman Thirsts — Frederick C. Davis
36. The Sorcery Club — Elliot O'Donnell
37. Tales of Terror and Torment Vol. 2 — Edited by John Pelan
38. Mistress of Terror and Other Stories — The Selected Weird Tales of Wyatt Blassingame Vol. IV
39. The Place of Hairy Death and Other Stories — An Anthony Rud Reader
40. My Touch Brings Death — The Weird Tales of Russell Gray Vol. II
41. Echo of a Curse — R.R. Ryan
42. The Finger of Destiny and Other Stories — Edmund Snell

CLASSICS OF SCIENCE FICTION AND FANTASY

1. Chariots of San Fernando and Other Stories — Malcolm Jameson
2. The Story Writer and Other Stories — Richard Wilson
3. The House That Time Forgot and Other Stories — Robert F. Young
4. A Niche in Time and Other Stories — William F. Temple
5. Two Suns of Morcali and Other Stories — Evelyn E. Smith
6. Old Faithful and Other Stories — Raymond Z. Gallun
7. The Alien Envoy and Other Stories — Malcolm Jameson
8. The Man without a Planet and Other Stories — Richard Wilson
9. The Man Who was Secrett and Other Stories — John Brunner
10. The Cloudbuilders — Colin Kapp
11. Somewhere in Space and Other Stories — C.C MacApp

DAY KEENE IN THE DETECTIVE PULPS

1. League of the Grateful Dead and Other Stories — Day Keene in the Detective Pulps Vol. I
2. We Are the Dead and Other Stories — Day Keene in the Detective Pulps Vol. II
3. Death March of the Dancing Dolls and Other Stories — Day Keene in the Detective Pulps Vol. III
4. The Case of the Bearded Bride and Other Stories — Day Keene in the Detective Pulps Vol. IV
5. A Corpse Walks in Brooklyn and Other Stories — Day Keene in the Detective Pulps Vol. V

THE FINGER OF DESTINY

AND OTHER STORIES

Edmund Snell

Introduction by

John Pelan

RAMBLE HOUSE

Written: 1938

Introduction: © 2013
by John Pelan

Cover Design: Gavin L. O'Keefe

Preparation: Fender Tucker

This work has been determined to be in the
Public Domain.
.

ISBN 13: 978-1-60543-718-7

Dancing Tuatara Press #42

THE FINGER OF DESTINY

The Omnipresent Edmund Snell		9
John Pelan		
I	The Finger of Destiny	13
II	The Magic Mosquito	47
III	The Gift of the God	61
IV	Way Back	87
V	The Chance	101
VI	Fate's Instrument	115
VII	Coulson and the Kerbau	127
VIII	The Man Who Stole the Head	135
IX	The Cure of Koomanis	147
X	Lonely Valley	159
XI	The Terms of the Contract	191
XII	Hari Besar	201
The Black Spider		209

The Omnipresent Edmund Snell

There aren't too many authors who can claim the level of popularity that Edmund Snell had throughout the 1920s and 1930s. Best known today for his novels such as *The White Owl*, *The Yu-chi Stone*, *The Sound Machine*, and *The Back of Beyond*; many readers would be surprised to learn that Snell's output as an author of short stories and novellas far exceeded the wordage of his published novels. During the 1920s it was next to impossible to pick up a British fiction magazine and not find an Edmund Snell story therein. When the story papers came along with the format of *The Thriller* calling for a full-length novella every issue, Snell was really at home, producing an astonishing amount of work of mystery/adventure fiction ranging from the supernatural to tales of American gangsters to weird tales set in exotic locales such as Borneo and Singapore.

What makes Snell's work so compelling today is the veracity of his tales from the Far East. Snell wasn't an armchair traveler like Harold Lamb or Frank Owen, but like Talbot Mundy he wrote about places he had actually lived and incorporated local legends into his tales. What is truly surprising today is how little of his output has been preserved in book form! Not counting the present volume that was originally published in hardcover, I've assembled some half-dozen collections of weird and suspense tales for publication under the DTP rubric. When this is accomplished, Edmund Snell will rival Wyatt Blassingame and Mark Hansom as our flagship author, a position that is well-deserved!

One comes to Dancing Tuatara Press and/or Ramble House Publishers to find unusual books . . .Whether they be the lunatic webworks of Harry Stephen Keeler, the rare science fiction published under Dick Lupoff's Surinam Turtle Press or the oddball British thrillers and weird menace tales here at Dancing Tuatara Press, the one constant is that the mundane and routine is eschewed in favor of the esoteric and unusual. The book that you hold in your hands is one of the most unusual that it's been my privilege to introduce. Edmund Snell is, by any standard that one wants to apply, a Ramble House author, in fact, if you were to ask me to name a *typical* author in this sanctuary of the atypical, Snell would be one of the first examples that comes to mind, for he fits a lot of the criteria that one tends to associate with our books. First and foremost, he wrote "thrillers", that wonderful anything-goes genre that existed before "mystery", "horror", "science fiction" became marketing categories, and books wherein these genres seamlessly melded together were the norm and not the exception. With Edmund Snell you never knew exactly what you were going to get. You might find supernatural horror such as *The White Owl*, straightforward gangster action, bizarre science fiction such as *Kontrol* or *The Sound Machine* or murder and mayhem in exotic locales (something that the well-traveled author was superbly equipped to write about.)

However, it was in the area of the "Asian Menace" tale that Snell really excelled, whether dealing with warring tongs or aboriginal magic, Snell's tales of the Far East such as those collected in the present volume are of a level far surpassing the quality of most of his contemporaries. For years many of the bibliographies have published erroneous data about his books, labelling *The Finger of Destiny* as a novel and *The Back of Beyond* as a short story collection, when in fact, the reverse is true. While the collection *The Finger of Destiny* stands well on its own, I couldn't resist the opportunity to expand the book by one story and include his horror tale "The Black Spider" as a bonus. Originally written for Charles Birkin's "Creeps series", this is one of those gems that for some reason has eluded anthologists over the years. As a matter of fact, all of Snell's short fiction seems to have suffered the same fate, and there doesn't seem to be any clear reason as to why . . . There's certainly nothing to indicate that the author or his estate was ever difficult to deal with and considering the overall high quality of his work, it remains puzzling that his work has been so universally ignored in the last forty years.

That said, I have to thank our Grand Poobah, Fender Tucker for leading the charge in the Edmund Snell revival well before I came on board with the publication of *Dope & Swastikas* and *The Sign of the Scorpion.* Going forward we'll be handling Edmund Snell much the same way that we're dealing with Walter S. Masterman; we plan on reissuing a number of his books and issuing several new collections, the material that ventures into the weird, sfnal, or Asian Menace arenas will be issued from DTP with new introductions. The material that is more straightforward crime/mystery will come out under the Ramble House imprint. As it stands, there are at least seven novels and a half-dozen collections that seem perfect for DTP and about the same number of volumes that would be more appropriate issued by Ramble House. In any event, prepare for a major renascence of Edmund Snell. Sadly, until Mike Ashley completes his index of the British magazines, there's really no bibliography to speak of. *The Thriller* has been pretty well indexed as has *Detective Fiction Weekly,* but there are literally dozens of fiction magazines (mostly British) that we know (or suspect) that Snell contributed to that haven't been indexed at all and are fairly rare today. Considering how prolific the author was, it's very likely that there exists as much quality material that I don't *know* about as there is of material that we do know of . . . Sadly, one volume that is very high on my list is the collection *Yellowjacket: The Return of Chanda-Lung.* The Chanda-Lung stories feature the title character, one of the most memorable super-villains of the pulp era. Rather than merely another clone of Fu-Manchu, lurking in the background while assorted henchmen carry out his plans. Chanda-Lung is more closely akin to A.E. Apple's terrifying Mr. Chang (who also stalked through the pages of *Detective Fiction Weekly.*) We anticipate being able to gather all the material necessary to release the Pennington trilogy sometime next year. Of course, this is just one of several projects with three or four collections already in hand and going through the editorial process. If you're an Edmund Snell fan already, than rest assured, there's a lot more to come; if you're just discovering this fantastic author for the first time, do check out the other titles available here at Ramble House and stay tuned for many, many more volumes . . .

John Pelan
All Hallows 2013
Gallup, NM

I

THE FINGER OF DESTINY

I

THE GREAT LINER lay at anchor off Aden—that bare, baking, cheerless hell-on-earth that marks the spot where the Red Sea ends and the Indian Ocean begins. It was night, the air was close and oppressive, and at the gangway a stout German sailor stood on duty with strict orders to admit no native traders, but from a series of furtive actions in connection with one grimy hand and a trouser pocket it seemed likely that to-night instructions were not to be strictly adhered to. However, the passengers did not complain, but distributed themselves in little knots all over the first- and second-class decks, deeply interested in the wares of tall, coal-black Somalis, with scanty clothing and bleached, fuzzy hair. Sharks' jaws, saw-fish saws, an occasional ostrich egg, feathers, fans, cheap bangles of doubtful origin, coral necklaces, glass beads—masquerading as amber-bottles of lime-juice (with corks not tamper-proof), Turkish delight, figs, dates, and here and there a basket of pomegranates.

In a corner of the second-class deck wild, incoherent cries and loud stamping of many feet announced that a crowd of natives, employed to carry melons on board, had suddenly formed themselves into an impromptu corps de ballet.

All round the ship traders' dhows were crowding in the dark waters, their occupants passing goods up for inspection by means of baskets on ropes thrown with marvellous precision for the intending purchaser to catch.

"How much, sah? How much you give? Ten shillin'? What you say? Two! Bah! Give them me back. Real ostrich feather fan! Ten shillin'! No! Now much you give? Six shillin'? Here you are, sah! Put money in the basket."

Occasionally a receptacle laden with fans, unskilfully handled, would fall suddenly into the water, its contents floating away amid a torrent of oaths in many languages from the infuriated owner.

A tall, clean-shaven, fresh-looking Englishman, in a suit of nicely-cut whites, stood airily puffing at a Turkish cigarette, idly watching the crude antics of the dancing natives.

He was firm of character, and entirely self-possessed, for, though on his first trip East, he had steadfastly refrained from speculating in the doubtful rubbish offered for sale by the wily tribesmen. His only purchase was a beautifully-worked Somali water-bottle.

A grinning native approached him, a dozen necklaces suspended from one arm. "Buy pretty necklace, sah?"

"No—damn you!" He turned away and surveyed the twinkling lights of many liners reflecting in the water.

"Real amber necklace, sah!"

"Real glass, you dirty thief!"

The native grinned amiably, revealing a perfect set of white teeth, and hurried off in search of some customer more easily plucked. Suddenly the young man waved his arm and shouted to him to come back.

"Hi! you dirty black devil—here!"

The young trader hastened back, followed by two of his dusky *confreres,* scenting business.

"Want amber necklace, sah?" he inquired, in a voice far more hopeful than before.

Harris, the Englishman, did not answer him directly. "What's that?" he asked suddenly, pointing at a queer leathern pouch suspended from the trader's neck by a couple of hide thongs.

"What, sah?" asked the bewildered native, not quite comprehending his meaning.

Harris tapped the pouch with his forefinger.

"Oh, that, sah! Him ju-ju!"

"Oh, ju-ju, is it? Well, what d'you want for it?" A hand in a trouser pocket jingled silver coins temptingly.

"No sell that, sah!" replied the Somali, his face suddenly assuming a serious expression.

Harris tapped the deck impatiently with the sole of a smart brown shoe. "I know all that darned bunkum! What'll you take for it?" He spun a florin in the air, and knew that three pairs of dark eyes watched its flight.

A dusky trader close at hand suddenly stretched out a long black forefinger. "He no sell that, sah, for twenty t'ousand pound. Him ju-ju! You know the Mad Mullah? He gib it him—dribe out debbils, sah! No sell him, sah—any money!"

"Dribe out debbils, sah!" chimed in two other guttural tongues.

Harris shrugged his shoulders and laughed. "Very well," he cried, pocketing his coin, "you may keep it!" He turned on his heel suddenly and strode away from the little knot of dark salesmen chattering together beneath the glare of a strong mast-light. Strolling across the second-class deck he encountered his cabin-mate—an elderly planter returning to his way-back estate after a six months' furlough in England.

"Any bargains?" inquired the older man, sucking at a well-coloured calabash.

Harris grunted. "Bought a pretty basket-affair for a shilling," he said; "but the only damn thing I wanted to buy the dirty rascals declined to part with—a stupid little bit of leather on a necklace! Rather quaint, though; look nice on a lady's drawing-room table. Some silly yarn about ju-ju and driving out devils. Get a superstition into their thick, black skulls, and, by Jove! you never get it out again. Dribe out debbils, indeed!" He tossed the fag-end of his cigarette overboard, and taking another from his silver case, tapped it mechanically on the lid.

The other man puffed for a moment in silence.

"There's a deal more in these native superstitions than meets the Western eye," he said at last. "They can cure fever by a few weird incantations quicker than any amount of quinine can do it. Ju-ju, or whatever they may call it, sounds all tommy-rot to you, but after studying the natives and living right amongst them for a time, you can't help becoming a little less sceptical. You'll find all that out before long; but take it from me, never believe a thing isn't as they say until you can prove it. There's a great deal more to be learnt in the mysterious Orient than you matter-of-fact Westerners could possibly conceive."

Harris tapped the ash impatiently from his cigarette and laughed. "Live and learn," he said. "Well, maybe I shall, and maybe I shan't! But ju-ju—oh, rot! Here, I'm off to bed!"

Palm-grown islets studding a bright blue tranquil sea that merged suddenly on to a broad expanse of very yellow sand; a background of virgin jungle fringing the base of one enormous slope of growing rubber trees, their well-kept regular lines waving gently in a soothing southern breeze; overhead a cloudless azure sky and the blazing, scorching, tropical sun of mid-afternoon.

Three native women, in bright sarongs and huge, conical-woven hats, strolled idly by the waterside, carrying fruit in large home-made baskets, worked in all the hues of the rainbow. A tall, wiry Sikh, in turban and khaki uniform, sat astride a sturdy little Borneo pony, barebacked, urging it to meet the gentle wavelets.

On the verandah of a long, flat bungalow, perched high on the summit of the overlooking slope, a sunburnt, clean-shaven Englishman lounged in a long cane-chair, wearing the usual Eastern *negligé* costume—a sarong and a singlet of Indian gauze. On the floor of the broad verandah a kitten played havoc with a pile of overseas papers; two dogs, a black chow imported from Hong Kong, and a sharp-faced terrier lazed underneath the bungalow, one eye just open for chance intruders on their master's privacy. A score of clucking hens picked ceaselessly, here and there, and on a line at the back of the house hung a miscellaneous selection of tropical garments.

Half-way up a distant slope the glint of changkols (hoes) in the sunlight drew attention to a scattered band of some fifty Chinese coolies, in red loin-cloths and huge, round hats, busily weeding between the growing trees. On a stump twenty yards higher up the slope sat a wizened, dark-skinned man, in a suit of dirty blue and a double Terai hat, sheltered from the sun by a weather-worn Chinese umbrella of oiled paper. This was the mandor—the overseer—whose duty was to take instructions in Malay and enforce them in the Hakka dialect.

Suddenly, just as the changkols seemed to lag, a huge khaki-clad, white-skinned figure appeared unexpectedly on the top of the rise and stood for a moment surveying the toiling coolies.

"Hi! Fi-te-lah! Kau damn kiti! Mandor! Apa matcham imi? (What's this mean?)"

The khaki-clad newcomer swung down the slope, a long malacca grasped tightly in one brown hand; the mandor sprang swiftly from his perch, and the hoes rose and fell with wonderful alacrity. The first assistant—the mighty Tuan-kechil—had come upon the scene, and the hand that wielded the cane was heavy!

A torrent of oaths, a score of well-delivered blows on a sweating brown back, some shouted instructions, and the Tuan-kechil was away again to urge on another gang whose axes could be heard from some obscure hollow some little distance away.

The manager of the estate sat up in his long chair and knocked an impudent cockroach from his gorgeous sarong.

"The damnedest, unluckiest blighter that ever walked God's earth—and that's me!" he muttered.

A shadow fell suddenly across the path, and Atkinson, his first assistant, mounted the steps.

"Phew, Harris, it's hot!" he gasped, and, removing his enormous planter's topi, threw it on the table.

"I s'pose that's your polite way of askin' for a drink," replied the other. "You'll have to put up with 'Kunchi' beer—the damn railway's still got my soda locked up in their dirty go-down in Api-Api, and if I don't raise hell when I next see Masters—"

"Owe him a good bit, don't you?" remarked the assistant, helping himself to a biscuit from a recently-opened tin.

The other eyed him for a moment. "Your memory's darn sight too good," he said. "I owe everybody money. I owe you a hundred odd dollars for roulette. I tell you, I wish to God I'd never set eyes on that bally wheel! Anyhow, I'll never take the bank again! Everything I turn my hand to seems to fizzle out. Never saw anything like it! Cards, billiards, races—it's all the same to me—damn bad luck! And that kind of thing sort of gets on one's nerves, y'know, Atkinson. Eh? Thirsty? Dash it, I forgot! Boy!"

"Dua beer, you hoonoon!" he shouted, as the white-suited kechil-boy hurried in.

"One thing—it's cool," he added, as the servant went out. "In the refrigerator, y'know."

The other man took off his coat, hurled his boots into a corner, and lit a cigarette. He threw himself at full length on a chair opposite his companion, and lay for a long while watching the wreaths of faint blue smoke curling skywards.

"Yes," he remarked presently, "the only bit of good fortune I ever remember you having was when you got the manager's billet after you'd only been here fifteen months. That was a bit of real good luck."

"And what have I gained by it?" asked the other. "Blackguarding letters every mail from a pack of the most ignorant, pig-headed, doddering directors that ever disgraced a London board-room. Pah! I'm sick of it! I wish to heaven I'd stayed at home and fretted my soul out on an office stool!"

"Still, it can't last for ever, old man. The tide must turn some time!"

"I'm sure I wish it would," said the other bitterly. "For it's left me pretty stranded just now. My rubber shares in Singapore are worth just about the paper they're written on. Dabbled in cocoa-nuts, and hit wrong 'uns every time! Hullo, here's the beer!"

The assistant raised the glass and glanced across at Harris, a look of real kindness and sympathy in his clear brown eyes.

"Here's to the turn of the tide," he said.

"Thanks, old man—and may it come quickly!" added the other. They put down their empty glasses, and both dozed off where they lay, till the pigtailed boy hurried in to announce that tea was ready.

Atkinson swallowed a banana, and poured half a cup of almost boiling tea down his throat. "I must be off," he said.

"I wanted you to hear my latest record on the gramophone," said the other, flicking the ants off his sugar before he dropped it in his cup.

"Can't now, old man! Sorry, but must give those cursed mandors their instructions for the morning. They'll be knocking off work in half an hour."

He strolled out on the verandah and fetched his coat and boots. A lace broke as he pulled at it, and he knotted it neatly, swearing amiably all the while.

"You want a shave," said the manager suddenly.

"Once a week is all the time I can spare now, with young Rock down with fever. Eh? Oh, he's better to-day, thanks! He'll be out and about again by Monday, I hope. Bye-bye!"

He seized his topi, rammed it on, picked up his malacca from a corner, and vanished down the path.

"Works like a horse! Damn good man!" said Harris, and poured himself out a second cup of tea.

"Hullo! Apa mahu? (What do you want?)"

A bearded face, surmounted by an enormous turban, suddenly appeared between the bars of the verandah.

"Man wants to speak to you, sir," reported the watchman briefly, in Malay, saluting stiffly as he spoke.

Harris shook the crumbs from his sarong on to the floor and strolled out.

A dirty, undersized Dusun stood by the side of the tall Pathan, one hand grasping a heavy-looking sack.

"Kelapa (cocoa-nuts)!" he explained shortly in Malay, and drew one out for the Tuan Besar to see.

"Prima-kasih (thanks)—take 'em round to the kitchen," ordered the manager. "Anything else?"

"A message, Tuan, from an old man down there in the Kampon, baniak sakit (very ill). He will die very soon, Tuan, and wishes to see you. I have told him it is impossible that the white Tuan would come, but he asks nevertheless—"

"Who is he? What's his name?"

"His name is Danudin, Tuan; and he has done much work for you when first you cut down the jungle. Many thousand acres has he felled for you—"

"I remember! He is dying, you say?"

"Yah, Tuan. He is very old, and cannot live many hours, and he says it is important that he sees you."

The manager looked away across the sea and stroked his chin thoughtfully. "Nanti (wait)," he said, and went into his room.

He laughed at himself as he drew a clean set of clothes from the cupboard and threw them, piece by piece, upon the bed; but, somehow or other, something seemed to prompt him to accede to the last wish of his old employee. He shrugged his shoulders, and called for the boy to put the buttons in his coat. At least, it would be something out of the ordinary routine of work, meals, and bed, with an occasional gramophone concert all to himself between tea and the evening makan.

He strolled out on to the verandah, fully dressed. The day was drawing swiftly to a close, and soon darkness would fall. Already the long lines of tired coolies were crossing the opposite slope, their chang-kols on their shoulders.

"The Tuan Besar is going down?" inquired the waiting watchman.

"Yah, sihaya pergi (yes, I shall go)," replied the manager, and, shouting for lamps, descended the short flight of wooden steps to the path.

II

DARKNESS FOLLOWED the sinking of the glowing orb into the sea, leaving a sky of ever-changing colours. Three figures carefully picked their way over the hills, by the light of hurricane lamps, to the little Dusun Kampon in the valley. They balanced on narrow paths between flooded padi-fields, skirted the sago-swamp, passed through a belt of closely-woven trees, and entered the native village beyond. The Kampon was very still and dark, except for the faint crackling and occasional glow of a smouldering watch-fire, somewhere between the clustered houses perching on poles high above the ground. Now and then a distant pariah-dog would bay the moon, and from the coolie lines rose an intermittent chorus of muffled shouts. But the village itself was still—old Danudin, the wood-cutter, was dying.

The native guide led the way between a veritable forest of house-supporting bamboo poles, halting at last at the foot of a tall, rickety ladder. The watchman saluted, and stood at attention outside. Harris followed the Dusun up the ladder, and crawled in after him through the tiny opening that served for a door.

In an inner room, stretched on a coarse native mat, lay the figure of a very old man. His swarthy face was one mass of tiny wrinkles, and the flesh fell in abruptly under the prominent cheek-bones. A highly-coloured blanket was drawn partly over him, and his long, bony fingers plucked ceaselessly at its ravelled edge.

"Who is that?" he inquired faintly of a young Dusun woman who crouched by his head.

"The white Tuan has come, bapa," she replied quickly. "He has deigned to come in the night across the dark Kabun. The Tuan Besar is very kind."

Harris wondered why on earth he had ventured out at all. It seemed so out of keeping with his principles. He rarely had dealings with natives, and, if he did, it was their custom to come to him, not he to them. Still, he was there, and must make the best of it.

"I was told you wanted to see me," he said hastily in Malay. "I heard you were very ill," he added.

The old man sat suddenly up on his mat and caught hold of the manager's white sleeve.

"Tuan Besar," he cried, in a queer, quavering voice, "I felt within me that I must see you before I died. You were generous to me when we felled the trees—very generous—when others around were hard. I have not forgotten that, Tuan. And now that all is not well with you, you have come to me a long way in the dark—to a black man who is dying very swiftly."

Harris started.

"Who told you all was not well with me?" he demanded in surprise.

"No man has told me, Tuan, but I can feel it," replied the old man, sinking back and gasping for breath.

The dark-skinned maiden by his side poured some milk into a gourd, and the dying man drank it eagerly.

"I have little time left," he continued hoarsely, "but I would like to reward you for your kindness to me—one of a supplanted race. You are surrounded by evil spirits, Tuan Besar; ill-luck besets you on every side. I would use my dying powers to alter this—in return for all you have done for me. Accept a small token of me in the same spirit that bade you come down to me to-night from the comfort of your great bungalow."

He fumbled beneath the blanket for a moment, and suddenly uttered a queer grunt of satisfaction. By the light of a smelling oil-lamp which swung from a blackened beam the manager could just follow the movements of the shaking hands. The old man produced something from beneath the coverlet and held it before him. It was a leathern purse, cylindrical in shape, and discoloured with age, fastened to a necklace of large blue and red glass beads.

"A small thing, Tuan Besar," said the old man in a far-away voice, "but it is very valuable to you—because I have made it so. It contains a finger—the finger of your destiny. May I place it on your neck?"

The planter, unable to refuse so simple a request, and heartily wishing that the whole business would soon be over, removed his topi, and the Dusun girl guided her father's quivering hands. The necklace caught for a second in his hair, then fell round his sunburnt neck, the purse resting over the second button of his coat.

The old man looked at him for a moment, and then whispered: "Tuan Besar, therein is a finger—wonderfully preserved. It serves as a symbol—the Finger of the wearer's Destiny. Wear it beneath your coat, and all that you do will succeed. It is a very powerful charm, although you white men believe not in charms and spirits. But, Tuan Besar, be very careful, and guard it well, for if ever the light of day shall fall on the finger which lies within"—the old man rose in his bed, and a queer light danced in the almost sightless pupils—"all your fortunes will vanish—disaster must surely fan on every venture. Guard it well, Tuan Besar, and no friend in all the world could be so true as this—the dying gift of Danudin—the wood-cutter."

The voice grew weaker and weaker until at last it ceased abruptly. The old man dropped back on to his mat, and, suddenly, the lamp flickered, flared up—and then went out. The girl uttered a shrill cry, and ran across the room.

Harris, a queer feeling stealing down his spine, struck a match and held it over the old man's face.

The light had gone out of the wood-cutter's eyes, the firm jaw was tightly shut, the palsied fingers were still—very still.

Harris burnt his fingers, swore softly, and struck another match. He bent forward.

"P'rempuan!" he cried hoarsely, "Danudin is dead!"

A wailing cry broke upon the stillness of the tropic night, and the ataps above him rustled weirdly in a sudden breeze.

Harris felt for his topi, and, groping his way towards the door, hastened softly down the steps to where the patient watchman held the lantern.

"Sudah habis (it is finished)," he said hoarsely, and they hurried silently away.

As he went to bed that night his hand fell upon the leathern purse suspended from his neck—the dying gift of the aged Danudin.

"It's like," he murmured thoughtfully, "it's very like something I saw at Aden a couple of baking years ago. 'Juju,' they called it there—and it drove out devils."

He laughed, and threw off his clothes; but somehow he still wore it under his gauze singlet when he blew out the lamp and tumbled into bed.

III

"Say, Atkinson, how much money have you got to spare?"

Harris was leaning over the broad verandah, smiling cheerfully, as his second-in-command strode sweating up the steep path.

It was morning, and the clock on the verandah was just on the point of striking ten in its wheezy, damp-affected voice. Overhead a huge brown hawk was hovering with a view to securing an early meal of chicken. A stream of soapy water gushed merrily forth from the concrete-floored bathroom, and, within, a toiling teucan-ayer hummed discordantly over his work. Away down the path towards the railway a couple of natives were leading a huge, unwilling kerbau to the little bare patch under a tree, which constituted the estate slaughterhouse. A Chinese carpenter was sawing busily at the back of the kitchen, and, by the line, a white-topied, black-skinned k'rani-clerk was carefully checking a consignment of goods from Api-Api, which the puffing and snorting goods-train had recently delivered.

"Money?" gasped the astonished Tuan Kechil. "Why, damn it all, man, you're mad!"

The manager denied the insinuation pleasantly.

"I'm as sane as yourself, old chap, and a deal more hopeful. Lend me a thousand dollars till Thursday. I'll pay you twenty per cent. It's a fair deal."

The other man gazed at him pityingly.

"Lend a thousand dollars to the most unfortunate man on the West Coast of Borneo! Why, man alive, you told me only a week ago you were absolutely cursed with bad luck!"

"A week ago—yes; but the tide has most providentially turned, as you so cleverly predicted. You may be surprised to hear it, but I've just had a wire from Singapore to say that my rubber shares are simply booming."

Atkinson mounted the steps and sat down suddenly on the verandah floor. He cocked his soiled topi well over one eye and looked up at the exultant Harris.

"Joking?" he asked slowly.

"Not a bit of it! I've simply cabled instructions to sell as soon as they reach a respectable figure. I am now appealing to you to lend me a few paltry pieces of Borneo paper just to help the tide on a bit. Races to-morrow, you know, in Api-Api, and I'm off to have a look at them."

"Yes, old man, I know all about that, but you surely don't expect me to finance you to back that pot-bellied old crock of yours your antiquated watchman is vainly endeavouring to train?"

" 'Mata-Mata' (Policeman) is all right—don't you fret. We were timing him last evening by stopwatch on the sands at low-tide. Had everything cut and dried, you know, and he's a certain win. I tell you, there's nothing on the coast, in the shape of horse-flesh, can touch him. Boy—Bo-oy! Dua beer—lakas!"

The bewildered Atkinson removed a dripping handkerchief from his neck and whistled.

"One of us is clean dotty!" he said.

Harris laughed, and handed him a glass of sparkling lager.

"Here's to 'Mata-Mata'!" he cried. "And may your thousand dollars become ten thousand tomorrow!"

"More likely ten," growled Atkinson. "Still, it's worth the money to see you so jolly bucked with your damned silly self, and I'll send 'em over by boy before you leave this afternoon. Put a couple of hundred on for me, if you will. I s'pose I may as well write the whole lot off as a bad debt. Rubber's lookin' well on your side. Think it must be the sea air does it. It's improved a good bit since I saw it last."

"Turn of the tide, old man!" explained the Tuan Besar, a roguish twinkle in his eye.

"Turn of me gran'mother!" growled Atkinson. "Still, it is better—and you're better, and I'm damn glad to see it. So long!"

Harris watched him descending the path with long, swinging strides. He remained leaning over the rail many moments after the tall form of his assistant had disappeared over the farther ridge. He was thinking. Could it be that the charm which he wore beneath his singlet was responsible for this ease of mind, this new feeling of sheer light-heartedness? He felt like a schoolboy with all the deep responsibilities of life lifted from his broad shoulders.

The idea was ridiculous, he told himself. It was merely the natural order of things—Nature's law of averages—the turn of the tide. Shares were part and parcel of a material, matter-of-fact, business world, in which the influence of native twaddle could not possibly exist. He had had his lean years, and now, surely, the fat years of prosperity must come as certainly as sunshine follows rain. As for the pony, under careful training and dieting its form had naturally improved. It was merely a strange coincidence that things had suddenly changed for the better on the very day after Danudin had died.

Just before the shrill whistle of the afternoon train announced its departure from Pinarut—the next station down the line—Atkinson's boy ran up to the bungalow, carrying a bulky envelope. Harris took it from him, and strode down the path to the railway. He felt confident that this short holiday of a couple of days was going to witness the certain mending of his sadly tattered fortunes.

The train squeaked, bumped, and pulled up. Harris mounted the high step and strolled into the long "European" carriage. MacDermott, the Government doctor, greeted him heartily, throwing the old copy of *Punch* he had been reading on to a seat in front of him.

"Lookin' well," he remarked jocularly.

"I'm fine, thanks!" cried Harris. "Never felt better in my life. How's the Mem?"

"As usual," said the doctor. "Rubber doin' well?"

"First rate! Everything I planted this week started off splendidly. Just the right amount of rain in the night to give the cuttings the required nourishment."

The doctor sat up and looked at him hard.

"Somethin' new for you, isn't it?" he said.

Another planter in a far-off corner chimed in suddenly:

"I've never known a worse year for the young trees," he said decidedly. "Mine are dying off by the score. It's damn sickening."

"Just luck, I s'pose," murmured Harris absently.

"Luck!" thundered the portly Scot. "Luck! Why, hang it all, man, who are you to lecture us about luck? It's the one standin' joke all along the line—your luck!"

Harris laughed out loud, and, picking up the discarded paper, turned its pages over placidly, chuckling every now and again as some subtle witticism caught his eye.

They reached the town only an hour behind time, and Harris followed the coolies with his barang (luggage) to the Rest House, where he had wisely secured a room a good month before. Api-Api is apt to be crowded during Race Week.

He dined at the doctor's bungalow, and the two men repaired afterwards to the more congenial atmosphere of the Sports Club. On the way Harris suddenly challenged the doctor to a hundred up for a wager of two hundred dollars, and the doctor, about the best billiard player around, modestly told him not to throw away his money. Harris insisted, nevertheless, and when the news of the bet had gone the rounds, the two players had a hilarious audience of nearly thirty planters and government men when Harris called upon the doctor to "break."

The game finished 100—33—for Harris!

The doctor laid down his cue, passed a clammy hand over his brow, and mechanically felt in an upper pocket for the notes. "Get me a drink, someone!" he gasped. "There's somethin' wrong here!"

Harris left the club shortly after, and walked on air back to the Government Rest House, where his bed awaited him.

Certainly the tide had turned with a vengeance. How long, he wondered, would it last?

The little racecourse—a mile out from the town—was as crowded as it had ever been when Harris strolled in with the portly doctor. Everyone knew whose pony was going to win the first race of the day, and everyone was equally certain that Harris' dumpy little piece of horse-flesh was not going to win anything. That was the reason he managed to secure such very long odds—and that was also the reason why he mounted the path to the bungalow next day several thousand dollars to the good.

There was a great reception held in his honour at Atkinson's bungalow, and the hornless gramophone shouted its choruses into the tropic night till the day was almost dawning.

Atkinson and Rock—the second assistant—shared the same bed that night.

As he fastened his sarong in true Eastern style, Rock turned to his companion.

"Extraordinary run of luck—what?"

"I told him his chance would come," said Atkinson, yawning, and he banged the hurricane lamp on the floor till it went out.

In the other bedroom Harris was turning the strange talisman over and over in his hand. The night was very still, and through the open window he could still see the myriads of twinkling stars which seemed so near. A rat was creeping stealthily through the ataps above, and a cricket called shrilly from the adjacent bathroom.

He drew back the mosquito curtains, blew out the lamp, and springing quickly into bed, tucked the thin gauze well in under the mattress. He lay at full length—a rug at his feet—for Borneo mornings are often cold in the hours before sunrise. He turned over suddenly, and the charm flapped against his chest.

"The Finger of Destiny" he murmured sleepily. "Everything you turn your hand to—will succeed. Finger—of—Destiny." He started. The weird leather-bound memento seemed quite warm. Perhaps it was only from the heat of his body? Perhaps—He sat up in bed. Pressed against his chest, he distinctly felt the pendant throb for a moment like the regulated pulsations of a human heart—and then—it was still again.

He looked at one bare foot very hard, and moved the toes thoughtfully.

"The Finger of Destiny! I believe there's something in it, after all," he said.

He fell back on to the pillow, and soon the dawn rose over a household of slumberers.

IV

Two years had passed—two long, lonely years—and the great Borneo Rubber Kabun, once bare as a ploughed field, with regular lines of green shoots scarcely showing against the sombreness of the soil, now presented a vast, shady forest of tall, spreading, green-leafed trees, stretching from the little railway line over the slopes and away—apparently to infinity.

Harris, the tall, handsome Tuan Besar, stood on the verandah of his hill-topping bungalow, surrounded by every possible modem convenience to enable him to tolerate his exile from a country where riches spelt enjoyment and luxury. Windows, that had once offered a free entry to all and sundry of the insect world, were now glass-paned; easy-chairs of every description abounded, soft cushions, fibre-matting on the erstwhile bare, boarded floor. Many white-clad Chinese boys, with long tow-chungs tucked into side-pockets, were busily laying the table for the evening meal in a style that vied with the splendour of the most up-to-date hotel in Singapore; and there was champagne waiting somewhere at the back in a pail of Sandakan ice.

The planter stood by the rail and smilingly surveyed the tranquil scene before him, a fat Borneo cigar between his teeth. "I am monarch of all I survey," he might have cried, and no one could have come forward to dispute his claim. Two years had seen great changes in the Karadin Estate. Soon the trees would be ready to tap. Already, just over there, in the dip, great buildings were quickly rising to house the huge, up-to-date machinery already in the hold of some great East-bound steamer.

Prosperity! How strange it all seemed! And two years ago—was it so short a time back as that?—his unluckiness was the one stock joke of planter and D.O. alike.

The most unfortunate man on the West Coast. He laughed aloud as these memories floated back to him across a short gulf of fleeting time; and then, suddenly, he felt the throbbing of the hidden talisman lying snugly on his breast, and he remembered that one eventful tropic night in a Dusun village on the evening Danudin—the aged woodcutter—died and left him—all this that he surveyed—the secret of prosperity.

Another memory came back to him as he smoked—a little scene, almost lost in the haze of time and fever. A liner's crowded deck and the sound of a Somali war-dance. Three black figures and an amulet—ju-ju, that was the term—and how he had laughed when the dear old planter who shared his cabin had talked so seriously about the possible truth lurking behind these native superstitions.

The memory of the liner took him back from Aden to Port Said, and its queer conglomeration of all races; the Suez Canal, long caravans crossing the desert; little Arab boys running alongside the ship shouting for "baksheesh," weird, awkwardly-moving pelicans, clumsly-looking camels, and flies—scores of flies. He remembered a strange-visaged little boy at Port Said who produced live chickens from nowhere, in the centre of crowded tables outside an open café where music was playing. He could see Messina rising out of its recent ruin, Naples, Genoa, Algiers, Gibraltar, The Needles, the jolly white cliffs of the Isle of Wight, the still waters of the Solent, the great British battleships at anchor. How his heart ached for it all again—home and bright lights and fair, white faces.

"I shall see it all before long," he told himself. "After five years' solid sweating the fruits of my toil will buy me everything I desire. I shall have a car and a big country house, plenty of neat, fresh-faced servants. I shall marry and settle down, and, perhaps, when the call of the East becomes a little too hard to bear, a trip, *en famille,* to revisit familiar scenes."

How pleasant it would be to travel out East again with just the one woman one loved! To point out the dirty quayside buildings, the queer railway, the Chinese shops. "That is where I landed—a mere boy. That is where I bought my first suit of khaki—my first sarong."

He flicked the ash from his big cigar on to the sandy path and dreamily watched the flight of a beautiful brown Pergram pigeon.

"Vale Borneo!" he cried suddenly, "Yes, I must go home very soon."

He strolled into his bedroom and stood for some time gazing absently at a green, cockroach-bitten trunk.

"Atkinson," he said suddenly, as the two men sat at dinner that evening, "I am going to resign!"

"Resign, old man?" The second-in-command looked aghast. His whole soul was centred in the source of his income—the great Karadin Estate. "Why, man alive! you're surely not thinking of leaving us—before we tap our first lot of latex—after all these weary years?"

The other nodded.

"I must go, old man! I love the old estate, every blessed inch of it. I know it all by heart, and could tell you each detail of its progress from the very commencement till now; but I must go—and that soon. I'm sick—homesick, if you like. I want to see the lights of a decent town—to talk to a pretty clean-skinned woman—to wear nicely-cut clothes. It's calling me every moment of this damned existence. Besides, dear old chap, what's the use of riches hoarded up in a Singapore bank? Look here, I've sold all my shares at a profit—a good fat margin over, I can tell you; I've settled all my cash affairs, and to-day month my contract expires. I've cabled home my resignation, and recommended you for the billet. You'll get it, of course—they think no end of you at home. I shall take the steamer for Singapore, and spend about a month there among the people I know. Then I'm off to dear old England."

Atkinson sipped his wine in silence for some time. He gazed at the clock on the wall, with its queer, damp-stained dial, the standard oil-lamp in one corner, the row of liqueur-bottles of all shapes and sizes—Maraschino, Kümmel, Hijau (Créme de Menthe), Curacoa. It was all so jolly familiar and comfortable, but it wouldn't be much without its present owner. He stretched out a huge brown hand across the table, and Harris gripped it hard. They were good chums, these two.

"Don't go," he said, "yet."

"I must, old man—I simply must. You'll see me in London when your leave comes along, and we'll drink to the dear old times together."

After dinner they strolled out on to the verandah, and stood, side by side, smoking and sipping their liqueurs.

Just beyond the rubber and the line, they knew there stretched that vast expanse of blue water which would soon form an almost impassable barrier between them. Perhaps they might never meet again.

Knee-deep in the tranquil sea, hundreds of native fisherfolk—men, women and children—stood in line, lanterns in their hands, spiking the foolish, inquisitive fish that must needs lose their lives from sheer, idle curiosity. All the two friends could make out in the inky darkness was the long, long row of twinkling lights.

To Atkinson these were accursed Will-o'-the-Wisps, luring his only friend away from him. To Harris they told of London and civilisation—theatres—merriment.

Atkinson broke the silence suddenly.

"The unluckiest planter on the West Coast!" he cried bitterly. "I almost wish the tide had never turned!"

V

THE LITTLE GRIMY mail steamer "Kudat" was moored alongside the wharf at Api-Api, loaded with coolies, fore and aft, fruit, cocoa-nuts, and gelatong rubber. Two sunburnt men sat in the saloon, a bottle of champagne between them.

"Harris," said Atkinson huskily, "will you do me a great favour?"

"Anything you ask, old man. What is it?"

"There's a little girl coming out by the German mail, and she's due at Singapore two days after you arrive. Her name's Molly Stevens, and she's in charge of a dear old lady I knew years ago, who's on her way back to Hong Kong. I want you to meet Miss Stevens, show her round Singapore, advise her as to what she's likely to want out here, and put it down to my account. She's thinking of changing her name to Atkinson.

The other man rose and slapped him warmly on the back.

"You tight old oyster!" he cried. "I've never heard a word of this before."

The new manager smiled.

"Didn't think you'd be interested," he said.

"Of course, I'll do everything I can for the lady!" cried Harris. "I'll introduce her to all the nice married women I know, and they'll go the round of the shops with her. I s'pose she's to leave for here by the 'Haufah'? She sails from Singapore about a week after Miss Stevens' arrival there."

The other nodded.

"That'll do fine!" he said. "By the way, here's her photo. You'll better be able to recognise her when you see her."

Harris took the portrait from him, and looked at the face of the girl intently. He whistled, and handed it back.

"Jove! She's pretty—damn pretty! Hearty congrats, old man!"

Atkinson rose and held out his great brown hand.

"Good-bye, Harris, old man—the best pal I ever had. Write to me sometimes—when you've a moment to spare. Think of us out here sweatin' away when you're a gentleman of means in town."

He choked, swallowed a lump in his throat, turned on his heel to hide his emotion, and strode away with affected nonchalance, down to the rickety gangway on to the quay. He waved his malacca in the air once or twice, and Harris, at the taffrail, waved back. He watched the solitary white figure disappear in the darkness, and then turned and crossed the saloon to bed. He felt that something vital had gone out of his life.

He woke before it was light, and knew by the swishing sound of water outside his open port-hole that the "Kudat" was already on her way. His heart throbbed tumultuously. He had actually started for home! He turned over and kicked the scanty bedclothes off him on to the floor. It was certainly devilishly close. Suddenly he thought he heard a voice whispering something in his ear.

"Molly Stevens—Molly Stevens! Damn pretty!" it seemed to say.

He pinched himself and sat bolt upright in bed. He listened for a moment intently.

"Nothing!" he murmured. "Nothing! But who the deuce is Molly Stevens?"

Then he remembered. That was the name of the girl Atkinson had asked him to meet in Singapore. Now he came to think of it, she was pretty; he remembered telling his friend so when he had handed him back her photograph. But why on earth should he think he heard her name repeated in the dead of night on a steamer on which he was the only white passenger?

"Dreaming!" he muttered. "Dreaming! That's all."

He tried to sleep again, but a second time the voice seemed to whisper at his side: "Molly Stevens! Damn pretty, old man!"

"Hang it all," he groaned, "can't you shut up?"

It was no use. It was far too hot to sleep. He fixed his sarong more securely round his waist, and, slipping on a pair of Japanese slippers, stumbled down the passage to the first-class deck. He gazed over the side at the oily waters as they rushed swirlingly by, idly following the movements of flaky wreaths of snow-white foam. Somehow they seemed sometimes to join and twist themselves into queer hieroglyphic shapes. Suddenly he distinctly recognised two of these strange formations.

"M.S. distinctly," he said. "I wonder what that stands for? M.S.! Why, Molly Stevens!" he cried, and in sheer desperation left the ship's side and flung himself wearily into a long cane chair.

As the five days' journey—including a two days' stop at Labuan—passed by with irritating slowness, Harris began to feel a most unnatural anxiety to meet his friend's fiancée. Her face and name haunted him in everything he thought or did, and, under it all, there seemed to be rising within him a fierce, almost savage, desire to have this woman Atkinson had chosen for his own. Argue with himself as he might, the desire became stronger and stronger as the little steamer drew nearer Singapore, until at last a furious, unquenchable fire burned within him that no possible amount of conscientious scruple or sense of honour could withstand.

He leaped out of the double-prowed sampan at Johnson's Pier, threw the native oarsman a silver dollar, and, hailing a passing rickshaw, drove off excitedly in the direction of Raffles' Hotel. Here he arranged for a room for the young lady's reception next to his own, and waited impatiently for the forty-eight odd hours to elapse before the liner was due to arrive. He drove to the shipping offices and made minute inquiries, but, somehow or other, did not remember to look up any ladies of his acquaintance to chaperone Miss Stevens after her arrival in Singapore. A mysterious spirit within him had suddenly forced him from his hitherto straightforward line of action into a rut of savage desire and cunning.

An hour before the "Kauffman" was due at the Borneo Wharf Harris dressed himself in a suit of well-cut, spotless whites, smart brown shoes, and new white topi, and, having ordered a motor to await him at the hotel entrance, drove down in it to meet the boat.

As soon as a gangway was placed in position he ran up swiftly on to the first-class deck, and, colliding suddenly with the portly purser, inquired hastily for Miss Stevens. The purser hailed a steward who was passing, and just at that moment the lady herself came out from the reading-room.

The planter stepped forward and removed his topi. He could see that the photograph in Atkinson's possession was an excellent one. "Miss Stevens, I believe?"

She started. "I am Miss Stevens," she replied.

"My name is Harris," he explained. "I was manager on the Karadin Estate before Mr. Atkinson, and he asked me to meet you and see you through Singapore."

They shook hands.

"I am awfully glad to meet you," she said frankly. "I was wondering what on earth I was going to do while waiting for the connection. You see, I have no friends here, and Mrs. Johns, my travelling companion, is in her cabin, not at all well. I have promised to look in to-morrow before the boat sails, just to see how she's getting on. How soon can we go on shore? It all looks so delightfully barbaric and quaint."

Harris rose to the occasion, commandeered her luggage, and sent it on to the hotel. Half an hour later they were driving towards the famous Botanical Gardens side by side.

The Malay driver took them along at a terrific speed, turning sharp corners with wonderful precision, steering the huge car without mishap through streets crowded with rickshaws, past highly-coloured open Chinese shop-fronts, and out through the fashionable European quarter beyond the town.

Harris gazed enraptured at his youthful companion as she eagerly scanned the passing landscape. She was tall and graceful, with hazel eyes and a wealth of rich brown hair.

Her costume was white, and beautifully cut, and her broad-brimmed topi suited her admirably. Her features were perfect, her forehead high, her chin determined. The planter sat by her side as one in a trance, mechanically pointing out each object of interest as they sped swiftly by. They strolled through the beautiful gardens together.

"How delightful it all is!" she said. "I think you are an admirable guide. I hope I have not bored you with so many questions?"

"I am only too glad to be of any service," he said, and they retraced their steps towards the waiting car.

All the way back to the hotel Molly Stevens was very silent, and Harris leaned back on the springing cushions and thought, and thought. The whirring of the engine hummed one never-ceasing refrain in his ear.

"All that you turn your hand to shall succeed."

Could it be possible that if he enforced his great desire, Molly Stevens, whether she willed it or no, would be compelled to obey? Nothing had failed him yet since that far-off tropic evening when Danudin—the native wood-cutter—had called him to his bedside.

"She shall be mine!" something cried within him, and the automobile pulled up suddenly outside the great hotel.

As they sat together at dinner that evening Molly suddenly stared across the room, and then looked quickly down at her plate. She glanced up again, and caught Harris' eye.

"There is a man over there whom I met on the boat," she whispered, crumbling her bread nervously. "He is such an idiot, and he made furious love to me all the way out."

Harris shifted his chair a moment later, and just managed to catch a glimpse of the man she indicated.

"I don't wonder at any man falling in love with you," he replied with a smile, and poured her out a glass of white wine. He hoped to goodness the fellow wouldn't endeavour to pursue his courtship further while they were living in the same hotel. He felt infinitely relieved when the man wiped his dark moustache with his serviette, rose, and went out.

Harris retired to bed that night feverishly absorbed in his mad infatuation. He threw off his clothes and slipped on his singlet and sarong, then he drew out the amulet from under his vest and gazed at it in silence.

"She must be mine!" he cried suddenly. "In the increasing of my fortunes you have always assisted me. Can you, I wonder, procure me the object of my affection?"

The leather case grew warm as he held it, and the finger within throbbed for a moment, and then was still again.

He turned out the light and stepped from the room on to the verandah. The garden lay below him, but the night was very dark, and he could not see the path. How still, how peaceful it seemed outside, and the heavens were studded with stars. A lizard was calling from some crevice in the wall, and a great flying beetle hummed suddenly by. A perfect tropic night, he thought.

A slight sound at his elbow caused him to turn. It was the opening of a window—her room. And then he saw that only a low partition separated her portion of the verandah from his. Everything seemed to be in his favour to-night. There was a light burning in her room—it attracted him strangely. He hesitated. Should he go to her? He must! The desire was too strong for him.

"Everything you turn your hand to will succeed." The voice was the same as that he had heard on board the little steamer pronouncing her name. It came from within him, but it was very clear. He strode across to the barrier and climbed it—deliberately. He knew now that nothing could resist him. She was his because he willed it so. He stepped noiselessly to the French window and seized the handle swiftly. Then he saw something moving through a chink in the blind. He stopped and peered into the room.

Molly Stevens was sitting on the edge of the bed, attired in a richly-flowered kimono, her dainty, bare pink toes just showing beneath it on the floor.

"My God!" he gasped. "How beautiful she looks!"

And still he hesitated, his shaking hand upon the china knob. A few bold steps—and she would be his for ever. He drew himself up.

Suddenly the girl turned and produced a large photograph from under the pillow. Harris started. He could just make out a figure in a broad topi and a planter's uniform, and he knew, deep within him, whose portrait it was she held.

She bent over the photograph with a long-drawn sigh, and showered passionate kisses on the handsome face.

Harris stood for a moment gazing in through the Venetian blind, stupefied with a sudden tumult of contrary emotions. Then, in a flash, he thought of Atkinson anxiously awaiting his beautiful bride, the estate, and everything he had known and loved. He reeled away from the window, and, scarcely conscious of what he was doing, climbed back across the slender barrier. Suddenly, utterly maddened at the thought of what he might have allowed himself to do, he drew the amulet from his sunburnt neck and hurled it wildly into the darkness below.

He turned on his heel, fled back into his room, and flung himself upon the bed, panting with suppressed emotion. The perspiration poured down his neck and arms, bathing his heaving chest. Then he grew calm and happy. The awful desire had fled with the falling of the discarded talisman, and his honour still remained untarnished.

He tucked in the flimsy mosquito curtains, rolled over on one side, and fell into a deep, calm sleep.

VI

Down in the garden a tall, dark Englishman strolled, bareheaded, smoking his last cigar before retiring. He was gazing anxiously up at the lighted window where he rightly calculated the lady of his dreams reposed.

Suddenly something struck his head and fell with a rattle on to the concrete path. He stooped and picked it up. It was a queerly-shaped leathern pouch on a chain of beads.

He pressed it to his heart in ecstasy.

"She does love me!" he said. "She is not so hard-hearted as I thought. She has thrown me this as a beautiful sign of her regard—a ray of hope in my darkness. Perhaps the chaperon influenced her on board. Anyhow, I will endeavour to speak to her to-morrow before I sail."

He slipped the necklace over his head, tucked the treasured token beneath his singlet, threw away his half-smoked cigar, and strode exultantly in to bed.

On the next day Harris left his charge in the company of some English ladies who were staying at the same hotel, and drove out to inspect a small rubber estate about thirty miles away from the town.

"Look after yourself!" he cried gaily, as he waved from the car. "I shall be back before evening."

He drew a prospectus from an inner pocket and scanned it eagerly. He little thought, as the miles multiplied between his friend's fiancée and himself that he would never see Molly Stevens alive again.

A quaint atap-roofed native police-station flashed by, and presently he passed a group of young Malay girls busily weaving mats. Occasionally a wild-eyed, long-haired native would come swinging along the centre of the tree-bordered thoroughfare, pausing to stare after the throbbing automobile as it whizzed by him in a cloud of fine dust. Nude and semi-naked children, playing in the road, ran screaming to the side, laughing aloud as soon as the danger had passed.

Harris suddenly became very thoughtful. He had spent a couple of solid hours early that morning searching in the garden for the talisman he had discarded in his fury, intending to burn it or throw it into the sea; but it was nowhere to be found.

Ah, well, it couldn't be helped! The thing was lost—and there was an end of it. Then the old man's words came back to him, warning him never to expose the contents of the leathern purse to the light of day, or his good fortune would be lost for ever. He laughed and shrugged his broad shoulders. Nothing could shake him now. Every penny he possessed was already safe with the Singapore and Shanghai Consolidated Bank. Shares could go up or shares could go down, for all he cared. He patted himself, metaphorically, on the back for his clever move, and once more became absorbed in the contents of the lengthy prospectus.

VII

It was late that afternoon when he returned to the hotel. A Chinese waiter brought him his tea, and then handed him a dainty note, addressed to himself, on a lacquer tray. It was in a lady's handwriting, and he slipped it into the pocket of his white coat in true casual, Oriental style. He stirred his tea absently, and dropped a slice of lemon into it. "Where's Miss Stevens?" he demanded suddenly. For the moment he had forgotten all about her.

"Mem makan hangin, Tuan (Out, sir)!"

"Out?" He suddenly remembered the letter and tore it open. He glanced through it hastily, then staggered to his feet, his brain reeling. He clutched at the table for support.

"My God!" he gasped. "What does it mean?" He read it through again slowly, his breath coming and going in short gasps.

"DEAR MR. HARRIS," it read,

"Forgive me! I scarcely know what I am doing; but I shall never see you or Mr. Atkinson again. Mr. Reynolds—the gentleman you saw at dinner last night—has asked me to go with him to Java—and I have consented. I have paid my own hotel bill. Please try and forgive me. You will never understand.

"Ever your grateful friend,
"MOLLY STEVENS."

And he had seen her kissing Atkinson's photograph in her bedroom only the night before. The letter dropped from his trembling fingers and fluttered away across the floor.

He ran into the hall and scanned the list of sailings.

"Great heaven!" he moaned. "Too late! Too late!"

The "Nymphius" had sailed for Batavia that afternoon at three.

He turned into the office and excitedly examined the clerk. There was no doubt about it whatever. It was no foolish joke, no wild, girlish freak. She had left with all her luggage early that afternoon, accompanied by the dark-haired Mr. Reynolds.

Harris fled to his room and fell exhausted into a long cane chair. He felt tired with existence—everything. Fate seemed suddenly to have laid violent hands on his inoffensive person and crumpled him up. He rang for a whisky and soda, and drank it eagerly to the dregs.

He racked his brain for a motive for so extraordinary a change in her affections, but failed utterly to discover a single rational clue. He went about town that evening in a state of coma, and came back to the hotel drunk—helplessly intoxicated for the first time for many years.

It was late when he opened his eyes the next morning and his head throbbed painfully, a natural sequence of the violent excess of the night before. He pulled aside his mosquito curtains and, jumping out of bed, plunged his aching head into a basin of cool, refreshing water. He drew it out after the third dip, and, his eyes smarting, felt blindly round him for a towel. Then, with a sudden shock the secret of the whole trouble dawned upon him.

"The amulet!" he cried aloud. "The cursed amulet—The Finger of Destiny! *He* found it in the garden—that night!"

He went down to breakfast a little calmer, and managed to eat a fair meal. Then he thought of something he ought to do. He must send off a cable to Atkinson—to break the awful news to the lonely planter.

"Poor old Atkinson!" he murmured. "Poor old devil! The irony of it all! The talisman that brought me wealth—and deprived him of the girl he loved—just at the very moment she seemed within his grasp!"

He smoked for a long while, turning the matter over calmly in his mind.

"No," he said at last, "I'll give the poor little girl a good long rope. Who knows but she may suddenly think better of it and come back? Poor little Molly! An angel in disguise up against the hidden powers of Oriental mysticism! No wonder she had to give in!"

VIII

That night Harris had a queer dream. He saw a boat speeding through a very calm, blue sea. It was mid-ocean, for there was no land in sight. He could see everything quite clearly, although he knew it was night, and that the stars twinkled brightly above him. It was the "Nymphius"—the little Java mail steamer. He had seen it often steaming from Singapore, but had he not known it well, the name was clearly painted on the stern.

Suddenly he found himself on board the vessel—he could feel the gently-swaying deck beneath his feet. He could see the officer on the bridge walking up and down, up and down, with almost monotonous regularity. It was all as clear to him as if his soul had been suddenly torn from his body and transported by some mysterious force to the very ship on which his beautiful charge had so unexpectedly eloped, and he knew that Molly Stevens lay sleeping somewhere near, beside the man she had told him she despised.

Something led him along the line of doors which opened into the many deck-cabins, and guided his hand suddenly to a handle which turned without any apparent effort of his own. He found himself inside a comfortably furnished cabin, which, in lieu of the usual port-hole, had an opening like the window of a house. There was a broad berth on each side of the compartment. On one he recognised the slender form of Molly Stevens—on the other the dark-haired man he remembered seeing one evening at dinner. The door closed softly after him, and he stood, with folded arms, waiting—waiting for something which he knew would happen.

The wall of the cabin was vibrating violently to the dull whir of the welcome electric fan. A watch was ticking somewhere in that heap of male clothing hung carelessly in one corner. He could hear distinctly the sound of the water without, and the measured revolutions of the powerful engines below.

Suddenly he started. What was that encircling the dark man's neck? Beads! Great heaven! Then his surmise had been correct! The cursed talisman—! Harris clenched his fists. It seemed a sacrilege—a personal insult to himself—that that dark-visaged stranger should be wearing on his slumbering breast that token.

How dark the cabin was, and yet he could see everything! He made a sudden step forward. He would tear the amulet from the usurper's neck—even if he had to strangle him in the attempt. He bent over the prostrate form.

There was a slight movement from the bunk opposite, and he stepped quickly back. Molly Stevens was stirring in her sleep. Supposing she should wake and find him there? He must go at once. He seized the door-handle, but somehow it stuck fast and would not turn. The girl murmured something in her sleep, yawned, blinked, then opened her eyes and sat up. She pressed something at her side, and suddenly a tiny spark of light from a neat electric hand-lamp flashed in the darkness. She was looking at the watch which hung by her head.

The light went out, the girl slipped from the bunk, and stood for a moment regarding the sleeping man earnestly. Harris tried to move the handle again, but still it failed to turn. Molly turned and looked towards the door. He caught his breath and pressed himself back against the wall. Then he began to realise that she could not see him.

Suddenly her eye lit upon the string of native beads which decorated her companion's neck. She bent over him, hesitated, then gave the beads a gentle tug. The charm stuck for a moment, and then slipped from its place of concealment and fell upon the sleeping man's chest. She gasped in wonderment, and held the purse for a second poised on the palm of her dainty hand. She weighed it carefully, and was evidently hazarding a guess at its contents. She sat on the edge of the man's bunk and examined it minutely, then she rose and felt in a small handbag on the rack above.

Harris gasped. He heard the sound of metal. She held a pair of scissors in her hand. Surely she was not going to cut the thing open? She mustn't do that, he told himself. He must prevent it at all costs. He tried to step forward, to take her arm and wrench the scissors from her; but somehow he was unable to move a muscle. He wanted to call out to her and warn her of the awful nature of its contents, but his tongue was tied. Great heaven! she mustn't do it!

Helpless, he saw the sharp blades sever each binding thread neatly. And still the unconscious wearer slumbered on. One—two—three cuts! Surely there could be no more required? The thing was so crudely sewn together.

She would scream. He felt certain she would scream. He wanted to thrust his fingers in his ears.

The last cut. A pause, and then something rolled out—something that seemed to light the whole cabin with a wonderful radiant blue light. A gem, no doubt, of priceless value. He had not the least notion what it was, but he felt that it must be very valuable—unique. And he had thrown it from him in a sudden fit of senseless fury!

The girl held the newly-found treasure between finger and thumb, gazing at it in mute astonishment.

And then—the day dawned in the East, and one white ray of light stole in at the open window of the cabin and fell upon the shining gem. In an instant the radiance was extinguished, and the object in her grasp was but a colourless stone.

He was no longer in the cabin. He was hovering between heaven and earth over a calm, blue sea. Suddenly the skies above him darkened, the wind caught his eye. It was something floating just below the surface, and the waves were bringing it swiftly towards him. It looked like a bunch of seaweed, a porpoise, or—Then he knew. It was the body of a man. Some fever-haunted suicide, maybe; some unfortunate victim of the recent typhoon.

He rose and made a step towards it. Suddenly a wave, stronger than the rest, lifted the inert mass. A dark head rose for a moment above the swirling waters.

Harris uttered a wild cry, and, burying his face in his shaking hands, staggered towards the town, striving to shut out from his gaze the vision of a man's white neck encircled by a string of native beads.

II

THE MAGIC MOSQUITO

"IF WE DID all that those darned sky pilots told us," remarked Huson dreamily, jerking his topied head in the direction of a tall, lean, bearded figure by the taffrail, "I shouldn't have exceeded my limit of liquor, my pony's girths 'ud have been prop'ly tightened, and this damned arm of mine wouldn't have been broken. Still, I s'pose there's always somethin' to be thankful for, and, comin' to think it out seriously, if I'd have followed the preachin' of those worthy men I shouldn't have got a fortnight's sick leave, had a run into dear old Singapore, and been landed for two days in this damned thirsty abomination of desolation—tellin' yarns."

The tall man in the long chair opposite fingered his glass absently and looked drowsily around.

The S.S. "Haufah" was moored alongside the tumbledown quay at Labuan, between that sleepy little island and another of its kind, smaller and palm-girt. The water was as smooth as glass and as blue as a poster-sea, and the tropical sun was pouring down its full force on to the canvas awning of the little German mail steamer. Fore and aft, brown-skinned coolies, women and children, smoked and slept, their world's possessions under or around them. A large long-tailed monkey with fluffy bluey-grey fur was sitting in one corner of the first-class deck, cooing softly as it stripped the red, prickly skin from a luscious rambutan.

Occasionally a fish would leap suddenly out of the still water and disappear again, leaving an evergrowing circle of tiny bubbles behind it. Beyond the few ramshackle wharf-buildings ran the main street, comprising a Chinese temple, a drinking house with a billiard-saloon, and a score of open-fronted Chinese shops. To the right an open space, the Government Rest House, and then the post office—a magnificent white building, guarded by two stalwart brown-faced sepahis with loaded rifles, and ornamented by disused field guns pointing threateningly from either end of the garden out to sea. A kerbau, tethered to a stake on shore, wallowed in the briny waters twenty yards from a tiny reading-room—a sort of miniature club house. Farther inland lay the Eastern Telegraph Co.'s station. White faces have been getting fewer in Labuan since the coalfields ceased working.

"If we did all those darned sky pilots told us," continued Huson, mopping his sunburnt face with a bright red square of silk, "instead of killin' this impudent little niamok (mosquito) whose infernal bad taste has prompted him to mistake my wrist for a newcomer's, I should either let him go with a molecule of my valuable blood, or politely offer him the other wrist to nibble at. But, seein' I'm not of the psalm-singin' brethren—"

He imprisoned the tiny interloper by tightening the skin suddenly, and squashed it unceremoniously between finger and thumb.

The tall missionary left the rail and the scenery he had been absently contemplating, patted the monkey on the head, gave it a couple more rambutans to discuss, and crossed the saloon to his cabin. He reappeared a few moments later, wearing his big white topi, and descended the rickety gangway to the shore.

"Ah!" remarked Huson, uttering a long-drawn sigh of relief, "I never feel quite my proper self when close up against a sky pilot. Not that there aren't some of the real pukka white men among their kind; but somehow or other the mere look of one of 'em makes me feel uneasy. Thirsty ship this, eh? Well, I think I will, thanks. Boy!"

The white-clad Chinaman appeared mysteriously from somewhere close at hand, and the tall man in the long chair shouted an order.

"Yah, Tuan!" came the brisk response, and the "boy" disappeared into the tiny saloon. The two men puffed at their cigarettes in silence for a while until a welcome rattling of glasses on a tray announced the arrival of the much-desired liquor.

"Chin, chin!" said the tall man.

"Chin, chin!" replied Huson, eyeing the bubbles as they danced merrily upwards through the pink liquid. "A gin-sling is a luxury you don't often see at home—what!"

"Ah!" The empty glasses appeared almost simultaneously on the deal table.

"You seem to be up against parsons in general," remarked the tall man suddenly. "Any reason in particular?"

Huson handed him a cigar, and bit the end off another for himself. He placed it between his lips and slapped all his pockets in turn in search of matches.

"Ah! Thanks!" He bent forward, puffed, and then sat back in his chair again.

"Sky pilots," he murmured reflectively. "Well, they are all very good in their way, I s'pose, but there was one I happened to run up against once who altered my whole opinion of their order—and his name was Talbot.

"I was a young assistant in those days on a mixed plantation way back from the East Coast—the name of it don't much matter, and I've drunk so many stengas since then that I should have some trouble in recollectin' it myself. The Tuan Besar (manager) was Cunningham—and a nicer man to work under never came out East—or, if he did, I never had the good luck to run across him. We grew a little rubber, and pineapples between-wise, a good many cocoa-nuts, and one or two other useful little catch-crops, and, under Cunningham, dividends were good. Yes, that plantation marked my *debut* in the East, and I shall never forget its influence on my small fortunes as long as I breathe.

"Believe me or not, as you will, but that manager insisted on the directors supplyin' us with gramophones, a piano, and—just before my contract ran out—a full-sized billiard-table! You know how valuable books are way back. Well, we had a case out from home every three months. And pay was good.

"It was damn lonely up there with jungle all around, and not another white face for miles—except just one—and that was this man Talbot. You could sit on the steps outside your cattle-shed that served for a bungalow and think and think, with not a sound to disturb your thoughts but the rustlin' of the wind in your ataps and the shrill singin' of ubiquitous 'squitos.' There was everythin' that bit, and plenty of those that curled themselves up in a corner of your room with awful death lurkin' in their ugly fangs. Talbot had a school of native kids somewhere about seven miles between us and civilisation, but sometimes he'd just run across to sort of register our respective progresses towards the devil. He was clean-shaven, with a long, hatchet-shaped face, made miserable-lookin' by many years of trying hard to be good, and he'd sit down to makan with the other assistant and myself with all the airs and graces of a Daniel in a den of roarin' lions.

"He never called on Cunningham if he could possibly avoid it, because Cunningham had studied for the Bar once, and could argue damn sight too well; besides, they didn't seem to hit it together at the best of times.

"Just as the strain of utter loneliness was becomin' too much for the Tuan Besar, his favourite fox-terrier died. It's just times like those that drive a man to drink, drugs, or the inevitable desire for companionship—human companionship! Cunningham was as clean-livin' a man as the East can hold, but it was just a pull between his sense of decency and madness, with a five years' contract pushin' behind him all the time.

"At last one evening he called up his watchman No. 1—an old Pathan soldier—and told him to go down into the Kampons around and find him a wife. The old man saluted, and marched over the hills into the darkness, and Cunningham went back to his room and looked up a photograph of a girl with fluffy hair he used to know at home. He's often told me about that night. In his way of thinkin' it seemed like cutting himself off forever from all that was good and pure and holy—not that Cunningham was a religious man—but he had his views.

"The stalwart old watchman No. 1 walked back that night with a story of a Tamil family he had run across with a beautiful young maiden, black as coal, and stated the tune of the bill Cunningham would have to settle. Cunningham knew the old man's taste was sound, and, soon after, the bargain was made and the girl took up her residence at the little bungalow the Tuan Besar had just had built. That girl was a veritable dusky queen—tall, erect, and perfect of feature, with the barbaric ornament business not overdone—just a little knob of gold let in each nostril and a couple similar in her upper lip and ears, to relieve the blackness of her skin. Cunningham limited her strictly to this—exceptin' for a pair of solid gold anklets he had ordered from Singapore specially for her; but he refused to let her adapt Western articles of female underclothin' as skirts—a general failin' with most Tamil girls I've seen. And so Cunningham settled down to tolerate his new existence, and found his desires for drink, and the lights of a decent respectable town with a theatre, more easily quelled.

"How was he to know that Marani, as he called her, had been one of that Talbot man's pet pupils? But, sure enough, she had, and as soon as that worthy gentleman heard of it he was up at Cunningham's bungalow, kickin' up the devil's own row, and threatenin' him with imprisonment for abduction as soon as a letter from his pen could reach the Commissioner of Police.

"Cunningham didn't worry himself very much about Talbot. He just let him go on rampin' and splutterin' for the matter of half an hour, and then trotted out the receipt signed by Marani's father. That finished the Reverend Talbot. He rammed on his topi, took up the red Chinese umbrella he always carried, and bounced out of the house.

"Cunningham inquired very politely whether he would stay to makan, but Talbot was deaf to all entreaties, and marched off home in all the heat of the midday sun, and it can be damned hot just then, as you know.

"He never forgave Cunningham, but that didn't worry the Tuan Besar. As for Marani, she heard of the row through her father, who had had a very unpleasant interview with the sky pilot himself.

"Now, a black girl, even if bought and sold like any article of household use, can learn to respect her lord and master a great deal more than most people would imagine, and I fully believed this Marani really loved the man whose property she had now become. Anyhow, she'd no particular affection for Talbot, and whenever that red umbrella came over the hills a queer light would burn in her coal-black eyes, her hands would clench and unclench, and her bosom heave to the mysterious dictates of some hidden emotion. One mornin' I reached the Tuan Besar's bungalow just as old Talbot had passed, and I distinctly saw that girl spit fiercely as she watched him disappear. And Cunningham—he was quite fond of her in his own queer way, and treated her damn sight too well for a native.

"One day, to Cunningham's surprise, he saw Talbot come suddenly along the path and walk straight up to the door of his bungalow. He mounted the steps very deliberately, and raised his hat as solemnly as a Chinese shopkeeper.

" 'Tabi!' he said, in almost a friendly way.

"Cunningham bowed very coldly, and waited to see what the old fool had to say.

" 'You have a new consignment of coolies, I believe?' he started. 'Is any preparation bein' made for their welfare?'

" 'The usual preparations have already been made,' replied the Tuan Besar; 'though I must say I cannot see what business of yours it is to interfere.'

"The sky pilot coloured up a little and coughed. He had a most irritatin' cough.

" 'You see,' he continued after a bit, 'I have lately been considerin' the advisability of conductin' a weekly mission among the coolies of adjacent plantations, and I thought—'

"That was just about enough for Cunningham. He got up from his chair and crossed the verandah.

" 'Here!' he shouted, white with fury, 'get out of this before I kick you out. I'm sick of you—you meddlin' old—'

"Talbot didn't wait to hear the rest, and perhaps it was just as well he didn't, for the Tuan Besar wasn't in one of his best moods.

"The big red umbrella bobbed away down the steep hill-path, and Talbot, white with fury and indignation, vowed he'd avail himself of the first opportunity of turning the tables on Cunningham.

"As it happened, that opportunity wasn't long in presentin' itself.

"One day, about a year after he'd bought Marani, Cunningham, feelin' considerably run-down in health, resolved to take a few weeks' leave and run up to Colombo for a trip. He left the estate in our hands, gave us all possible instructions, and asked us just to see that Marani was looked after safely at night. He added a rider concernin' keepin' an eye on Talbot when he was prowlin' round, packed his barang, and, with a list of orders from the other man and myself in his breast-pocket, and a wad of fifty-dollar notes, started off by the only train to the coast town.

"I saw him off, and although I knew it was only for the matter of a month or so, I'd worked alongside him for pretty near three sweatin' years, and I tell you I didn't like that last hand grip. I just loved that man. Dumb animals liked him; the cook's children—little dusky girls in red trousers and grimy little boys, their heads all shaved but for a comic-lookin' little tuft of hair—would all trot up when he came by, sure of a bottle of sweets between 'em from the estate kedei (shop), or the price of one.

"Marani stayed on alone at the bungalow on the hill. Other ngi (housekeepers) would have gone home to their people in their masters' absence. But I rather fancy Marani was afraid of runnin' into her old teacher with the red umbrella; anyhow, she stayed on, and any time of day you might see her, seated on the steps in front of the bungalow, hummin' softly to herself as, with deft fingers, she wove ugly bits of rotan into beautiful-lookin' baskets. Sometimes she'd disappear for a few hours, returnin' always at dusk with a bundle of ripe fruits on her back. I don't think she feared anyone but Talbot, and at night she had Cunningham's two dogs on the verandah and watchman No. 1—the straightest thing I ever struck in a black skin—walkin' about outside all the time. The other man and I worked hard and slept hard—three men's work is quite enough for two to do!

"Well, Cunningham went down to the town, won a few dollars at the pony races, and shipped by this very boat for Singapore. Nothin' excitin' happened to him on the way, except this damn little cockleshell ran into the tail-end of a typhoon, and pretty near capsized with all aboard. However, he reached Singapore with a whole skin, and put up, as usual, at Raffle's. He met a lot of old friends stayin' there, and they did the town pretty well between 'em; had a look at the Chinese theatre, and, another evenin', had the luck to see an English opera company doin' somethin' almost up-to-date from home.

"He left the theatre, said good-bye to his pals, and, hailin' a passing rickshaw, drove off in the direction of the wharf where he had to board the steamer for Colombo. The coolie that pulled him was a bit unsteady on his feet, and, comin' suddenly round a corner, collided with another goin' in the same direction. There was an awful bang, a tearin' of spokes, and both cars upset, tippin' their occupants into the road. There was a girl in the other rickshaw, and she fell right across the tramline. Both coolies looked a bit dazed, and sat on the ground, one rubbin' his tummy, tryin' to get back some of the wind the other man's shaft had knocked out of him, and the other rollin' from side to side, holdin' his head. Cunningham was a bit shaken, too, but his bein' the quickest brain of the lot, he came round in time to realise that there was a slight, white form right across the tram-line, and a damn drunken native driver bringin' a tramcar along at full speed—an' you know about how fast a native driver can go when he's worked up!

"Cunningham sprang to his feet and nearly sat down again, for one leg had got a bad twist in the fall. He staggered across the road, bent down, although it was absolute agony to move at all, and, pickin' the young lady up in his great brown arms, just pulled her clear before the long, open car whizzed by. Jove! it was a near shave! And the girl knew it, too, for she just sort of woke up and gave Cunningham one of those grateful, tellin' looks that tug at a man's heartstrings, and that cunning Mr. Cupid must have been hangin' round in the cocoa-nut trees just by, for Cunningham felt somethin' go snap inside, and then his leg gave way; he lay down suddenly, an' for a few minutes he didn't know any more.

"One of those queer-lookin' native police guys was bendin' over him when he came to, and someone in a private motor was offerin' to give 'em both a lift home.

" 'Where for?' asked the newcomer, a red-faced, jolly sort of man, with white whiskers and a perfect suit of whites.

" 'Prinz Heinrich,' said the Tuan Besar, mechanically, and then he nearly jumped with delight—the girl was bound for that boat too!

"The next mornin', after breakfast, Cunningham was limpin' along the first-class deck, swearin' at a German steward who was followin' behind with his deck-chair, when he spotted the girl of the previous evenin' sittin' all alone in a corner, readin' a sixpenny novel. He hadn't had much opportunity of lookin at her before, his leg had given him too much to think about, and a girl don't naturally look her best when she's tryin' to stop herself from cryin' with pain. But now he could see her as she really was, and, gad! she did look fine! Small, and just sufficiently plump she was, with pretty, fair hair, and a wonderful complexion—for the East.

"She was wearin' a broad pith topi, and beautifully-cut white costume, and the ankles that just peeped out from under her skirt were perfect—perfect!

"Cunningham stood for a moment spell-bound, and then she turned and caught sight of him. The stolid German steward had been on trips like this before, and, dumpin' the deck-chair down right next to hers, cleared off, almost forgettin' to put out his hand for the forty-cent piece Cunningham chucked at him.

" 'Tabi!' said the Tuan Besar after an awkward pause. He felt quite out of place standin' there with those clear blue eyes seemin' to look into his very soul. And Cunningham wasn't a bad thing to look at, either—as men go. He was tall and broad, and as strong as a bull-kerbau, his face was tanned, and his moustache neatly trimmed.

" 'How can I thank you?' she said at last. 'You saved my life!'

"Cunningham was every inch a gentleman, but the East isn't the best school for manners.

" 'If my coolie had been sober,' he said, 'there would have been no need for what I did.'

" 'Had it not been for you,' she replied, with a smile, 'I should not have been here at all.'

" 'May I sit down?' asked Cunningham—and he did.

"When two young people of opposite sexes are thrown together on a seven-days' journey, with nobody else about to matter, things are apt to progress somewhat rapidly.

"Well, these two breakfasted, dined, and tea'd together, listened to the band, and talked together all day and a good part of the night. At Penang, where they arrived next day, they drove round together in a car Cunningham managed to hire, and dined at a club he had once been a member of. They bought all kinds of little rinchik-rinchik (odds and ends), and Cunningham made her a present of a queer little bangle in silver, with three moonstones, beautifully set. They returned to the boat that night, each thinkin' the other the nicest friend they'd met, and Cunningham nearly ruined the deck-steward's table by hackin' open a green cocoa-nut with a native axe in order that she might taste the juice.

"On the way to Colombo he learnt how it was she was trav'lin' alone. She was holdin' the position of governess in a colonel's family, and was takin' the trip while her employer was makin' a friendly call in Hong Kong. She had been asked to accompany the family, but preferred a few weeks away from her charges. Incidentally she mentioned that she hated the children and her work, and but for the prospect of unemployment would have journeyed home months before.

"They hired another motor when they reached Colombo, and drove out to Mount Lavinia together. They did the native quarters and the Cinnamon Gardens the next day, and finished up with dinner at the Galle Face Hotel. He insisted on her acceptin' innumerable presents of native silks and laces and table-centres worked in metal and coloured thread. He bought her one of those great, shinin' blue beetles, mounted in gold, and both were very sorry when the time came for them to go aboard the 'Zeitman' for the return journey.

"They stood together at the stern and waved a long farewell to that spicy-smellin' pink-an'-white city, with its beautiful fringe of palm-girt shores, and, somehow or other, when they both turned to find their chairs—they suddenly discovered they were holdin' hands!

"She blushed, and drew hers away, and Cunningham found somethin' peculiar he hadn't noticed before in the colour of the sea.

"It was dark when they reached Penang again, about a week later, and they stood together watchin' the phosphorescent light dancin' on the waters and the crowd of native-manned, double-prowed sampans below them. Suddenly Cunningham put his arm round her and drew her to him. Nothin' was said, but she just yielded to his strong embrace, and their lips met. They stayed like that for fully a minute, till, suddenly, they heard a sharp cough comin' from somewhere near at hand. They sprang apart, and Cunningham clenched his fists and turned. He seemed to recognise that cough.

"There, standin' full in the glare of an electric deck-light, was the long, spare form of Talbot, whom he'd imagined potterin' about in his native school on the East Coast.

"He bowed to Cunningham, a nasty light in his cold grey eyes.

" 'Let me be the first to congratulate you, sir,' he said. 'It is certainly an improvement on your black wife in Borneo!'

"Barbara Stones, the girl he had held in his arms only a moment before, uttered a low moan an' fainted. He caught her before she fell, and the parson stepped off the gangway into a waitin' sampan, and rowed away shorewards, or I'm fully convinced Cunningham would have wrung his scraggy neck and thrown his ugly carcass to the sharks.

"It's just when everythin' seems desolate and blank that Nature has a queer way of assertin' herself and puttin' matters on a proper basis. Cunningham, sore at heart, and feelin' certain that Barbara would never look at him again, was pattin' her hands and throwin' water on her temples from a glass he'd collared from the bar, and she was just comin' round nicely, when a tiny little mosquito settled on his wrist, and bit! It was just that one kind of benatang (insect) that gives a man malaria, and Cunningham had been on the verge of it so long that this last bite sort of put the finishin' touch, and next day he was down in his cabin, absolutely ravin'. It's queer how soon a dose of fever can bowl you over.

"Barbara Stone was very shocked, of course, at what had leaked out about the man she loved; but she wasn't the sort of girl to run away and leave him without a chance of clearin' himself. She missed him next day at breakfast, and when midday makan came along and he hadn't put in an appearance, she went and found his steward, and, after that, the ship's doctor.

"In short, she appointed herself his nurse, superintended his removal from the boat to Raffle's when they reached Singapore next day, and resolved to hear his explanation as soon as he was well enough to offer one. If the parson's story were true, she told herself, she would leave him for ever and go down to a sour old age, teachin' other people's bad-tempered kids things they hadn't the least desire to know. But as it turned out, that knowin' little mosquito had just looked in at the right moment, for Barbara learnt from his lips, when in fever, what he'd have been too proud to confess when well. Lyin' in his bed at Raffle's, he raved almost incoherently about the plantation and the loneliness of it all, about his long struggle against circumstance, and his eventual defeat. Then he talked about her—and the difference her comin' into his life had made, and soon she understood and was satisfied. She bent down over him, her pretty cheeks streamin', and kissed his burnin' forehead many times.

"About a week later, towards evenin', a red umbrella bobbed up the steep path from the railway and stopped outside Cunningham's bungalow. Marani, surprised at her work, gathered up her rotan and a half-finished basket, and retreated hastily across the wide verandah, a wicked light in her dark eyes. Talbot either did not notice how she looked, or failed to understand how much she hated him. He mounted the steps and came towards her, smilin' in his queer, unpleasant manner. She shrank back against the wall, and Talbot, in his maudlin' kind of way, suddenly put his hand upon her shoulder, intendin' no doubt, to tell her all he'd seen when in Penang.

"Marani was no longer a shrinkin', cringin' little school-girl; she was a woman grown, with a woman's fears and feelin's—and I think she must have suspected somethin' evil. Anyhow, no sooner had those long, cold fingers touched her naked shoulder than her hand flew swiftly to her hair, and—well, I don't know if you know it, but Tamil girls carry daggers in their hair!"

The tall man whistled. "And so Marani never heard about Miss Barbara?" he said.

"Never a word, for as soon as she realised the awful thing she'd done, Marani gathered up her barang (luggage) and fled into the jungle—and Cunningham never set eyes on her again."

III

THE GIFT OF THE GOD

I

WAY BACK WHERE white man's foot had never trod, nestling in a clearing hewn out of the dense jungle by shining native parangs, lay a sleepy village of short, dark-skinned Muruts. There were perhaps thirty houses in all, half raised on poles firmly founded in the soil, half standing high out of the muddy waters of the winding Ayer river in a long irregular line like a clumsy flock of antediluvian creatures cooling their long thin legs in the stream.

Between the river and the dense tropic forest on the other bank stretched a long narrow strip of flooded padi-land, and there, standing knee-deep in water, eight or nine Murut women, with neatly coifed hair and sarongs gathered carefully up, rapidly made the necessary holes in the mud for the young green shoots and planted them with marvellous rapidity and exactness. All were short and broad-faced and very plain, according to Western notions, except one. Kami was taller than her toiling companions and very erect. Her features were finer and her nose less broad; her lips were thinner and her figure more supple. She worked far ahead of her dusky sisters, and her deft fingers plied the planting stick unerringly.

As she laboured all through the intense heat of the tropic afternoon she hummed a plaintive native air, occasionally breaking forth into a wail, now loud, now dying down again, rising and falling until the sun went down in the west. Then the women gathered up the few remaining shoots which lay in their folded sarongs and laughingly raced through the brown water to the bank.

A man was leading a water-buffalo across the river, splashing the stream with a flat piece of wood to keep lurking crocodiles away, a big hawk wheeled overhead, and a score of almost nude wood-cutters, their parangs hanging from their waists, appeared suddenly in the clearing by the houses. Occasionally a woman would stagger in with a sack of cocoa-nuts or jack-fruit, followed by two or three naked children. The work of the day was finished, and an old wizened figure was fidgeting with the material for a watch-fire. A pariah dog sniffed at the root of a cocoa-palm, and then began digging furiously with his front paws.

The sound of a gong broke upon the night, and the booming of its deep, rich note caused a sudden hush among the chattering Muruts.

"Kami is playing," they said. "She is sad to-night."

It was a wonderful sound, soothing and yet mournful, like the deeper notes of a harp. The loiterers in the clearing sank to the ground, and, huddling round the blazing watch-fire, smoked queer bamboo pipes and listened. Two young girls seated near one another beat their hands together in time and laughed.

A wizened form, his bones twisted with acute rheumatism, climbed awkwardly down a rickety bamboo ladder and joined the figures squatting in the circle of light from the fire. One of the girls sprang nimbly to her feet and ran to assist him. She held him gently under the arms and lowered him tenderly to a sitting posture.

"There, bapa," she said. "You will feel better where it is warm."

The old man's clawlike hands fidgeted with a blackened bamboo pipe and a bag of fibrous tobacco which was suspended from his waist.

"Kami is playing," he muttered suddenly. "She is beating the old, old gong that I can remember her mother playing on feast days; yes, and her grandmother before that. Nobody knows how old that gong is, but the story goes that once, when the jungle was young, a god was passing on his way through the woods towards the riverside. He was tired and hungry—very hungry—and forgot the perils lurking in the shadows. And there came from a cocoa-palm an orang-outang—the wild man of the woods—and he followed the god in the tree-tops, hurling branches down at him. He threw many kelapa (cocoa-nuts) as well, and the god fled from the fury of his attack. There was a young Murut called Samarin ploughing his field of padi, and he heard the roars of the infuriated orangoutang and the cries of the fleeing god. He left his kerbau (water-buffalo) and his wooden plough and crossed the river to his house. Here he found his sumpitan and crept with it into the dense undergrowth. The huge orang sprang down to the ground, his terrible claws buried in the neck and breast of the god—and then Samarin puffed a poisoned dart with aim so true that the creature loosened his grasp and with a mighty roar fell dead."

The listeners in the warm glow of the firelight gazed at the dusky patriarch in wonder. The two girls had long ceased playing with their hands, and now sat very erect, their plump black arms about one another, their mouths opened, eagerly taking in every word that fell from the aged lips. A monkey slipped from a bough above with a shrill cry of fear, caught a lower branch as it fell, and scrambled back again. A huge flying beetle wheeled into the circle and was gone. A hen clucked sleepily on its perch under an adjacent house.

The old man puffed for a few moments, coughed wheezily, and then went on again.

"And the god rose from the ground where he had fallen, and his eye fell on Samarin, who stood, sumpitan in hand, surveying the monster he had slain. He took him by the hand and told him that for his bravery and skill he would be well rewarded; then he went on his way soon after with food and milk Samarin had given him. Samarin returned to his work, and later in the day he skinned the huge orang. When he was cutting it up in portions, so that he could more easily carry it away, he saw something bright protruding from the enormous ribs—"

The old man stopped suddenly and puffed. His pipe had gone out while he was talking. He slowly drew a lighted piece of wood from the fire and inhaled deeply. One of the girls looked at the other and smiled.

"It was a jewel," she said, "a precious stone."

"What was it, bapa?" asked her companion.

"It was not a jewel, my child, but a huge brass gong, and how it had come there nobody knew; but Samarin handed it down to his son, and he, in his turn, to his, until at last it comes that Kami is playing it to us to-night. Listen, my children. Is it not richer far in tune than the others she beats? It is the gift of a god to his preserver, and it brings its possessor good fortune."

The old man dropped his pipe, his head fell suddenly upon his breast, and he dozed. The Muruts drew closer to the blaze, and the two girls rose swiftly and ran to their dwellings.

"It is a wonderful story," whispered one man to another. "I have never heard him tell it before."

"It is better seldom told," said an older man meaningly, "or the gong would not remain long where it is, and luck would leave the village."

Beyond the circle of light, balancing carefully in a large dug-out canoe pushed in among the tall river reeds, a dark figure was standing erect, listening eagerly to the conversation. He was too brown for a Murut, but he understood their dialect, as he knew all others around, for he traded in cloths and pretty trinkets and strings of many-coloured beads. He told wonderful tales, too, of men with white skins who came from afar in ships without sails; but this story he had heard as he hid in the rushes was far more interesting to him than any he had ever told or heard tell of before.

"The gong brings its owner success," he murmured to himself, "and Kami is very beautiful. I must think well over this."

He sat down suddenly in the bottom of his boat and puffed thoughtfully at a metal pipe.

The Muruts crept into their houses one by one, the watch-fire died slowly down, and still he smoked and thought. There was no one watching in the clearing now, but a solitary watchman dozing on his spear quite fifty yards from the bank.

Again he heard a low throbbing sound just audible in the intense stillness of the tropic night.

"The gong!" he muttered. "The gift of the god!"

From a hut rising out of the still waters on eight thin poles, the figure of a girl suddenly emerged. She held the heavy instrument by leathern thongs, and drummed softly on its surface with the fingers of the other hand.

The silent watcher in the big canoe gasped.

"Kami!" he said under his breath. "How beautiful she looks!"

The girl came half-way down the frail ladder and seated herself in such a position that one foot could just dip in the dark waters. Her black hair she had undone, and it fell in great waves over her neck and shoulders. She brushed it away from her lustrous eyes with a dainty hand and then commenced drumming softly on the gong once more. It was an old piece of metalwork, as the aged Murut had said, bluey-grey with rust and mould; but it fascinated Mamut, the trader, as he gazed from the reeds by the riverside. An hour passed, and still the maiden drummed softly on the ancient gong, and Mamut watched, drawing his sarong closer round him.

He could not sleep for sight of her and for the knowledge of what he had heard the old man say. A spirit within him murmured incessantly: "The gong! The gong! It will bring you success!"

He started. The girl was nodding sleepily, lulled by the music she herself was playing. Gradually her fingers ceased to move. She was asleep. Surely this could not be his chance, his opportunity, so soon? The gong was lying in her lap, the leathern thongs twisted twice round her supple wrist. He dug the paddle into the bank and pushed out into mid-stream, then he softly manipulated his canoe until it stopped at the foot of the ladder on which the beautiful Kami dozed.

Should he cut the thongs? Perhaps she would wake and give the alarm. And she looked so beautiful as she slept—so tempting. He swore under his breath and sprang nimbly on to the ladder. He could not help it—he must take the player with the instrument.

Kami opened her eyes and started up. A lithe, dark form was bending over her. She opened her mouth to scream, but a cloth was suddenly flung over her face, almost stifling her. Then two strong arms lifted her easily and bore her down until she lay uncomfortably on some hard surface. She felt a gentle rocking, and then the swishing of swiftly passing waters broke upon her ears. She tried to rise, but a strong arm pushed her back, and still the swirling waters rushed by. The cloth around her nostrils smelt strangely, and soon she was dozing gently off to sleep again.

When she awoke it was broad daylight and the birds were singing in the overhanging trees. There was no cloth on her face now, and opposite to her, paddling vigorously, between densely wooded banks, sat Mamut, the Dusun trader.

He smiled as she gazed at him in astonishment.

"So it was you," she said softly.

"Yes, my Kami. It was I who took you so roughly from your father's house. I heard you playing on a gong, and your music fascinated me; and then you fell asleep, and the sight of your beautiful hair blowing in the night wind tempted me too sorely, and so I stole you away."

The girl put one dark hand over the side of the canoe and let it trail in the bubbling waters.

"If you had asked me," she whispered, "it would have been just the same, for I was weary of the Kampon and old men's tales."

She laughed suddenly aloud and drew a necklace of bright beads from a bundle at her feet. She dropped it over her head and lifted the flowing hair till the ornament fell lightly round her neck. Then she skilfully rolled her hair into a queer cylinder and fastened it in position with a strip of rotan.

"Am I not beautiful?" she asked, looking at him from beneath half-closed lids.

"Very beautiful, my Kami," said the Dusun trader, and plied the primitive paddle still more vigorously. Suddenly the girl started, a troubled look came over her face, and she felt about her in search of something.

"My gong!" she cried hoarsely. "What have you done with it?"

"It is here," replied the trader calmly. "I feared you might lose it in the water as you slept."

Kami stretched out her beautiful arms and took it from him.

"It is old," she said, "and worthless—except to me. I love its beautiful note. Listen."

The deep rich throbbing of the beaten metal echoed in the stillness of the jungle on either side. The girl stopped suddenly and bent down.

"I am your slave," she said, and kissed the hem of his sarong.

II

Hubert Connolly lay at full length on a long cane chair by the flight of steps which led from his broad verandah to the ground. He wore a bright sarong of Java dye and a gauze singlet open at the neck. Every now and then he dropped the magazine he was reading into his lap and scratched his calves furiously. At last he rose impatiently and went in search of another sarong. He flung himself into his chair again and wrapped the second cloth round his feet and legs.

"Now bite, you little devils!" he muttered savagely, addressing the myriads of tiny sand-flies hovering thirstily round him.

"Never knew such a year for the brutes," he said, filling his briar from an open tin by his side. "I'm one darned mass of itching lumps and sores. I wish to heaven I was on my way home. Let's see. What's to-day? Friday, May 14. H'm! Fourteen long boiling months yet before that six months' furlough comes along. Ah, well, I suppose it'll pass by somehow. Eh? What d'you want?"

This last remark was addressed to a blue-coated Mandor (Chinese overseer) who stood, hat in hand, his fingers twitching nervously on the brim.

"Orders, Tuan, for to-morrow."

"Orders? Oh, I forgot. Well, take your gang of men and weed between the trees on that slope—ci-blas-sana (right over there). Tahu?"

"Yah, Tuan."

Connolly sprang to his feet, and, seizing a boot that happened to be handy, hurled it full at the Mandor's head. The Mandor dodged and then ran humbly to pick the missile up.

"Undo that tow-chung (pig-tail), you kiti!" he bellowed. The trembling Mandor saluted, and, loosening the offending tow-chung, stole softly round the corner of the bungalow. It is a terrible insult to address a white man with the pig-tail rolled up.

The planter returned to his chair and smoothed his fair hair placidly.

"I suppose the idiot forgot," he said, "but it doesn't do to tolerate anything of that sort. Hullo! More trouble!"

A turbaned Pathan in a brilliant uniform—khaki with red facings—was leading an unfortunate coolie towards the bungalow by the ear. In one hand the watchman carried a long bamboo pipe.

"Makan chandu, Tuan Besar (smoking opium)," he explained shortly.

"When?" asked Connolly, looking round for his malacca.

"This afternoon, Tuan. He feigned sickness in the konzses (coolie lines) and did not go out to work."

The manager found the heavy cane and came down from the verandah. He seized the wretch by one arm and thrashed him unmercifully, heedless of the torrent of uncouth cries. He confiscated the pipe and some opium screwed up in a strip of palm-leaf and gave the unfortunate Chinaman back into the watchman's charge.

"Cut him three days," he said.

This is an illegal custom occasionally practised. A coolie is engaged by contract for three hundred days. To cut him three days actually means the addition of three days to his contract time without extra remuneration. On many Borneo plantations opium smoking is a dire offence.

The dark-skinned wretch who slunk away from Connolly's bungalow was frightfully emaciated. His bones seemed about to protrude through the parchment-like skin, and his clothes were badly patched in materials of every hue in the rainbow.

"Ugh!" ejaculated the Tuan Besar. "It's a dirty job and demoralising, but it's got to be done. Kindness is lost on the brutes."

The sun was fast disappearing into the sea a couple of miles to the westward. Connolly shouted for whisky and a syphon.

"I hope to goodness there are no more disturbances tonight," he said. "I'm sick of it all."

The sound of heavy footsteps broke upon his ear, and a huge white figure strode into view, whistling gaily, a couple of dogs trotting after him.

"Hullo, Connolly!"

"Hullo, Bates!"

The newcomer stepped on to the verandah just as the boy hurried in with the whisky.

"Thirsty house this!" he remarked.

The manager laughed.

"Bring another glass—lakas (quickly)," he said. The boy disappeared and the assistant threw off his coat. He sat down in a heavy contraption of wood and canvas, known as a "Borneo chair," and reached for the manager's tin of tobacco.

"I like a properly equipped bungalow," he said. "Decent-looking baccy this, too." He filled a very blackened briar and put the tin down again.

"Nice and cool this evening," said Connolly. "I hear your men have been doing well with the planting of the new slope."

"Not so dusty," replied the assistant, puffing amiably. "I also had Ah-Kit's forty-two weeding—padjak-work (piecework), you know. Gave them each seventy trees. Pays that way, I find. Ah, here's my glass."

They drank to the prosperity of the new slope of rubber, and Bates threw his topi neatly on to a nail on the wall some distance away.

After a moment he said: "I've pretty near finished the building of the new bungalow over there, and I intend occupying it shortly. When the third man comes out he can have the one I am now living in. You see, now the work's so far away, it means such a devil of a journey before I can sail comfortably on to the scene of action."

The manager nodded.

"It's lonely enough here," he said, "but what it'll be like over there I scarcely like to think."

"I know, old man. I've thought of that. Still, I've got my dogs and a new gramophone."

"I often wonder you don't buy a ngi (housekeeper)," said Connolly. "You do get a sort of companionship then, you know."

"Haven't seen anything I fancy yet, old chap. It'd have to be a jolly pretty black face that'd attract me. By the by, I intend burning that four-hundred-acre bit I've just had felled. If all's well I'll put a few men on to it next week."

"Not more than six coolies each end, then," said the Tuan Besar, "and put a watchman in charge of half of them. You know what damned idiots sinkies (unskilled coolies) are. They'd be sure to burn one of their number if you left 'em to themselves."

Bates knocked out his pipe on the heel of his brown canvas shoe and nodded.

"I know," he said.

III

Two days later the burly assistant twirled his long moustache and surveyed the landscape from his new abode. The wood smelt fresh and resinous, and there was a strong odour of tar into which all the poles of the house had been carefully dipped to prevent rot. It was a neat, well-made bungalow, and the furniture, constructed by the convicts at Sandakan, was strong and very solid. A square deal table stood in the centre of the verandah, and blue sun-blinds covered the front and sides, leaving only the doorway open to the light. A large clock ticked high up on the wall, and a crowded collection of horns formed a kind of barbaric frieze.

Bates stood by the door and gazed around him. All the hill on which the house stood was as bare and desolate as a ploughed field, carefully weeded and only requiring lining-out and planting. To the right, on a farther slope, the jungle had been recently felled, and a long string of coolies was winding its way from that side to the path which led to the recently constructed coolie lines. To the left was the end of the older portion of the estate, and there the trees were green and some almost eight feet high. Straight ahead, at the foot of the slope, was a sago-swamp, a strip of virgin jungle, and then the turbid waters of the Ayer river. On the nearer bank there rose a solitary native hut, surrounded by cocoa-palms.

Something was moving on the roof above him. He went out on to the step and looked up.

"Lord!" he ejaculated. "A snake already!" A venomous-looking, orange-coloured reptile, a yard and a half in length, was creeping stealthily along the freshly thatched ataps.

The assistant seized his malacca and struck it smartly on the head. It rolled off the roof, and an axe brought its career to a sudden termination.

The fox-terrier came out from under the house and sniffed at it suspiciously, then turned tail and ran quickly back.

"You don't like 'em, and I don't like 'em," said the brawny Bates. "Thank heaven it'll be dark soon. The atmosphere may be a trifle cooler then."

He mopped his brow with a coloured silk handkerchief and went indoors.

It was dark when he again came on to the verandah.

"Supposin' we have a song," he said, and started to wind up the gramophone.

Suddenly he stopped and listened. Far away in the valley a gong was throbbing, softly at first, and then gradually getting louder and louder. It was just one single note, but it held the listener spellbound. It was so rich, so mellow. He sat with his hands clasped between his knees, and the record on the machine remained unplayed.

"Gad, what a fine tone!" he cried. "I should like to have that gong for the people at home. Fancy having that to summon you to dinner. It'd give a dyspeptic old colonel an appetite."

And then he was silent again, for across the silent valley there came the faint, sweet notes of a woman's voice—singing. The air was plaintive and sad, but very sweet, and all the time the gong throbbed out a hushed accompaniment.

As Bates turned into bed that night he made a firm resolution.

"I'll track down the dark minstrel," he said, "and if her face is as sweet as her playing, I swear by all that's holy I'll bring her here to share my solitude."

He kicked his rug to the foot of the bed and listened to make sure no impudent mosquito had stolen into his curtains unawares.

"Anyhow, I want that gong," he murmured, turned over, and went to sleep.

The following morning he strode out and superintended the commencement of the day's work, allotting a task to each toiling gang. Having assured himself that everything was going as well as possible on his side of the wide Kabun, he left the estate and made for the bank of the Ayer river. He followed the stream, pushing his way through reeds and lalang and coarse undergrowth—always with a keen eye for lurking reptiles—until at last he came to the little palm grove, in the centre of which stood the native house he had seen from his bungalow the night before.

He advanced boldly towards the ladder which led up to the tiny doorway. He was about to shout to the master of the house to put in an appearance immediately, when he caught sight of a bright green sarong beyond the building. He strolled leisurely in the direction of the brilliant piece of colouring and eventually came face to face with a beautiful, dark-skinned woman seated on the ground weaving a mat.

She looked up, half shyly, half in fear; but his frank smile reassured her, and she revealed a perfect set of white teeth.

"What is your name?" he asked in Malay.

"Kami," replied the girl, casting down her lustrous eyes.

"Kami, eh? That's a pretty name. Where do you come from?"

A shadow crossed her face.

"S-a-ana, Tuan." She waved her hand vaguely to indicate infinity. Bates leaned against a post of the little house and surveyed the progress of the woven mat.

"Who is it plays so prettily on the gong?" he asked suddenly.

The girl smiled and looked down again.

"Sihaya (I), Tuan," she said.

The assistant picked up a fragment of rotan and began tying it into knots.

"Are you married?" She looked up sharply.

"Yah, Tuan," she whispered. "Mamut, the trader, is my husband."

Bates twisted the rotan into a figure eight and squinted thoughtfully at it, then he flicked an ant from his sleeve and stood away from the wall.

"Are you happy with him?" he ventured after a long pause.

The girl did not answer for a moment. From under her long lashes she swiftly surveyed the white Tuan, his powerful physique, his handsome face, the gold watch on his strong wrist.

"He beats me sometimes, Tuan," she said.

"Does he, the brute!" muttered Bates to himself.

He threw her a cigarette and strolled away.

"I shall come back again—soon," he cried, waving his long malacca. The girl sighed, watched until he was out of sight, and then turned to her mat-making again.

"He likes to hear me play," she said. "He is rich and powerful, and perhaps white men do not beat their p'rempuan (women). Yah, I shall play to him every night till he returns."

And Mamut, as he paddled his big canoe from village to village, selling his wares for much more than they were ever worth, dealing in kind or cash transactions, according to the distance of each Kampon from civilisation, was beginning to tire of wedded life. In the first instance the old wizened gossip of the camp-fire must most certainly have lied, for the trader found himself not a whit more prosperous than when he trod the blissful paths of bachelordom. As a matter of fact he found himself, with a wife to provide for and a home to keep up, rather poorer in pocket than he had even been before. And so, when able to spend a few days with Kami, he found her society boring, and then he beat her and told her she was useless to him and a drag on his purse, and threatened often to leave her altogether.

So Kami, when her lord and master was away, beat her gong with a cloth-bound bamboo rod and sang her plaintive lay to the desolate jungle, the deep swamps, and to a certain white Tuan who dwelt in a beautiful new bungalow on an adjacent hill-top. And Bates remembered what his chief had told him—that he ought to seek a companion in his solitude. Every evening at sundown the full rich notes throbbed out across the valley until an intense longing seized him, and he heartily wished the dark-skinned trader might never return. One evening he strolled down to the solitary house by the riverside. He was too wise and too wary to think of stealing the wife of a native neighbour, but he saw no harm in talking with her when her brutal husband chanced to be away.

He tiptoed through the lalang and under the shady palms, looking eagerly round him for his dusky charmer. She had seen him coming from afar, and, darting suddenly out from behind a broad tree-trunk, ran a few paces and laughingly glanced round at him, expecting him to follow.

Her flesh shone like ebony, her hair was like a raven's wing, her teeth were white as pearls, and the silver ornaments jingled temptingly on her dainty ankles and graceful neck.

The planter stood, dazzled with her loveliness, in the centre of the little clearing, his fists clenched, his breath coming and going in short gasps. Her beauty had him fast enthralled. Prudence was flung to the winds. Darkness fell. He cried out aloud, sprang forward a few paces, caught the fleeting form in his strong arms, and, lifting her from her feet, rained passionate kisses on her lips, her eyes, and her neck. She clung to him unresistingly, lifting her beautiful face like a child for his caress.

IV

As the dawn came up Mamut rested on his paddle and thought very deeply. Should he go home to his beautiful plaything or turn his back on married life for ever? It was but a simple thing to reverse the big canoe and paddle away into the beyond. He could have a p'rempuan at every village if he chose, for they all loved to hear his wonderful tales and to handle his bright wares. His eye fell suddenly upon a brass dice-box of Chinese pattern. Within there was a tiny cube of wood, half black, half red.

"This shall decide," he said, and shook it vigorously. "If the red is towards me, I go home; if the black half, then I shall never return to Kami and the little house beneath the palms."

He rattled the box again and lifted off the brass cover. "It is the red—I shall go home."

He took up the paddle again, and, rounding the bend, pushed the canoe in among the reeds. Then he leaped nimbly ashore, and strode towards his house.

He stopped and listened. Voices—and one was that of a man! Fury surged into his breast. A man in Kami's room! She had betrayed him! He spat furiously and felt in his sarong for something. Then he stole under the house and listened again.

A white Tuan was speaking. A cold shudder ran down Mamut's spine, great beads of perspiration stood out on his dark forehead. And the Fates had told him to come home. It was in order that he should witness this—his wife's unfaithfulness. And then Mamut went mad.

It was six o'clock by Bates' watch as he strapped it on his wrist after giving it a few careful turns. He tapped sundry creeping things from his topi, seized his malacca, and, ignoring the steep bamboo ladder, leaped to the soft soil below. Kami knelt by the doorway watching him. The waiting Mamut crouched, sprang suddenly upon his white rival with a furious inarticulate yell, and struck him in the back with his sharp kris. The undulating blade pierced the khaki coat, and by a stroke of good fortune encountered the brass plate at the back of the webbing braces the planter wore in preference to a belt.

The kris slipped and gashed the flesh badly. Bates uttered a wild oath, turned, caught up his assailant, and hurled him several yards. The trader fell half against the foot of a tree and half along the ground and curled up with a groan.

Kami ran screaming from the house. She did not even glance at the silent form by the palm tree, but turned to assist her white lover, whose khaki coat was stained with fast-flowing blood. She flew back for water and white cloth from the trader's store, and Bates, dizzy from loss of blood, crawled into the shadow of the house, stripped to the waist, and allowed her to bathe his wound. He gave her instructions how to form an efficient temporary bandage, pulled on his stained singlet, and buttoning up his khaki coat strode across to look at his assailant.

"He's only stunned, I think," he cried in Malay. "What are you going to do?"

She stood by the ladder looking shyly at him, and then laughed. "Do you still wish for me?" she asked.

Bates cocked his topi over one eye, looked hard at his cane from end to end, and nodded.

"It's lonely up there," he said.

"Bi-la! I shall come soon," she whispered, and ran into the house. He was about to turn away in the direction of his bungalow when she called. He swung round on his heel as she hurried after him. In one hand she held a Chinese cup of samsu; in the other the wonderful gong, the tone of which he had so admired. She made him drink the hot native spirit, which burned his throat considerably, and then handed him the gong.

"Take it," she said, "and keep it safely for me, or he will steal it again." She jerked her thumb in the direction of the form beneath the tree.

"Tuan, you must go," she whispered, and, pushing him gently, ran up the steps and disappeared.

Bates, feeling less faint since drinking the strong spirit, stepped briskly out in the direction of his new home.

Kami waited till the planter was well out of sight, then, tying her barang into a bundle, slipped down the ladder to the ground. She seized a large kerosene tin and dipped it into the river, then she ran across and hurled the contents over her husband's face and neck. The trader stirred and presently rubbed his eyes. Kami stole softly to where her bundle lay, threw it across her back, and disappeared into the jungle hard by.

Mamut staggered to his feet twenty minutes later and looked vacantly around him. He crawled to the river and dipped his head many times in the cooling waters, then he drew himself up, and remembered. He found his kris stained with blood lying on the ground where it had fallen, and he called aloud:

"Kami! Kami!"

There was no answer.

"Bi-la!" he said wearily. "She has gone to the white Tuan's bungalow. I shall find her soon."

He regarded his weapon lovingly, wiped it in the grass, and hid it carefully in his sarong, then he crept indoors to eat. Two hours later he climbed an ill-frequented path among the recently felled trees to a spot where he could command a good view of the planter's house.

"I shall strike again, O white Tuan," he muttered hoarsely, "only this time my aim will be sure."

A sudden drowsiness stole over him, and he hid himself between two parallel logs and slept. All unwittingly he had placed himself in the hands of his enemy, for it was this very morning that Bates had given orders to burn the recently hewn jungle. Hidden carefully from sight, the trader slept on as the two bands of coolies fired the grass at either end of the slope. In the absence of the assistant, two stalwart watchmen kept the coolies well in hand, and soon a raging furnace blazed to the very heavens.

Bamboo spluttered and exploded on all sides like the ceaseless rattle of musketry, monkeys shrieked and fled where they could, and huge snakes, hissing venomously, stole swiftly through the fast-blazing grass to the ever-increasing circle of flame and death.

Lying on his side in his long chair, heavily bandaged, the planter watched with keen satisfaction the progress of the jungle fire. It burned merrily all that day and far on into the night, and Bates knew it would be by far the most successful "burn" he had tried, and would save the estate many thousand dollars' worth of labour.

As the darkness fell a slender form stole on to the broad verandah, and a dainty hand fell upon the planter's arm.

"I have come," she whispered, "forever."

She sat at the foot of his chair and regarded him tenderly.

"Tuan is ill," she said soothingly; "but the kris was clean, and the Tuan will be better in the morning."

Bates bent forward and stroked her luxuriant hair.

Two days later a watchman approached the bungalow at breakfast time. He saluted and waited respectfully till the assistant chose to address him.

"Apa mahu? (What d'you want?)" demanded Bates, his mouth full of banana.

"Native man burned in the fire, Tuan," replied the Pathan.

"Sure it wasn't a coolie?"

"Yah, Tuan. It was Mamut, the Dusun trader."

Bates started back and whistled.

"Are you certain?" he asked.

The watchman handed up a blackened kris.

Bates took it gingerly and then tossed it on to the table. He looked at the Pathan keenly.

"Mind, not a word to anyone of this," he said. "It would not sound well in Api-Api."

The watchman saluted and disappeared, and Bates stood by the verandah rail for a long while thinking deeply. He had been not a little uneasy since Kami had come to him, fearing the many unpleasant consequences he felt certain must ensue—to say nothing of a law-suit brought by the enraged husband and the scandal it would cause in Api-Api. And now Mamut was dead and his mind set at rest. He tapped a cigarette on the rail and lit it mechanically, then he turned and called:

"Kami!"

"Yah, Tuan." The reply came from an inner room.

"Mari sini (come here). I have news for you."

The girl came slowly from the bedroom, still fastening her sarong.

"Mamut is dead," he said, looking into her eyes.

She laughed merrily, and sat on the end of a long cane chair. "Of course," she replied shortly.

Bates was puzzled.

"Why of course?" he demanded, his brows contracting.

She played with her necklace of big glass beads for a moment and then said:

"I told you he beat me—many times."

The planter did not reply.

"My gong—the gift of a god to my ancestor—is always looking after me," she whispered. "It is I who play it, who look after it well; and, while I am kind to it, it will surely take care of me. The wise men of my village have always told me so."

"That's all damn nonsense!" Bates cried out in English, then in Malay he said: "Kami, I do not believe you. The gong is brass, a beautifully toned instrument—but that is all."

The girl shrugged her shoulders.

"Still, Mamut is dead," she replied obstinately.

"Mamut is dead," cried the planter irritably. "He was imprisoned in the circle of fire and could not escape. He might have known I don't have four hundred acres felled for the mere fun of the thing. He was sleeping more likely than not."

"He was hiding in the trees," said Kami very slowly. "He was waiting till evening and watching the Tuan to kill him—and Kami also. I know him well, Tuan. He would never forget."

Bates started.

"Perhaps she's right," he muttered.

He took up his stick and topi and went out across the estate towards the bungalow of the Tuan Besar.

Connolly heard his heavy footsteps on the hard path and threw down the paper he had been reading. The assistant climbed the steps and sat down in the nearest chair.

"You look a bit seedy, old man," said the manager. "What'll you have to drink?"

"I am seedy," agreed Bates, "and I'll take lager, thanks. Some of that fresh lot you had in last week from Api-Api, if you don't mind."

The manager laughed. "Well, what's the trouble now?" he said.

Bates waited till the beer had put in an appearance and then told him the whole story—the fascination, the temptation, the murderous attack by the enraged husband, and Mamut's subsequent death in the jungle fire.

The manager listened patiently and then whistled.

"It was you who put the cursed idea into my head," declared the assistant. "You told me I wanted a companion in my loneliness."

"I know. And are you sorry you took my advice?"

Bates shook his head. "Not exactly," he said.

"Then what in the name of heaven have you to worry about? The girl's yours, the husband's dead, and you didn't kill him. He was in all probability waiting to give you your quietus when he fell into the trap. I know the man you mean, and a pretty fine specimen of native blackguard he was, too. Serve him damn well right, I say, and good luck to your new ngi."

"You're very cheerin'," said Bates, wiping his moustache as he put the empty glass back on to the deal table, "but you must remember I've still got a most unpleasant gash in my shoulder, and I'm scarcely able to see things in such a rosy light. However, perhaps you're right."

"I know I am," asserted Connolly. "Have some more beer." He poured out the sparkling lager.

"Funny thing is," continued Bates, "she seems to have expected her late husband's tragic end. When I told her about it she grinned, and said, 'Of course.'"

"Cold-blooded little devil!"

"Said something about her darned gong being an heirloom, endowed with most extraordinary powers."

The manager leaned back in his long krosi (chair) and laughed.

"They all talk like that," he said. "It's as natural to them as sentiment is to our women. Tell 'em the tallest ghost yarn and they'll take it all in—and add to it, in all probability. Don't you think any more of that, old man. And now to business. I want to congratulate you on that last 'burn' of yours. It's saved the estate no end of money. I glanced down your new slopes of rubber, too, as I rode past the other day. They're simply A-1. I'm putting a special word about you in my next mail home. You ought to get another fifty dollars a month—if the directors are feeling generous."

V

Bates toiled all the baking tropic days, rapidly improving his portion of the broad estate until at last the desolate landscape was lined with the rich, fresh green of thriving rubber-trees.

Line upon line they stretched from the bungalow steps to the sago-swamp, the commencement of the jungle, to the very riverside.

One dark night a kerbau (water-buffalo) broke the wire fence and trampled down many promising young trees. A watchman brought the news next morning, and the planter swore himself hoarse. He ordered the fences to be heightened and strengthened, but again the beast broke in, until at last every fresh morning brought news of further havoc.

Bates visited the neighbouring Kampons and threatened to shoot any kerbau he should find wandering untethered, but still the trouble continued. At last he summoned a trusty Pathan watchman and discussed with him all preventive measures he could think of.

The dark ex-soldier saluted humbly as he left the bungalow.

"Will the Tuan leave it in my hands?" he asked. "I have a notion, Tuan. I have trapped many wild animals in the Himalayas years ago."

Bates' brow straightened.

"I will give you a free hand," he cried, "and a hundred dollars into the bargain if you catch the brute."

The watchman went away and found a body of coolies busily weeding between the trees. He borrowed a dozen from the Mandor, and, arming them with spades, led them to where the greatest damage had been caused. Bates was on the other side of the slope all through the heat of the day, and when he returned the coolies had gone back to their weeding, and nothing of the proposed trap could be seen from the hilltop.

A touch of fever had made the planter very irritable.

Bates bawled lustily for whisky, and drank for some time in silence. Then Kami raised her cloth-covered bamboo rod and began to strum. The planter fidgeted with his feet in the long chair, swore, and then got up.

"Kami, stop that idiotic row!" he shouted suddenly.

The girl looked up at him, laughed, and went on playing. The blood flew to his head, and for a moment he stood watching her, growing more angry every minute.

"I told you to stop!" he roared. "Why the devil can't you do what you're told?"

The girl glanced up again, stopped playing, and then, a wicked little smile on her face, beat the old gong obstinately once, like a naughty child.

Bates seized his malacca, advanced a couple of steps, and struck her furiously across the shoulders. He had never raised a hand to her before. The girl started to her feet, stared strangely at him, and, bursting suddenly into tears, buried her beautiful dark face in her hands and fled from the broad verandah into the darkness outside.

Bates, a queer feeling within him, lurched into his krosi, and lay gazing stupidly at the wooden ceiling. He was heartily sorry for what he had done. He was ill, and he had lost sudden control of himself. He would tell her when she came back, and all would go smoothly again. Little rows of this kind often served to clear the air, he told himself. He waited many hours anxiously listening for her soft footsteps on the path, but dawn came up in the east and still Kami had not returned.

"She has gone to Mamut's house," he said. "I will go at once and bring her back."

He went into his room and bathed his aching head. There were large blue rings under his eyes, and his hand shook with fever. He swallowed a tabloid of quinine, washing it down with a glass of lager; then he took his topi and stick and strode down the steps.

He took the path between the rubber which led towards the Ayer river. Suddenly a break in the surface of the soil to his right attracted his attention. The watchman's trap, he told himself—a pit covered with frail poles and concealed by turf and bushes. The kerbau must be trapped within, for the cover had been newly disturbed. He ran across the well-weeded slope in sudden excitement.

"Now we've got you, you brute!" he muttered to himself, and peered into the deep pit. It was dark within, but he knew there was no kerbau there. He tore away the matted boughs and looked again. Then he staggered back, uttered a wild cry, and covered his face with his hands. He had seen the figure of Kami lying cold and still, impaled on the bamboo spikes a dozen feet below.

That evening he sat on his broad verandah, rocking to and fro in silent agony.

"My beautiful Kami?" he cried at last. "It was I who drove her to her death!"

The darkness came on and the lamps were lit, and still Bates sat gazing absently across the desolate verandah.

Suddenly he started and sat sharply up. His hair rose on end and the blood ran cold in his veins.

The gong was throbbing softly where it hung, and there was nothing visible to cause the sound. Louder and louder its deep note resounded, and Bates thrust his fingers in his ears, striving vainly to shut out the ghostly music.

"Stop!" he cried in agony. "Stop! Oh, my God! Stop! For heaven's sake, stop!"

But the gong throbbed on as it had been wont to throb when Kami had beaten it at the time they had been accustomed to retire. Then the booming ceased abruptly, and the frenzied planter staggered wildly to his lonely bed. As he lay awake the words of Kami came back to him across a short space of fleeting time. "My gong—the gift of an ancestor—is always looking after me." And he remembered the awful fate of the wretched Mamut.

The following evening as Bates waited, his eyes fixed strangely on the rusted gong, the booming commenced again.

"Oh, for pity's sake," he moaned, "not again."

The beating grew louder.

The huge assistant, maddened with grief and fever, sprang to his feet and tore the offending instrument from its thongs. He plunged with it under his arm down the steps and dashed into the darkness. Even in his grasp the hollow note resounded. He covered it with his khaki coat and ran for more than a mile. Then he stooped down and, digging with his hands in the soft soil, buried the gong at the foot of a rubber tree on Connolly's side of the Kabun. He turned and fled back to the lamp-lit verandah, the haunting music still playing in his ears. His nerves were strung to breaking point, and he sought solace in many glasses of strong spirit.

On the following evening Connolly was returning from a tour of inspection on his sturdy Borneo pony. Darkness had overtaken him, and a watchman walked by his bridle carrying a hurricane lamp. Suddenly the pony snorted and shied. Connolly, almost thrown from his seat, pulled furiously at the animal's head.

"What's that, watchman? Snake?"

"No snake, Tuan."

"Then what on earth's the matter with the brute?"

He pulled up and listened.

From somewhere below him there came a muffled boom. It sounded like a gong from the Kampon below, but the sound seemed close at hand.

The Pathan heard it too, for he put his ear suddenly to the ground. "In the earth, Tuan," he said at last. Nothing appeared to surprise him.

"In the ground? Impossible. It's a native gong beating."

The watchman said nothing, but shifted the soft soil with his stick. The loaded end struck something, and he scooped the earth away with his black hands.

He drew from its resting-place a large rusted gong, blue with age. He held it up in both hands. Suddenly it throbbed loudly, and he dropped it again at the foot of the rubber tree.

"What's the matter?" cried Connolly. "It's got a beautiful tone. I wonder how it got there."

"Tuan," gasped the unfortunate Pathan, "it is playing by itself. I have not touched it."

The instrument was humming softly now like an enormous flying beetle.

"It is the gong the Mem Kami used to play. I have heard she is dead, but the music still plays on. It is haunted, Tuan Besar."

The watchman clung to the pony's bridle in terror, and the startled beast snorted and pawed the air.

Connolly started. Kami was the name of Bates' woman. She was dead, and he had had no word of it from the assistant. What was the meaning of this strange phenomenon? Then he remembered a chance remark of Bates', when he had told of Kami's queer beliefs. "When I told her of her husband's death," a chord of memory brought back to him," she said, 'Of course.'"

A sudden fear seized him. He sprang from his mount and lifted the reverberating gong.

Then from the other side of the hill the loud echo of two pistol-shots in quick succession broke upon the intense stillness of the tropic night. There was a blinding flash—the gong bounded from his grasp and shivered into a thousand pieces.

IV

WAY BACK

I

A HUGE, SUNBURNT, heavily-bearded man sat by a pile of books on the open verandah of a Borneo bungalow. He wore riding-breeches, puttees, and a khaki shirt open at the neck. A gramophone with an enormous, much-battered horn stood on a small table in one corner, a scattered heap of records, some broken, some whole, lying on the boarded floor around it. The house was old and ramshackle, dirty inside and out; lalang, waist-high, surrounded it, through which a path had been trodden to the little railway line below. Lalang grew, in fact, everywhere. It had been allowed to spread and thrive among the ill-nourished, neglected rubber-trees. Occasionally a fast-diminishing band of emaciated coolies was ordered to clear a slope of the dread scourge; but soon the weed had grown as bad again, and now the great estate, once so promising, was fast falling to ruin under the sluggard hand of Alexander Grimwade.

He turned over half a dozen pages with a grimy finger, and then slammed the cover furiously down.

"By God!" he cried. "No one must ever see those. It'd mean gaol for me."

He drew himself up to his full height and thumped his broad chest with a great brown fist.

"Nobody shall see 'em!" he shouted, and, taking the pile in his arms, he shot them into the open safe and slammed the iron door.

He strode to the rail and looked gloomily out over the waving lalang and impoverished rubber trees to the wide stretch of virgin jungle which extended between the solitude of the Jelumpur kabun and the comparative civilisation of the tiny coast town.

Nine long years in Borneo without a single break! Seven years of struggle and hardship, then a chance stroke of luck bringing him the managership of the new estate.

Luck! Was it really that? Had not that sudden change in his affairs marked the commencement of his decline? Drink, then fever, and drink again, until at last the very day's programme spelt nothing else but these two. Then followed neglect of the kabun, and afterwards the secret use of the money entrusted to him, to meet the constant calls on his account that resulted from his ceaseless debauchery.

They had sent him two assistants. One came in April, and left again in October, vowing to expose him when he again reached London. Grimwade recollected with some satisfaction that he had pegged out before he saw even Singapore. The other man was quiet and uncomplaining. He tried hard to make things shipshape on his side of the slope, but Grimwade had been too much for him; he had stolen away at last during one of his master's prolonged periods of debauch, leaving the copy of his contract, torn in two, on the steps of Grimwade's verandah. After that he had cabled home asking them to send him no more help, as he had obtained two men locally. Of course he had not done so, but he drew their salaries, and there was nobody there to see. His mails, when he sent them, contained wonderful descriptions of a most promising estate, up-to-date buildings, and everything, in fact, that could delight a director's heart.

A tall, coal-black Tamil woman crept suddenly on to the verandah.

Grimwade turned.

"Apa Mahu (What do you want)?" he inquired savagely.

"Tida Mahu apa-apa (Nothing)," the woman wailed, and was about to disappear into an inner room when her master suddenly picked up a gramophone record and hurled it at her.

It whizzed past her head as she bent instinctively, and was shattered to atoms on the adjacent door-post. A fragment struck her face, causing the blood to flow. She uttered a low moan, and, one hand on her cheek, ran from the verandah, slamming the door after her.

"Temper, eh?" snarled the tyrant. "Temper—with me—you kiti! I'll teach you to slam doors!"

He strode across the floor, kicked his way into the room, and looked quickly round him for a suitable weapon. A heavy portmanteau caught his eye.

He seized a brass buckle and drew out a long, broad strap. The woman was stretched on the bed face downwards, moaning and rocking to and fro, a fragment of dirty rag over the recent cut. She uttered a shrill scream as the leathern strap rose and fell three times, cutting into the flesh where her highly-coloured sarong had slipped from her dark shoulders.

Grimwade strode out again, tossing the strap into a corner. He filled his pipe, struck a match, and puffed thoughtfully. The directors at home expected that in two years the trees would be ready to tap. Two years—that was the utmost length of his tether. He must amass as much money as he could in the time and then disappear. Where?

The deep blue of the tropic sky brought back to him a memory of palm-girt islands he had once seen in the South Seas. Yes, he would make his way to one of those havens of ceaseless sunshine as soon as he found Borneo becoming too hot for him. Lonely, certainly, but a great improvement on a British prison, anyhow, he told himself.

A sudden mouthful of nicotine caused him to splutter and spit into the lalang below. He looked up to find a timid Mandor (Chinese overseer) bowing and scraping on the overgrown pathway, his stained double terai hat in his hand.

"Well?"

"Coolie dead in the konzses (houses), Tuan."

"What in the name of hell d'you want to come and worry me for? Bury him—lakas (quickly)."

The Mandor fled hurriedly round the house as the Tuan Besar (manager) loosened his bootlace meaningly.

Grimwade smoked and thought till darkness fell. Leaning over the verandah rail, heedless of the shrill humming of many mosquitoes, he did not hear the bedroom door open behind him.

The Tamil woman stood in the shadow, an evil look on her dark face. She was feeling for something in her hair. Suddenly Grimwade glanced towards the clock, which ticked loudly on the wall by his side. The woman started back, glided noiselessly down the passage, and was gone.

The manager poured himself out a stiff glass of whisky, and shouted for soda and a lamp.

He did not know how near he had been to death that night.

Out in the lalang behind the house a tall Tamil woman was slipping something sharp and shining back into her coils of long black hair. She stood for a moment, her lips parted, revealing two rows of very white teeth, then she waved her hand menacingly in the air and disappeared into the darkness.

"Mirima! Mirima! Where the devil have you gone?" came a bellow from the broad verandah. "When I do catch you, I'll flay you alive, you she-devil!"

Grimwade swore himself into and out of every apartment in the little bungalow in vain. Then he came back to the table and his square bottle of yellow liquor. He drank himself into a sullen stupor, and did not realise that the last human companion in his solitude had left him for ever.

He fell asleep in a long cane chair, and nobody dared to wake him until late next morning, when a turbaned watchman brought the mail to the bungalow. Grimwade started up, rubbing his heavy eyes.

"What's that?"

"Mail, Tuan."

The Tuan Besar grabbed the bag, unlocked it, broke the huge red seal, and, thrusting in one brown arm, groped until his fingers closed upon a long, fat envelope. He knew there would be only one; he could scarcely remember when anyone had written to him privately.

He tore off the top edge neatly, drew out an important-looking headed page of typewritten matter and perused it rapidly, muttering to himself all the while.

Suddenly he started, looked at the page more closely, then crumpled it up in a fury and hurled it over the side of the verandah. He bit his nails and began pacing restlessly to and fro.

"Send a visiting agent!" he cried. "Send a chartered accountant to look through my books! Not if I know it! Let him set foot on my verandah, and I'll wring his cursed neck!"

He tore wildly at his beard and stamped the gramophone records to powder beneath his heavy heel. Then he caught sight of the half-empty bottle. He disappeared into an inner room, and returned carrying a heavy cardboard box of cartridges and a wicked-looking magazine pistol. He banged the box down in the centre of the wooden table and filled the magazine. Then he laid the weapon by his side and started to drink.

As the day drew on his fevered brain began to picture visiting agents coming to expose him from behind every blade of lalang, from every charred stump on the slope. Then he grew mad and fired wildly in all directions, and his servants fled in fear from the kitchen at the back to the shelter of the jungle below the hill.

II

About a month later a wild-eyed figure in white drill clambered on to the long train at Tembakut, the nearest station to Grimwade's estate. He staggered into the car marked "Europeans Only," and sank into a seat by the window. The sun was strong on that side of the car, so he pulled down the blind and contemplated the ruin of what had recently been a new shikar topi. There were two neat bullet-holes in the crown, and it was covered with earth.

The only other occupant of the car—a short, wiry, clean-shaven D.O.—looked up from the magazine he had been reading.

"Been in the wars," he remarked, and opened a silver cigarette-case invitingly. The other man crossed over and helped himself.

"Thanks!" he said, tapping the cigarette on the palm of a very white, well-formed hand. He shook a wooden match-box, and, finding it empty, looked at his companion. The D.O. handed him his already lighted pipe.

"Yes," admitted the man with the damaged sun-helmet, surveying the end of his cigarette to assure himself it was evenly lighted, "I have been in the wars, and I wish to heaven I'd never taken the job on at all."

The D.O. appeared interested.

"I came out here," continued the other, "with instructions to call at a certain estate, peruse the accounts—I'm a chartered accountant, you see—and report to my directors by cable. Well, I reached the estate and saw the manager—a most eccentric sort of fellow. I just put one foot on his steps, and the blackguard was grinning down at me, a revolver in one hand.

" 'What d'you want?' he demanded. I told him. I don't remember much more, except that pretty well every article of furniture within reach came at me at once, and I ran for dear life, followed by a volley of pistol bullets. It's a wonder I got here at all."

The D.O. whistled and then smiled.

"Looks a bit fishy, don't it?" he said.

"It certainly does," admitted the chartered accountant. "Anyhow, it's far too unpleasant a billet for me, and I shall cable home my resignation to-morrow. I consider the directors have treated me abominably. I came out under the distinct impression I was on a soft job."

III

In the Rest House at Jesselton, John Tyrningham lay in a long Borneo chair in the uttermost depths of despair. He was tall and very broad, with a heavy, fair moustache and a fine forehead. He was young—about thirty-five—and his skin was tanned a deep brown with many years' exposure to a tropical sun. He had arrived in Borneo only a bare month ago, with about twenty pounds' worth of dollar notes in his coat pocket, looking for work. He now found himself face to face with the alternative prospects of starvation or humiliation. In a word, he was "broke to the wide," and a heavy Rest House bill for a week's accommodation still awaited payment. He tapped out his pipe on the heel of his canvas boot and swore softly.

"My luck's dead out," he muttered. "Every job there is going is filled by a youngster from home. They don't want old hands here; they're lookin' for kids—to teach! Everything's gone against me since—since I—"

He passed a huge hand in front of his clear blue eyes, and shuddered.

Suddenly he started. In the farther corner of the long verandah two men were talking. Tyrningham remembered them coming in just after the arrival of the afternoon's train.

"What the directors want is a man," someone was saying, "and a real smart man at that." The conversation died down again so low that the listener in the long chair could not catch what was said.

"Wanted, a man!" murmured Tyrningham. "Jove! that sounds like something in my line. I wonder what the job is?"

"It's so humiliating, having to go back straight away and confess oneself a failure." The voice became loud again. "But what in heaven's name is a fellow to do? It needs something superhuman to tackle an armed lunatic!"

Tyrningham sat up straight and felt for his khaki coat. He slipped an arm into the wrong sleeve and drew it out again. Then he put the right arm in and felt behind him for the other sleeve. He drew the garment on and fastened the two top buttons. Then he crossed the verandah towards his fellow-occupants of the Rest House.

"Excuse me, gentlemen," he remarked suddenly. "You've been talkin' rather loud, and I couldn't help overhearin' what you said. Did I rightly understand there was a vacancy somewhere for a man?"

Both men looked sharply up, and the D.O. smiled and offered his hand.

"Been out here long?" he asked.

"Not here," said Tyrningham, feeling for the arm of a chair and drawing it to him. "Seen about fifteen years, on and off, in Colombo, Assam, and the F.M.S."

The third man extended a slim white hand, and a brown paw gripped it like a vice.

"My name's Price; I'm a chartered accountant," he said. "I came here two days ago, and went up to a certain estate as visiting agent, don't you know. I found the manager practically a homicidal maniac, and came away what I believe you call 'baniak lakas' (very quickly). I was just recounting my adventure to my friend here." He indicated the wiry D.O.

Tyrningham began to see daylight.

"Thanks!" he said, and took the speaker's pouch. He pressed the mixture into the bowl of his blackened briar very carefully. He mentally decided the tobacco had cost its purchaser some money in London. "So you don't hanker after the idea of goin' home and facin' the board with nothin' to show for money spent?"

He shielded the burning match with his hand.

"That's just it," said Price. "It's not my fault, but I wasn't built for a job of this kind."

Tyrningham brought a huge fist down on to the table. An empty glass wobbled and fell on its side. He picked it up and looked from the D.O. to Price and back again.

"But I am!" he exclaimed. "It's very life to me! Here have I been waitin' and waitin' and kickin' my blessed heels about in this God-forsaken hole lookin' for a billet of any kind, and there's yourself with the very thing on offer that'd just make or break me, and that's what I'm game to try. Do we understand one another?"

There was a pause, and then a white and a brown hand gripped.

Price thought for a moment.

"What do you propose?" he asked at last. Tyrningham puffed for a few seconds and then said:

"I want two hundred dollars for a start. If I fail—well, you'll be two hundred dollars out and I'll be a dead man. If I succeed, you take the kudos and recommend me for the managership. That's fair, I think, gentlemen?"

The D.O. nodded. "Sounds straight enough," he agreed.

A boy stepped out from the dining-room below and rang a bell.

"Maken!" said Tyrningham.

"You'll sit with us, of course?" asked Price.

"Thanks, I will. We'll talk of something else, and you'll think things over and let me know your decision in the morning."

The three men rose, and each disappeared in search of soap and water.

IV

"This is a case where tact is required," remarked Tyrningham grimly.

He was sitting on a disused trolley wedged between the ruin of a railway go-down and a couple of disused sleepers, which heavy rains and time had caused to become embedded in the soil.

Above him rose the weed-covered slopes of the Jelumpur kabun. He had strolled there from Tembakut—much too wary a hand to stop the train anywhere near the bungalow of the terrible Grimwade.

"Price'd have a blue fit if he saw me now," he chuckled thoughtfully. "He'd expect me to go at a thing like a bull kerbau at a white man!" He slipped the hot pipe into his pocket and, drawing out another, filled it deliberately and fit it. He noted with much satisfaction that the sun was fast setting. "Be dark in an hour or so," he said. "I wonder how that bearded blighter up there is gettin' on?"

He removed his topi, and, rising suddenly to his feet, peered warily over the waving lalang.

"H'm! Still goin' strong!" He sat down again. The Tuan Besar, totally oblivious of the presence of another, was pacing the verandah, his head down, occasionally glancing at the path, as if expecting every moment to see the slim figure of the chartered accountant making a second attempt to audit his books.

"Wish I had some of that liquor down here," soliloquised the patient Tyrningham. "Phew! What a constitution he must have had. Lived on nothin' else but whisky for the last few weeks, I should say. Hullo!"

He sprang to his feet and felt for his revolver.

"My God! Was I dreamin'? I could have sworn—"

He bent low and walked a few paces into the tall grass. Then he came back and sat down again.

"I could have sworn I saw a black head lookin' at me over there!" he declared. He let his hand rest on the weapon in the side pocket of his khaki coat. "Won't pay 'em to meddle with me, anyhow," he muttered, and pensively watched the flight of a huge brown hawk.

Darkness fell.

Tyrningham rose to his feet, stretched, and then stooped. From behind the trolley he drew a new hurricane lamp, made sure that there were plenty of matches in his pocket, and slowly mounted the path to the bungalow. He thanked his stars there was no moon. An ideal night for a surprise visit, he thought.

Half-way up he stopped and shivered.

"Lord! What a desolate spot!" he whispered. "Ah! No light in the house yet." He stooped down and crept round to the side of the bungalow, then he peered on to the verandah.

"Asleep!" He removed his boots carefully and stole silently towards the low flight of wooden steps. Still no sound from the man on the verandah. He pressed forward, one hand in his pocket. His fingers were on the rail now. "One step—two, three!" he counted softly.

"Thank you! Hands up!"

An electric torch flashed suddenly in his face, and the hand in his pocket closed on the pistol too late. A blotched, bearded countenance was thrust close to his own, and his eyes were looking into a gleaming barrel.

"Come in! Come in!" cried the manager, with a brutal laugh. "Welcome to Jelumpur!"

Tyrningham stepped on to the verandah, and his host waved him with mock ceremony into a long cane chair.

"Let me see—you have a pistol?"

Tyrningham swore softly and threw it on to the table.

Grimwade, one eye on his tall prisoner, slowly and deliberately lit the swinging lamp, using only one hand.

He replaced the glass chimney and turned.

"Neat bit of work that, eh? All on whisky, my boy, good old Scotch! Thought I was napping, didn't you?"

He picked up Tyrningham's pistol, slipped it into his pocket, and crossed over to the safe. Tyrningham watched him, eagerly awaiting an opportunity, but none came. Grimwade was returning with two books in one hand. . "My journal—my ledger, Mr.—"

Tyrningham did not answer.

"Very well—Mr. Accountant, shall we say? You have come here to see these things I believe? Well, well, you are welcome! Come, draw up your chair."

The prisoner obeyed. Grimwade threw open the books at the required pages.

"See!" he cried wildly. "There, and there, and there! Defalcations! Salaries to assistants who don't exist! Faked pay-sheets! False commissions! I'm a rogue, a swindler—d'you hear? Why don't you sack me! Why don't you have me arrested?"

He broke into a peal of awful laughter, that made even Tyrningham's blood run cold. It echoed weirdly in the stillness of the tropic night. Heavens, how lonely it was! And what a fine mess he had made of it all! Ah, well, he had tried and failed! Sudah habis (it was finished).

"Look well, young man," bellowed the madman suddenly. "Look well, for when that book closes—you die!"

He laughed wildly again, and lifted the cover to close it down.

And then Tyrningham sprang!

There was a flash, and something like a red-hot iron grazed the younger man's side. They closed and fell heavily to the floor together, knocking over the table and the two heavy books. The cardboard box of cartridges rolled across the verandah, spreading its contents broadcast; a square bottle crashed against a post and broke, and Tyrningham heard its contents dripping steadily on to the ground below.

The manager fell first, with the younger man on top of him, his hands on Grimwade's throat. Grimwade dropped his weapon and clutched at Tyrningham's neck, and for an endless period they seemed to rock to and fro, neither gaining any advantage. Then there was a pause—two fierce, panting beings gazing into each other's eyes. Then the Tuan Besar made a sudden effort, and the pain in Tyrningham's side became intense. He held out for a while, and then collapsed with a grunt. He closed his eyes. The madman was on top of him; he could feel his breath on his face. His fingers were slowly closing over his windpipe. It was the end!

Suddenly the grip relaxed, and Tyrningham opened his eyes.

The manager was looking behind him, apparently momentarily deprived of the power of his limbs, and there, full in the circle of light from the swinging oil-lamp, stood a tall Tamil woman. Even as Tyrningham strove to rise, something bright flashed in the air, and a black arm rose and fell. Grimwade staggered to his feet, one hand endeavouring to find the wound.

"Mirima!" he gasped, and crashed to the floor.

The other man sprang to his feet, but the black figure had vanished into the lalang.

He turned Grimwade over with one foot. A glance sufficed—the planter was dead. He picked up his revolver and slipped it back into his pocket; then he turned calmly and glanced down the columns of the ledger.

Suddenly a queer smell caused him to look up. The verandah was full of smoke. He sprang for the open, and almost immediately the ill-supported front portion of the roof crashed in. He ran a few paces down the hill as a case of whisky exploded and flared to the heavens.

"There's no hope for that bungalow," he remarked. "Lord, how thirsty I am! What a wicked waste of good liquor!"

Suddenly he gasped. In the light of the conflagration he caught sight of a solitary figure seated calmly on the roof above him.

He rushed as near as he dared.

"Jump!" he cried wildly. "Jump, you damned idiot!"

The woman shook her head, stood suddenly erect, and plunged head foremost into the blazing ruins.

V

THE CHANCE

TADAK, WHICH, as all the world knows, is a small coast town somewhere about the north-east corner of the island of Borneo, consists of a squat railway station, a little white post office, and a handful of neat bungalows occupied by civil servants of the British North Borneo Company. Before the rubber boom—that great volcanic disturbance which burst suddenly forth upon the peaceful citizens of civilised cities, making rich men paupers and poor men persons of some importance—Tadak was unknown except to the handful of officials whose duties kept them there, and their relatives whose duty it was to write to them more or less frequently. The papers at home reeled off article upon article, companies cropped up in every city building, bits of unsurveyed jungle assumed suddenly the dignity of estates, millions changed hands—and one blazing tropic morning Tadak woke up. There was a stirring as of bees in honey-time; athletic young men in white suits and equally white sun-helmets strode easily from the gangways of little steamers and presently took train inland. There came seething crowds of Chinese coolies from Hong Kong and Singapore, and then boatloads of rubber seeds, shoots, changkols, axes—everything was rubber—and it was with that sudden springtide that Ronald Sayers came. Ronald Sayers was tall—something approaching six feet in his socks—broad-shouldered, thin, and wiry. His hair was of no particular colour, nearer brown, perhaps, than anything, and his eyes were blue. His nose was straight and his chin pretty firm, and, pandering to the prevailing fashion, he was clean-shaven. He was clean-shaven when he arrived, and wore a decent collar and neat tie; after he had been way back in the interior a month he had forgotten what neck-wear was like, and he shaved once a week—if he felt that way inclined. The second son of a prosperous fanner, he had left the snug homestead nestling in a hollow sheltered by the Sussex Downs to assist John Braham in the management of the Tankap Kabun. He could ride and shoot; on the voyage out he discovered, too, that he could dance as well as most men, and sit out dances a good deal better—at least, so Doris Rothingham thought. They had made friends, these two, on the first day out from Southampton. At Port Said, where Doris, her aunt, and Sayers had gone ashore together, they were inseparable, and people on board were beginning to whisper. Somewhere in the Indian Ocean, between Aden and Colombo, when the sea was calm and the great twinkling stars seemed to smile on them, a pair of strong arms, for a second only, held a soft, trembling form to a thirty-eight inch chest—and then the patter of hastening footsteps on a wooden deck broke upon the dream of happiness, and an anxious chaperon found two young people in two separate chairs vainly endeavouring to appear interested in two separate novels in a portion of the vessel where deck-lights were scarcest!

Before they parted at Singapore each had promised many things, and she had asked him to call and interview her parents when he obtained his first period of leave three years later. And so Ronald Sayers had landed at Tadak full of hope and happiness with still another name upon the list of friends and relatives he had faithfully promised to communicate with weekly. As time went on this last name on a crisp foreign envelope with an oblong red stamp was the only epistle which constituted his regular outward mail, and his people at home, after many remonstrating letters, thought themselves singularly well favoured if they received a four-line scribble once in three weeks.

Ronald Sayers lived in a rough wooden bungalow, thatched with sago-leaves and raised high above the ground on stout, long poles. It had a broad, open verandah, a couple of bedrooms, a dining-room, a compartment where he kept scores of bottles of light lager beer and other things, a small office where he wrote figures in his check-roll, and a kitchen twenty yards to the rear. He had a Chinese cook-boy and two water-carriers, and he lived much the same life as any other rubber assistant in any other lonely, baking, fever-ridden portion of the globe. He kept his health better than most men and drank a good deal less. He was liked in the club at Tadak, for he was a good hand at billiards, tennis, and cards; but he had one weak line in his harness—his powers of imagination were too strong. When danger was brewing, as was not infrequent in these early days at Tankap, he saw too far ahead. If the coolies rose and swept in swarms down upon the bungalow of the manager, John Braham, that heavy, blundering, cheerful worthy would sally forth like an enraged water-buffalo, relying only upon his two great fists, and after that there would be no more thought of rebellion for many a long sweltering day. But on Sayers' side of the estate it was different. When things went wrong his imagination pictured results so vividly that he hesitated, and the coolies thought him a coward. Presently he began to rely on the assistance of Braham, who loved a fight, and gradually his power of initiative weakened—until the thoughts of John Braham were his thoughts, and he became almost a pawn at the beck and call of his superior. True, he worked as hard as any man; he carried out his orders to a letter; but the pity of it all was that, should a manager's billet come his way, he would never be qualified to step into it. Unless something wonderful happened, he would remain an assistant until his hair turned grey and his muscles failed him, or until he sickened of the East and went home to lead an idle life on the slender allowance of a second son. He knew that he was losing his hold over his men, and he foresaw the day when John Braham would be absent, himself alone in his way-back bungalow—and the clouds which had long been gathering in the Chinese konzsies would suddenly burst.

Two long sweating, toiling years had passed since Ronald Sayers first set foot on the island, and one day he took the little rackety train down to Tadak to spend a couple of days in the coast-town. The visit was partly in connection with the work of the estate, partly pleasure. He arrived, at the station at about half-past five in the afternoon and shouted to his boy to take his barang down to the new hotel. There was an hotel in Tadak now, quite an improvement on the little bare Government Rest House; Tadak was looking up with a vengeance. The last few weeks had been a nightmare to the young assistant. His Mandors were getting insolent, his coolies laughed and talked about him behind his back—this he both knew and felt. He was glad of these two days to take his mind off his work a little. Had it not been for a promise to a certain pretty girl, he would undoubtedly have drowned his troubles in the way other planters drowned theirs. He had come down to the coast-town, too, for strength. After dinner was over he left the others who were staying at the hotel and went out alone into the night. There were shouts of laughter coming from the direction of the club, but for once he did not turn his footsteps in that direction. He wanted to be alone—alone with himself. Free for a short space from the troubles and trials of a planter's life—that of a pioneer planter, moreover—he wanted to reason with himself in solitude. He wandered aimlessly down the sandy road, taking a path which led from the Chinese shops and the lighted streets towards the seashore.

Out in the bay a seemingly endless line of paper lanterns revealed where dark-skinned Dusun men, women, and children, knee-deep in the calm waters, were busily engaged spiking inquisitive fish and thrusting them, still struggling, into the wicker baskets hung about their shoulders. The palm-trees waved softly in a slight breeze from the sea, somewhere a gramophone was playing a queer Chinese melody, and a woodpecker kept tap-tap-tapping in an adjacent tree. Ronald Sayers strolled along, his hands behind his back, until the sounds of the tiny township became faint, then sat down on a fallen tree-trunk, and, resting his chin in his hands, gazed moodily out across the dark waters. No one who had known Sayers in England, or had seen his jolly smile on waving farewell from a double-prowed sampan at Singapore would have recognised the same person in the dejected form who fought with himself that dark night on the lonely seashore down Tadak-way. The healthy cheeks had fallen in, the face was sallow and drawn; all merriment had been burnt out of those once twinkling blue eyes. He himself did not know he was so changed. He rarely looked in the glass except when the spirit prompted him to shave. He tried to analyse his feelings and that one fault within him which men who did not understand called cowardice. He tried to remember instances of pluck shown while he was in England, and then through the mist of years there came a picture of a remote millpond and a child drowning in the swirling waters. Someone had plunged fearlessly to the rescue—and that someone was Ronald Sayers. The thought gave him courage and assurance. If he could do this once he could do it again. He was but a young boy then, just leaving school, before his imagination had developed and made him appear a coward. Suddenly he clenched his fists, closed his jaw determinedly, and sprang resolutely to his feet.

"I must do it," he cried aloud to the stillness. "I must show Braham that there is yet some pluck left in me. When the crisis comes I must grit my teeth and fly to meet the danger. My God! I wasn't like this when I landed. I wasn't a fool, weak and without initiative. I must pull up."

A drop of moisture ran down his cheek, and he wiped it away with the back of his hand; another followed, and yet another, and he drew a damp handkerchief from the sleeve of his white coat. He tilted his terai hat back and mopped his brow. Perspiration bathed him from head to foot. The struggle had been a keen one, and he hoped—scarcely daring to do so—that he, his old strong, heedless self, would prove the victor.

As he strolled back along the lonely path he heard the siren of a steamer hooting mournfully, and remembered that the little German mail steamer was due in that day from Singapore.

"I wonder if there are any letters for me?" he muttered, and suddenly stepped on to the roadway he had left earlier in the night. Coming from the direction of the quay were two white ladies. They passed Sayers just as he gained the road, and left him standing rooted to the spot with astonishment. Then, recovering himself with an effort, he hurried after the retreating figures. He came upon them under the light from a large Chinese store. They both started as he raised his hat, and Doris Rothingham gasped.

"You—Ronald? Why, how changed you are! Isn't he, aunt?"

The older lady agreed and held out a welcoming hand towards the young planter. "You've lost a good deal of flesh since we saw you last," she said, smiling. "It's not the best of climates, I believe, but Doris wanted to come here, and as we were on our way to Yokohama and had plenty of time to spare, I thought we couldn't do better than pay a surprise visit to an old acquaintance."

"I'm awfully glad you came," he replied. "Three years takes a long time passing." He stepped between the two ladies, and Doris took his arm. "It's funny I should be in town at the time you arrived," he said. "Of course, you're staying at the hotel?"

They walked slowly towards Tadak's latest acquisition. The manager was a Dutchman—Van Eyck by name—and these few words of welcome were gaudily painted just inside the door, culled, no doubt, from the columns of an American journal:

"To trust is to bust;
To bust is hell!
No trust—no bust;
No bust—no hell!
In God we trust—
Everybody else cash down."

Doris laughed when she read the notice, and her aunt pretended to look shocked. Ronald had seen it too often to be greatly impressed, but he laughed because Doris did.

On the following evening, after makan, Miss Dane discovered that she had a letter to write, and so Doris and Sayers sat out on the verandah beyond the circle of light from the lamp and talked. That is to say, they discussed general topics of conversation very thoroughly whenever a chance after-dinner walker strolled, cigar in hand, towards their end of the verandah.

There had been a lull in the conversation for some moments, and the stillness around was so intense that the tiny gold watch on the girl's wrist could be heard ticking. Suddenly from the lawn below came the sound of two voices. Sayers knew who the speakers were—planters who had come down by the train that afternoon. Presently one of them said:

"Say, Rogers, tell you somethin' you don't know?"

"Well, what's that? Some cock-an'-bull yarn about your rubber trees? If it is, I don't want to hear it. Met people of your sort before."

" 'Snothing about rubber. I bar 'shop.' It's about young Sayers."

Doris looked at her companion. His face had turned deathly white. "They're talking about you, dear," she whispered.

"I know," he nodded faintly. "They're canned, I expect."

"Sayers?" repeated the man addressed as Rogers. "Sayers? Who in the name of goodness is Sayers?"

"You know. Assistant at Tankap—Braham's place."

"Oh, yes. Plays a good game of tennis. I remember now. Beat me in the singles last May. Well, what about him?"

"They say he's an arrant coward."

Sayers clutched at the arm of the long cane chair on which he was sitting, and dug his teeth into his lip until it bled. He glanced at Doris, and knew that she had heard what had been said. Her face was averted, and she was gazing steadfastly at the two shadowy forms pacing restlessly on the grass below.

"What!" ejaculated the second man, "Sayers a funk?"

"They say that his coolies laugh at him, that every week there's mischief on up there and he can't deal with it. Has to get Braham to pull him out of every little scrape. I hear old John's gettin' a little fed up with things by now. He won't ask that young man to help him after his time's up. Get rid of him before then, I shouldn't be surprised."

Ronald Sayers leapt suddenly to his feet, his fists clenched, his breath coming and going in short gasps.

The girl sprang up as well and caught him by one sleeve.

"Where are you going?" she demanded.

The young man looked full into her eyes.

"Look here, Doris," he cried hoarsely, "I know you're a sport, and so I'll tell you. If you were an ordinary girl I'd have put you off with some yarn—and done it behind your back. You heard what that man said about me—I want you to let me prove that it's a lie."

She sank down on to her chair again and looked up at him, her clear brown eyes fixed on his own: "Is it a lie?" she said.

Sayers did not answer her directly. "I am going to prove to him that it is," he said. "He must have known I was here. It's a deliberate challenge to me. It would mean ruin to me if I let it pass unheeded."

Doris looked down at one white shoe and shrugged her fair shoulders.

"Don't let aunt hear the row," she whispered—and Sayers was gone down the stairs. As he strode across the lawn to meet the man who had libelled him, he realised how much this evening's work would mean to him. He felt like a gladiator entering the arena, knowing that the woman of his choice was watching to see what manner of man her lover was. He knew deep within him that this was, in reality, no open challenge to him whatsoever. The others had come by that afternoon's train and had not appeared at dinner. Probably they had not even paused to scan the visitors' book in the hall. The news of Sayers' failures had gone the round at last, and the speaker was merely repeating idle gossip which would soon be the subject matter of all verandah conversations over after-sundown drinks.

Under the light from the verandah lamp the three men met. Rogers, the eldest, scenting trouble, stepped back a pace or two, and Duncan put out a slim hand, which Sayers ignored.

"You made a statement just now. Are you prepared to repeat your words?"

The other started. "I don't quite understand you, Sayers," he stammered. He was a shade shorter than the man who stood before him, of rather heavier build, and he wore a dark moustache which gave him a fiercer appearance than his general disposition warranted.

"I will remind you then," said Sayers bluntly. "You remarked to your friend there that I was a coward and likely to lose my billet for it. D'you remember now?"

The other was an older and more experienced man than Sayers, and he resented the attitude of the younger man.

"I repeat nothing," he replied a trifle testily; "but what I have said I stick to."

What happened after that Sayers scarcely remembered. A mist rose before his eyes and he hit out—straight from the shoulder, as he had once learned at school, down in dear old Sussex. Whether it was that Duncan placed such faith in the rumour he had repeated that he did not trouble to defend himself remained a mystery. Anyhow, a score of men from the smoking-room found Rogers and Sayers bending over a man with a broken jaw, and from the verandah, very white of face and apparently greatly agitated, a young girl was looking down on to the scene.

It was through the intervention of Doris Rothingham that the matter was hushed up and the two men eventually shook hands. The following morning Ronald Sayers took the train back to his estate at Tankap, Doris and her aunt promising to spend the next week-end under his roof.

"You'll find it pretty rough," he had said as the train moved off, and the ladies hastened to assure him that they would be content to forego a little luxury to experience the sensation of sleeping in a way-back bungalow in the midst of a plantation hewn from the virgin jungle itself.

As he leaned back in his seat and watched the varied scenery whirling by the open window, Ronald Sayers felt at peace with himself. He had taken the first step towards his salvation. In spite of the hushing-up of the incident—a secret is not long a secret in the East—presently every white man on the coast would know that Sayers had laid Duncan out for calling him a coward. John Braham would learn of it and marvel. It now remained to enforce his authority on his side of the Kabun and to put things a little more shipshape before Doris and her aunt arrived.

John Braham met the train at the little go-down by the line.

"Hullo, Sayers!" he growled amiably. "You have come back, then?"

There was a ring in the younger man's voice when he replied, and Braham looked at him in wonderment.

"Look here, Braham," he blurted out presently. "I've been an idiot these past few months, and you've put up with me as no other boss out here would have done, and I'm sorry you've had to—that's all. But all that's at an end. It's got to stop—and it's going to. I'm going to show you that I've still got a little grit left in me, and if in two months' time my side of the Kabun isn't as peaceful and respectful as yours—well, I'll resign and—and go home and learn skittles."

John Braham, bluff and bearded, beamed amiably upon his assistant, and then grabbed him by the hand with an earnestness that surprised even Sayers. "D'yer mean it?" he bellowed. Sayers nodded.

"Then just you listen to me. I've been scribblin' out my mail to-day, and I was just puttin' before the board my resignation to the managership, because somebody's been fool enough to die and leave me money. Well, someone's got to carry on the work out here, y'know, and until this very minute I was sure it wasn't goin' to be you. But here's my bargain: you do as you've just said, get those blasted sinkies of yours to learn their manners, and—there's my hand on it—you're my successor."

So Ronald Sayers, a fierce light in his eyes, his brows ever contracted, went doggedly about his task of putting fear into the hearts of his rebel coolies. He did not know that his sudden activity had come just a trifle too late, and instead of clearing the clouds which still hung about the scattered coolie-lines, only served to bring the storm closer and closer.

He was sitting at tea on his verandah with Doris and her aunt when the news came. John Braham was away for the day, and would not be back until evening. There were no guns on Sayers' side of the Kabun, and all the coolies in his lines were up in arms. A breathless watchman, who had run from the scene of action barely a mile away, hailed him excitedly as he rounded the side of the house. "Tuan, Tuan! The coolies are up!"

Fortunately he spoke in Malay, and the ladies did not understand the import of his message.

Sayers sprang to his feet, turned very white, clutched the edge of the table and recovered himself, then reached almost mechanically for his hat and stick.

"There's a slight disturbance down in the konzsies, that's all," he explained. "It'll all be over as soon as the beggars catch sight of me."

He contrived to appear at ease as he uttered the last words at the foot of the verandah steps, but deep in his heart he knew that he lied, and even as he hastened with the swarthy Pathan in the direction of the coolie-lines, he gave him instructions regarding the safety of the two ladies should matters go against him. He carried a heavy malacca cane, and that was all; the Pathan had a crooked stick, weighted with lead at one end. The coolies, Sayers knew, had axes and heavy hoes, and some even, during his period of weakness, might have procured weapons from the natives in the near-lying villages and hidden them among their barang.

Suddenly, on rounding a bend, they encountered a coolie carrying a wounded friend with gaping wounds, leaving a sinister trail of fresh blood as he staggered towards the rough hospital on Braham's side of the Kabun. Soon they came across injured men crawling along the path. Sayers shuddered and hastened onwards, the watchman at his heels.

He had learned that the riot was due to a religious difference in which some two hundred and fifty coolies were involved, but he knew also that the sudden rising had but one object—the swift extermination of himself. This interkonzsie strife was but a blind to deceive the authorities who would inquire into the crime. The actual murderer of the white man would disappear into the jungle. No doubt his name was already known among the men. Inveterate gamblers, they had probably cast lots for the honour on the previous night. The perpetrator of the crime would have all the money his companions could scrape together so that his escape might be made easier.

They came suddenly within view of the surging mob of rioters, and a howl of execration ascended to the very heavens as Ronald Sayers appeared. The planter did not flinch. The Pathan, an old cavalryman from India, glanced anxiously up at the man it was his duty to follow, and he saw that his teeth were firmly clenched; there was a war-light in those keen blue eyes that he had once believed capable of flinching in fear.

A huge Chinaman, smiling confidently, swaggered, axe on shoulder, to meet the white man. He was the biggest man on that side of the estate, to whom was entrusted the work of hewing the saplings left by the native contractor, because he knew how to use an axe to the best advantage. Sayers remembered this, but did not blench. In his mind's eye he saw for a fleeting fraction of a second a youth saving a child from a mill-stream at imminent risk to himself; he remembered the two women in the bungalow he had lately left, and he suddenly recalled the feeling of satisfaction as his fist met the jaw of the man who had tried to belittle his name.

The Chinaman was upon him with the axe whirled aloft. The Pathan uttered a weird war-cry and tried to dash between his master and the weapon, but Sayers thrust him on one side, leaped nimbly out of the way as the glittering gepok clove the air, and as the Chinaman stumbled with the impetus of the stroke, he sprang suddenly in upon him and felled him with his fist.

The watchman stooped and picked up the axe with a grunt of satisfaction. He knew that this thing he had just seen was nothing more nor less than a miracle, but he was not paid to evince surprise at anything, and so refrained.

The coolies, their leader cowed and beaten, hesitated—and were lost. For Sayers, followed by the Pathan ex-soldier, rushed into their ranks, slashing, punching, throwing, using nature's weapons against ill-wielded wood and iron, until presently there was no more rebellion, and black watchmen, summoned from all sides of the Kabun, stood on guard outside as peaceful a group of long, ramshackle houses as any manager would ever wish to see.

And Ronald Sayers, seated on a log, cigarette in mouth, glanced up to see the broad, bluff figure of John Braham beaming amiably down upon him.

"Lord, what a glorious fight!" he bellowed. "I dug my spurs into this little brute's flanks, but I simply couldn't get here in time to take my share in the festivities. Sayers, I'm proud of you—proud of you. You've turned up trumps, in spite of yourself—which is a devilish hard job for any man to do. Hi, watchman! Come up here and hold my horse."

"This is where you come in," laughed Sayers, and they strolled together towards the konzsies.

There were many sore backs that night on the Tankap Kabun, and, as darkness fell, two tired, white forms with splintered malaccas joined two anxious women on Sayers' verandah.

"Ladies," bellowed John Braham after evening makan was over, "let me introduce you to the best friend and the pluckiest man I've known in all my time—out East or anywhere. He met the strongest Chinaman on the estate armed with an axe to-day—he met him with his fists. Ladies, I leave Borneo in two months' time; Mr. Sayers here is my successor."

VI

FATE'S INSTRUMENT

A WHITE-CLAD Englishman stepped on to Hudson's broad verandah and woke the manager from his afternoon doze.

"Good afternoon, Tuan Besar (manager); sorry to surprise you like this, but I came up by trolley from Api-Api. Can you put me up for the night?"

The manager yawned, and rose from his long chair.

"Take a pew," he said, and waited for the other to introduce himself.

"I'm Pearson, y'know, just appointed inspector of labour for your district."

The broad, clean-shaven manager opened his mouth and then closed it again with a sharp snap.

"I'm Hudson," he said slowly. "How do?"

They shook hands, and Pearson threw his topi and cane on to the deal table.

"So you're the new inspector?" remarked Hudson after a pause. "Speak Chinese and all that, of course?"

The other nodded. "Lived in China five years," he said. "Still, I hope we shan't begin by quarrelling. It's not the nicest job I've undertaken, you know."

"Sort of buffer," laughed the manager. "Sandwiched between employer and employee, eh?"

He pushed a box of Borneo cigars across the table as the inspector sank into a comfortable chair. "What'll you drink?"

"Oh, beer, I think."

The manager bawled lustily for the boy.

"Bring a couple of bottles from the refrigerator," he said in Malay.

Pearson bit the end off his cigar, lit it, and looked up.

"Somewhat of a luxury—ice," he remarked.

"Well, it's about the only one I allow myself. Get it from Sandakan twice a week, you know. There's nothing in the tropics to come up to a nice cool lager. What?"

"Been out here long?"

"Oh, a fair time—about twelve years, off and on. This is my first managership. Jove! but it's lonely up here—at times. I've a couple of assistants. One lives about three miles over there." He jerked his thumb across the hills, just visible between the house and the blue sun-blinds. "The other, when he's not down with fever, superintends the clearing and burning another two miles beyond that. Not much company, you see."

Pearson puffed and thought.

"No," he said at last, "I don't think I should fancy a billet like yours very much. Still, the screw's good, of course, and you get your periods of leave just the same as the rest of us. Ever had much trouble with the coolies?"

The manager started. "Don't you think we might leave business till the morning?" he said, a trifle coldly.

"Sorry. I was speaking purely from a friendly point of view. As you say, I am postponing more serious matters till to-morrow."

"Well, as a matter of fact, we do have trouble now and then. Sometimes it's on a matter of religion. Occasionally they try and see what sort of stuff we're made of; but, generally speaking, I'm a deal safer here than you, for example."

"Than I?"

"Most certainly."

The inspector shrugged his shoulders and shifted uneasily in his chair.

"I always carry a pistol," he said.

"And I," said the manager calmly, "never do."

Pearson gasped.

"What!" he cried. "You control four hundred odd Chinamen and go about unarmed?"

The other nodded, and flicked the ash from his cigar over the verandah rail.

"And yet you say," continued the inspector, "that you are far safer here than I am?"

"I say it and I mean it."

Pearson leaned back in his long chair and laughed. "But it's ridiculous," he said.

"To you."

"But to anybody in his senses it would sound absurd."

"Perhaps; but—let's change the subject. Our beer must be pretty well boiling by now. Here's luck!"

A band of fifty coolies hurried past the verandah, some carrying axes, others hoes. Behind them, a few paces to the rear, an enormous, evil-visaged Chinaman in a suit of greasy blues swaggered idly along under the protecting shade of a large red umbrella of oiled paper.

Pearson gazed after him in astonishment.

"Gad! What a giant!" he exclaimed suddenly.

"The biggest Mandor (overseer) on the West Coast," said Hudson. "He's not been with me very long, but he manages to get more work out of those lazy devils than any other man I've struck. But I forgot—you're the inspector of labour." There was a merry twinkle in the manager's eye, and both men laughed heartily.

On the following day the inspector of labour for the West Coast accompanied Hudson across the estate to the bungalow of the first assistant, Hooper. It was a queer place of residence, coolie-built of rough timber and thatched with sago leaves. The verandah was broad and fairly solid, the furniture was good, plain, and the chairs comfortable. There was a gramophone on a small table in one corner with a pile of records, some in paper covers, some exposed to the air. A ginger-coloured kitten prowled about searching for insects, and a fox terrier basked in the early morning sun.

Hooper stood at the door with folded arms, his keen blue eyes on the sandy path. He was tall, broad, and handsome, a heavy brown moustache adorning his upper lip. He wore a white flannel shirt, open at the top, and around his neck a handkerchief was knotted. Khaki trousers and brown canvas boots completed his costume. His sleeves rolled up above the elbow revealed two powerful-looking sunburnt arms.

Suddenly he started and whistled—two white-clad forms appeared around a bend in the path.

"The new inspector," he said. "I saw him last week in Api-Api. Why in heaven's name did he want to poke his damn nose in here just now?"

He drew a cigarette from a silver case on the deal table by his side and lit it carefully.

"Ah, well," he murmured, sinking into a long cane chair, " 'twas ever thus!"

Hudson, with Pearson close on his heels, strode swiftly round the corner of the house and mounted the verandah steps.

"Mornin'," grunted the first assistant, rising. "Who's the friend?"

"This is Mr. Hooper, my first assistant, Mr. Pearson. Mr. Pearson's the new inspector of labour down here, y'know."

The two men shook hands, and the manager managed to kick Hooper's foot as he sat down by the table. The first assistant winked as the inspector turned.

"Pleased to meet you, Mr. Pearson," he said. "I think you'll find everything quite serene on our estate. Take a seat—will you?—and a cigarette."

They sat down simultaneously.

"I've never worked on a kabun before," continued Hooper, "where the coolies seemed so damn contented. On some estates you'll have rows every day, and never know whether your night's rest isn't going to be disturbed into the bargain. But here it's just the reverse. You—"

An almost naked Chinaman staggered suddenly up the steps and flung himself at the inspector's feet, howling bitterly. The first assistant looked across at the manager and pursed up his lips. Hudson crossed and uncrossed his legs, while the inspector ordered the coolie to rise.

"Apah mahu (what do you want)?" thundered the manager. Pearson waved a slim hand in the air.

"Leave it to me, if you please," he said. "The man has evidently been ill-treated."

It was a terrible tale of woe that poured like a ceaseless torrent into the new inspector's ears, and his face, as the recital continued, assumed a graver expression. At last Pearson put up his hand, and the coolie retreated humbly to the path below.

"It's a most serious charge this man brings against one of your Mandors, Ah-Kit by name. He accuses him of brutality, of defrauding the coolies, and many other things. I should like to interview Mr. Ah-Kit."

"It's the old, old story," said Hooper wearily. "There was a rumour of your arrival, and immediately the biggest liar in the konzies (houses) was chosen to perpetrate a baseless charge against an over-zealous officer."

The inspector said nothing, but drummed thoughtfully with his fingers on the deal table and whistled softly. An hour later Ah-Kit, the gigantic Chinaman, was tried, convicted, and dismissed. He took the money due to him, shouldered his red umbrella, and marched insolently away down the winding hill-path.

"Enemy number one," said the manager quietly.

Pearson started. "You think so?" he said.

"I know it," replied Hudson, and he wiped the perspiration from his sunburnt brow with a soiled handkerchief.

The inspector drew an automatic pistol from his pocket and gazed at it fondly.

"That's been a very good friend to me," he said musingly.

"Well," replied the manager slowly, "you need one now."

Pearson laughed, and, picking up a magazine, turned the pages idly.

When Hudson's boy drew aside the new inspector's mosquito curtains the following morning he found Pearson lying in a pool of blood with a long sharp knife through his heart.

Ah-Kit, a price on his head, fled into the jungle, the police hard on his trail. He lay hidden in the undergrowth by day and robbed native villages by night. Where he could not obtain food by stealth his great strength aided him, and soon the list of murders grew long and the price on his head rose higher and higher, till the name of Ah-Kit became a byword, in the mouths of coolies and natives alike, only to be mentioned in a terrified whisper.

In the skipper's cabin of the SS. "Haufah," bound for Api-Api, Leslie Berwick turned a heavy native weapon over in his delicate white hands.

"It's a pretty useful-looking article," he said.

The skipper nodded and laughed. He was a German of rather heavy build, but his English was perfect.

"That is a straight kris," he said. "The blade of an ordinary kris is undulating—you have seen them in museums in England. The sheath belonging to this one is made of wood, bound with strips of coloured bamboo. In war time, however, there is another kind of sheath, and it is made in this way: a narrow strip of wood is placed on each side of the blade, and then a few strips of rotan are bound lightly round. You notice how heavy the sword is? Well, a Bajau, say, is searching for his enemy, and he carries the weapon in its false sheath over one shoulder. His enemy approaches, and suddenly the kris whirls through the air, strikes the unfortunate man, the binding is severed, the false sheath flies off, and the naked blade is exposed. It is a cunning trick, is it not? My boy, if ever you meet a native carrying his sword over his shoulder, shoot at once, you may not have another chance."

Berwick shuddered.

"Bloodthirsty lot of natives round here, then?"

"Oh, no, not altogether. Occasional bouts of head-hunting; but on the whole they're fairly peaceful, especially near the coast. Inland they're more ferocious, I believe. There's the bell. Come along and have some makan. We shall be at Api-Api in an hour or so."

Four hours later Leslie Berwick surveyed the fading landscape through the window of his bare bedroom at the Rest House. He had come out East on spec, so to speak, and had found the trip from Southampton, via Suez, a great deal more expensive than he had imagined. There were so many interesting things to be bought, so many sights to be seen, so many unscrupulous persons lying in wait for the unwary; and now he found himself with but a few pounds in his pocket, friendless, in a wild, strange country where strength and stamina tell a great deal more than brain and high breeding. Berwick was short, thin, and good-looking in a weak kind of way. He could play a fair game of bridge or billiards, he could ride a horse and shoot a little; but he was not exactly the sort of man likely to impress a burly planter from way-back.

He strolled from his bedroom out on to the broad verandah and watched a crowd of slovenly convicts leaving their work for the day, guarded by two Sikh soldiers with loaded rifles. To his right was a white wooden clock tower, and beyond that again a little squat railway station. Above him the sky was fast changing from deep blue to grey, and out in the bay a native vessel was rocking at anchor in a light evening breeze. A fish leaped out of the water and disappeared again, an owl hooted in a tall tree not ten yards away, and behind the house a dog was barking. Native women in tall woven hats and coloured sarongs smoked cigarettes and chatted, standing idly in little knots on the sandy thoroughfare. A queer, clanking, screaming, primitive engine drew three loaded trucks from the quay to the town. A Chinese coolie, in white trousers and nothing else, was lighting a swinging lamp which hung from the verandah roof. Berwick lit a cigarette and sighed.

"So this is Borneo," he said aloud. "I'd often wondered what it was like."

A tall, broad-shouldered figure emerged suddenly from a bedroom door and fell into a long cane chair a few yards from where Berwick was standing.

"So you're just out," remarked the newcomer quietly.

The younger man started and turned.

"Yes," he answered, "I arrived this afternoon by the 'Haufah.' It gets dark quickly, doesn't it?"

Night had fallen suddenly, and the swinging oil lamp flickered and then burned brightly, casting heavy shadows from the scattered furniture on to the bare, boarded floor.

"What on earth made you come out here, of all places?"

Berwick crimsoned. "Oh, I don't know," he said. "People pegged out, and I thought I'd like to see something of the world."

Carter, the older man, snorted, and drawing a couple of dark cigars from the breast pocket of a white jacket, threw one across the verandah on to the other's knees.

"It's very good of you," said Berwick.

"It's a Borneo weed," replied Carter, "and you may as well taste all you can while you're here."

"I shall have plenty of time to do that, I hope."

Berwick was stooping down over a box of matches, and the cigar rendered his diction somewhat inarticulate.

Carter whistled.

"So you've come to stay?" he cried. "Man alive, what on earth are you going to do here?"

"I thought of learning planting. It's not difficult, is it?"

Carter laughed, and bit the end off his cigar.

"Difficult? There's nothin' difficult about the science of plantin'—whether it's baccy, cocoa-nuts, or rubber—to a practical brain; but it's the climate's the trouble. D'you feel equal to sweatin' up and down acres of steep hills in a broilin' sun? D'you fancy whackin' hundreds of dirty, coloured backs, of holdin' your end up in a native riot, of livin' on tinned foods and unhung meat as tough as kerbau hide?"

Berwick shrugged his sloping shoulders and laughed. "It sounds pretty stiff," he said, "but I mean to try."

"Jove! you've got some spirit for a young 'un," he said. "But I'm afraid it'll be too much for one of your build. However, there's a job goin' on my estate up the line, and you shall come along with me to-morrow and try your hand at it. I'll pay you a hundred dollars a month for a start, and the usual servant allowance."

Berwick crossed the verandah and stretched out a slim white hand.

"It's awfully good of you," he said, and then winced as he felt the vice-like grip of a huge brown paw. "Lucky I should run into someone with a billet to offer right away."

Carter flicked the ash from his cigar and gazed into the darkness.

"It all depends how you look at it," he said. "The other man pegged out last week—poor devil! He was a nice chap, too, and no end of a sport."

To his surprise Berwick's white face betrayed no signs of fear.

"One man's meat's another man's poison, and vice versa, I suppose. Anyhow, I'll do my best," he said.

As they sat opposite one another at the evening meal Berwick swallowed a mouthful of fish and then asked: "How did he die, did you say?"

Carter crumbled his bread and looked sharply up.

"How did *who* die?"

"Why, the fellow you talked about before makan."

"Oh—that chap!" Carter followed the pattern in the table-cloth with his thumb-nail. "He—was—killed," he said slowly.

"Killed?"

"Yes—knifed."

Berwick whistled and looked interested.

"Damn you!" cried the planter suddenly. "I can't make you out. Why the devil don't you look scared? Why don't you cry off?"

"Why should I? You haven't told me how he got knifed, by the way."

Carter cleared his throat and poured half a glass of lager down it.

"There's a Chinese murderer at large somewhere on the West Coast," he said. "He's killed no end of people. He began with an inspector of labour—Pearson by name—who got him the sack from the next estate to mine for brutality. I think he's mad now with the lust for blood. Anyhow, there's a price on his head of one thousand dollars—nearly one hundred and twenty pounds—y'know. Well, this man, Durward—my late assistant—was crossin' Hudson's kabun in the dark, and I rather fancy the beggar mistook him for the manager of that estate. Anyhow, he knifed him, poor chap! He was lookin' forward to six months' leave in England, too."

"Rotten bit of luck," remarked Berwick thoughtfully. Then he laughed heartily, leaning back in his chair.

Carter looked puzzled.

"Joke?" he asked wonderingly.

"Rather. I was just thinking that the blighter wouldn't mistake one of my build for a burly planter. So I'm pretty safe in that direction, you see."

Carter rose, a grim smile on his tanned face.

"I hadn't thought of that," he said. "Come across to the club. I'll introduce you to a few people, and we'll have a game of billiards. You play, I s'pose?"

Berwick nodded, and the two men strolled out into the intense darkness of the tropic night.

Insects hummed in the bushes by the road, a gramophone shrieked a weird Chinese melody to the blinking stars, a kerbau (water-buffalo) was grunting in a padi field, and from a gambling den came a chorus of hoarse cries.

Leslie Berwick looked up at his companion admiringly. His heart was very full. He had struck oil on his very first night in Borneo. The past had been comfortable; the present was quite tolerable, too; as for the future—well, he didn't worry himself much about that.

Two months later Carter met Hudson, the manager of the neighbouring estate, on the boundary line.

In a hollow, just out of sight, a gang of fifty coolies were toiling in the blazing sun, only the rhythmic thud, thud, thud of their heavy changkols (hoes) audible.

"Mornin'," said Hudson.

"Mornin'," replied Carter, puffing at a well-used pipe.

"How's things?"

"Oh, pretty fair, y'know. Got a new assistant."

"So I hear. What's he like?"

Carter screwed up his face and blew out a cloud of smoke. "Come over and see," he said.

They strolled together to a point on the hill-path where they could command a view of the Chinamen working in the valley. Every man was putting his utmost into the task. There was no smoking, no chattering, no pausing for breath, and a short, slim, white-skinned, khaki-clad Englishman, a malacca as long as himself under his arm, strode between the lines of sweating coolies, a fierce, set look on his young face.

"What a nipper!" exclaimed Hudson suddenly.

"He gets the work out of them, though."

"They'll turn round and eat him one of these days. That reminds me. Seen anything of that blighter Ah-Kit lately?"

Carter smiled grimly.

"Not since he knifed my late assistant—damn him!"

"Perhaps he'll look in and do the same for this one. I rather fancy he'll have another try at me shortly. I don't think it'll pay him, though. I should rather like to earn that one thousand dollars. By the way, I s'pose I ought to make the acquaintance of your new man. What's his name?"

"Berwick."

"Oh! Well, ask him to drop in to tea this afternoon, will you? Bye-bye."

He waved his cane and disappeared over the ridge, and Carter went on his way to urge on another toiling gang; but neither of them noticed a hideous face, contorted with hate and fury, peering out from behind a clump of lalang scarcely twenty yards from where they had been standing.

Ah-Kit gazed stupidly down at the blood-stained face of the man he had just killed. A dog ran up the steps, sniffed at Hudson's prostrate form, and then whined. The gigantic Chinaman sent it yelping from the verandah with one deft movement of a broad, bare foot. He had adopted native attire on the day when he had learned there was a price on his head, and his tow-chung (pigtail) was now quite a thing of the past. He slipped the sharp, straight kris, wet as it was, back into its wooden sheath, then he turned and strode jauntily down the sandy path. He was mad—mad with the lust for blood—or he would never have ventured from his jungle retreat in the broad light of mid-afternoon.

He waved his sheathed weapon thrice in the air and shouted aloud in the Hakka dialect, "Avenged at last!" And then he stopped, for a white form had appeared suddenly round a bend in the path. He swung his sheathed kris smartly on to one shoulder and laughed. He was not afraid of men but half his size. He swaggered on his way again with the air of a drunken butcher, then a dark thought came into his mind. A white man! All white men were his enemies now. Had they not hunted him down for many months—caused him to slink from tree to tree like a frightened ape? His dark fingers tightened on the handle of his sword and he quickened his pace towards the Englishman.

Leslie Berwick, tired, and looking forward to a refreshing cup of tea with the broad-shouldered Hudson, saw before him on the path a tall, ragged native. It was not until he drew near that he began to realise the enormous proportions of the hurrying newcomer. He appeared to be carrying something on his shoulder. Berwick found himself idly speculating as to its nature—a stick, perhaps, he thought, or a weather-worn Chinese umbrella. It occurred to him that the man was walking a great deal faster than was customary in Borneo in the heat of the day.

"Jove!" he cried suddenly, and stopped dead. He had seen that Ah-Kit was carrying a sword of a type he had seen once before. And then something floated across his weary brain, something he remembered hearing only a couple of baking months back:

"My boy, if ever you meet a native carrying his sword over his shoulder shoot him dead—you may not have another chance."

Berwick wrinkled his brows, clenched his teeth, felt in a side-pocket of his coat, and, as Ah-Kit thundered towards him down the steep path, coolly cocked his pistol over his elbow and shot him through the head.

VII

COULSON AND THE KERBAU

"Hi, boy! Dua whisky-soda—lakas!"

Two men lolled idly on the high verandah of a Borneo Rest House. The speaker was short and thick-set, his khaki coat open at the neck, displaying a small triangle of gauze singlet. On a table by his side was a huge planter's topi that had once been white, but was now grimed and blackened with the smoke of many a jungle fire. A long, unmounted malacca stood by his chair, splintered not a little at the smaller end through constant use. His face was tanned almost black, and a heavy, tangled moustache ornamented his upper lip.

The second man was tall, thin, and clean-shaven, neatly dressed in a suit of well-cut "whites," and his Shikar topi was almost aggressively new.

The white-clad "boy" hurried in with the two drinks; Huson, the first man, threw a signed chit towards him and lifted his glass.

"To your stay in Borneo," he said, "and may you make a damn big pile."

The other laughed, and both drained their glasses. It was almost unbearably hot.

"Sweatin' like a kerbau," said Huson suddenly. "Not that I've ever seen a kerbau sweat. Eh? What is a kerbau? Never seen one? Well, you've not missed a lot; but they're damned awkward beasts to quarrel with. If you don't believe me, ask Coulson—or rather don't ask him—that is, if you value your hide."

The tall man laughed, stretched his legs and waited for the other to continue. The day was drawing to a close, and a few paces off a semi-clad coolie-boy was tinkering with the oil lamp which swung from the roof of the verandah. A tongkong (native vessel) with a patched sail, rocked at anchor in the bay, and in a tree somewhere close at hand a brightly-hued woodpecker tapped monotonously. A score of sweating, dark-skinned convicts, closely watched by two huge, bearded Sikhs, with loaded rifles, toiled ceaselessly at some slow, crack-brained experiment at reclaiming land. A group of native women in large conical hats and bright sarongs—some chewing betel-nut, some puffing at long, handmade cigarettes—stood idly watching the progress of the work, occasionally laughing aloud at some whispered joke at the toilers' expense.

"A kerbau," said Huson slowly, "is a water-buffalo. It hates white men like poison. Most Englishmen funk 'em when they first come out—I did, I know, before I knew their ways. Ride 'em now often—when the padi-fields are flooded. Funny sort of mount, and unless you hold tight to their tails they'll slish any amount of muddy water over you.

"Well, Coulson—he was D.O. somewhere down Parpar way then—hated kerbaus just about as much as they hated him. He was a big chap, too, somewhere about six foot three, and pretty well sixteen stone in weight. He asked his boy one day how it was that the brutes were so damn ignorant—showin' respect for dirty, unwholesome natives and not caring a tinker's curse for a respectable, high-minded, God-fearin' Briton! The boy told him that it was because he washed in sabun (soap)—any native will tell you that—and for a whole month Coulson never touched a tablet! It was no good—it wouldn't jedi (do)—for at the end of his period of abstention he nearly broke his neck jumping a parret to avoid a couple of the brutes. He came home covered with mud and slime, with about eleven leeches clinging tenderly to his calves. He made his boy pull the devils off, and then kicked him round the bungalow out of sheer gratitude for his disinterested advice. The boy gave notice that night, and Coulson began to wonder how any Fate could have been so unkind as to stick on the same roasting island such an impossible combination as Coulson and kerbaus.

"Funny—well, I guess it was. There was nothing else that man did fear. It was a hobby of his to disguise himself as a Chinaman and wander into native drinkin'-houses and gamblin'-dens in search of evidence when any important native case came on. Brutal he was too at times. Known him string a Chinaman up by one ear to get a confession out of his unwillin' lips. Still he had his good points, and it was when one of these generous moods took him that the little incident occurred that I'm going to tell you about.

"The Parpar Rubber Estate was a bit short-handed, and the Tuan Besar (manager) was pretty well as busy as he could be, when Johnson—his right arm—got down with fever. He was a nice boy, was Johnson—not long out from home, but keen as mustard, and worked like a blessed horse. Well, the boss couldn't nurse him, and, even if he could he hadn't the time, and there wasn't a white doctor for miles around. A black apothecary they called Mr. Elijah—he styled himself Elijah pilai, which is about the same as Esq. with Tamils— was told off to dose the poor devil to the best of his ability, and all the good he did was to make him a darned sight worse. And then Coulson popped on to the scene, up on some native scare business, and he saw at once how low poor Johnson had got. Somehow he took it into his great clumsy head to do Johnson a real good turn. He chucked his traps into the spare bedroom, took off his coat, shoved a cigarette-paper and some quinine down the sufferer's parched throat, and waited on the unconscious Johnson hand and foot.

"Johnson was regularly delirious, and the language he indulged in at times was terrible. When you're really down for the first time you rave about sherbet and American soda-fountains, and everything nice and cool you remember drinking at home. Then you talk about the old folks at home, and pals, and then you branch off on to the girl tack.

"Well, this chap Johnson went through all those stages in strict rotation, till he finally got to the question of girls. Coulson listened to all he said, as he washed Johnson's face and changed his sheets like a certificated hospital nurse, and by-'n-by he learnt that there was a dainty, dark-haired little girl at home with all the proper qualifications for a perfect wife, and that the susceptible Johnson was pretty hard hit. When the invalid was again doin' the delirium business, Coulson was treated to a few further interestin' details. It seemed that the last letter from Johnson's adored one had been so far from satisfactory that he had given up all hope of matrimony in blank despair, and was now contemplatin' marriage—by purchase—to a handsome, dark Dusun maiden down in the adjacent Kampon. Shockin'? Well, perhaps it was; but it's done, y'know, ev'ry day of the week.

"Now, from what I've told you of Coulson's qualities, you'll not be surprised to learn he was not over-scrupulous in all his dealin's. In his own house, mind you, he'd treat you like a king—champagne *ad lib.,* an' all that. But once outside his door, his view of you changed completely, and he wouldn't hesitate to swindle you out of your last pair of socks.

"When he heard the words 'black girl' and 'Kampon,' he began to prick up his ears, and since he'd got rid of his own ngi (housekeeper) some time back, on account of thievin' propensities, he began to fancy no end this dusky charmer on whom his ravin' patient had got his eye. Then he caught the name—Maradi it was—and the pretty sound of it so appealed to him that he swore he'd have that black girl from her dirty Dusun father *baniak lakas* (very quickly), or he'd know the reason why.

"The next day Coulson put on his best suit of whites, crossed the Kabun, entered the Dusun village, crawled into a native hut with about as much comfort as an elephant getting into a dog kennel, and drank dirty milk out of half a cocoanut shell with the coveted Maradi and her father. He was rather forceful in his ways was Coulson, and before he left that evening he'd arranged everythin' very nicely, agreed on the price, and fixed up to take Maradi away from her father's home on the followin' afternoon. He went back to look at Johnson, feelin' pretty bucked, I can tell you, and to see him tend the suff'rer—who was now mendin' very fast—you would never have guessed at the treachery lurkin' in that D.O.'s soul.

"The next mornin' Coulson packed up his traps, sent 'em down by his boy to his official residence, such as it was, and prepared generally for the great elopement. He didn't stop to worry much over what Johnson would say when he was fit again, besides, how was he to know Johnson was thinkin' of buyin' the same ngi as himself? He bought a lot of coloured sarongs for Maradi that day, and a pair of elaborate silver anklets. He pictured her delight at puttin' the-gewgaws on, and the thought pleased him no end.

"Well, the afternoon came along in due course, and Coulson started out alone to fetch his intended wife to her new home. He swung his cane about like a boy of eighteen durin' his first love-affair, and started across the swampy fields as blithe and gay as a Java sparrow.

"At first he didn't notice the kerbaus. There were about nine of them in a bunch, and they'd smelt him coming a good way off. As he drew near they left off chewin' grass, and all stuck their great square snouts in the air, snortin' with indignation. Then they commenced strollin' across to get a better view, and then it was that Coulson spotted them. He started, stopped swingin' his stick, and looked nervously round for a suitable tree. He was about half-way between the Kabun boundaries and Maradi's home, and there wasn't so much as a damn bush for a good quarter of a mile. The kerbaus were advancin' in full strength now, their tails twitchin' and their noses protrudin' in a most ominous manner. Then a great old bull, with short, thick horns, sort of nudged his companions and said: 'Just you leave this to me!' He made suddenly for Coulson at a sharp trot. That settled it. Coulson dropped his stick, took to his heels and ran. Lord, how he ran!—and that damn animal ran, too. Over bank and hollow, through swamp and lalang they raced, till Coulson could almost fancy the brute's breath on his heels. His topi fell off, but he didn't dare look back. I don't suppose any man livin' ever beat Coulson's record for that quarter-mile sprint; but there was nobody there with a reliable stop-watch to time him, so Coulson never attained fame. But he did get to cover—only just in the nick of time—swarmed up the first tree, and sat there sweatin' and blowin' and cursin' like a blessed trooper.

"When he'd recovered somewhat from his exertion he glanced down. The kerbau, lookin' as cool as a juicy pomolo, was browsin' just under the tree, squintin' up every now and then to see how Coulson was keepin'. It went on hke that all the blessed afternoon, Coulson sittin' perched up in the tree, feelin' every moment that the branch was bound to give; and there was that cursed kerbau feedin' away calmly, and just waitin' till Coulson felt disposed to descend.

"Funny? It was that, only Coulson couldn't see the humorous side of it. Nice position for the local Tuan Hakim (magistrate) to be in, wasn't it? He began to wish he'd never set out on that cursed journey at all, and wondered whether Johnson had trained the damn brute to do this cunnin' sort of thing. Coulson sat there until dusk, and was just debatin' to himself whether it would be more comfortable to be torn in pieces right away or spend the night where he was, when there was a sound of footsteps, and a dark figure stepped out on to the jungle path. Coulson gasped—it was Maradi! Jove! she did look lovely. Her teeth were like ivory, and her hair shone like a patent leather shoe.

"She came along, holdin' herself very erect, as all these women do, and then she suddenly spotted Coulson. She started back in surprise, and caught sight of the blessed kerbau feedin' placidly close by. She looked from the kerbau to Coulson, and from Coulson to kerbau, and then the facts of the case dawned upon her, and she laughed aloud, showin' all her beautiful white teeth. Funny how quickly a fellow's taste changes. Coulson thought he'd never heard such a silly, idiotic, empty laugh before durin' the whole of his magisterial career.

" 'Tahan!' she cried out suddenly, and, believe me, that blessed kerbau turned right round and followed her down the path like a lamb.

"Coulson waited a minute, shifted his huge carcase from its perch, and slid ponderously down the tree to the ground. Then he had a good dose of cramp in two places at once, and swore himself pretty well hoarse. I don't suppose any man has ever felt more of a damned idiot than Coulson did then.

"A loud female voice broke in upon his blasphemous reflections, and he turned sharply to see the pretty, dark face of Maradi grinnin' roguishly at him through the bushes.

"She gave him a wicked little look and then disappeared, shriekin' with mirth—an open challenge for him to follow. But hide-and-seek wasn't appealin' to him just then, and he didn't.

"It seemed to him, on reflection, that Maradi wasn't anythin' like as pretty as he'd thought she was—in fact, at some moments she looked positively ugly, especially when she laughed. Then it began to dawn upon him that he hadn't really acted very decently towards Johnson. Anyhow, it wouldn't do to have a woman about the house who grinned at one like that on the least provocation.

"Coulson walked slowly back the way he had come till he'd found his stick and topi; then, as darkness had fallen suddenly, and he knew the kerbaus must be all safely tethered up, he strode back to Johnson's bungalow, feelin' a very different sort of man to the one who had started out earlier in the day. On one thing he was particularly certain—he didn't want Maradi. Johnson could have her and welcome, and her old Dusun father could go to the devil.

"Hullo! there's the makan (meal) bell. Well, I'm going in to have a wash-up. See you downstairs. Eh? What's that? Oh, did Johnson buy Maradi? Well, what do you think? Yes? Then you're wrong, for the next mail brought such a lovin' little letter from the girl at home that Johnson—well, I'm off in here, or I shan't be in time to get any makan."

VIII

THE MAN WHO STOLE THE HEAD

NIGHT, DARK NIGHT, had fallen over jungle and swamp and over the wide-stretching rubber-grown Kabun. Occasional swinging lanterns dotted the winding hill paths, and below, somewhere beyond the sago swamp, glowed the watch-fires of a Marut village.

From the adjacent coolie lines came a chorus of hoarse cries. The Sikh watchman, tall and bearded, halted outside the open bungalow and stood for just a moment, his turbaned head on one side, listening intently.

"Mine-mine (gambling)," he muttered to himself, and resumed his solitary tour of inspection. Gambling is quite allowable on Borneo rubber estates after business hours—it keeps the coolies out of mischief. Bull-frogs were croaking away down there in the swamps, and fire-flies flitted like minute fairy lamps through the inky darkness. Suddenly there came a wild shout from the native village, and a dozen gongs throbbed tumultuously in weird barbaric time.

"A native hari-besar (feast-day)," remarked Holliday from the depths of his long cane chair.

"Makin' a damn lot of noise about it," replied Gordon, the other assistant, drily. "Hope they don't do this sort of thing often."

"They do," said Holliday cheerfully. "Week a time when the padi-harvest comes along. Musical, isn't it?"

Gordon puffed thoughtfully at his blackened briar. Another chorus of cries broke upon the stillness of the tropical night.

"What's on now?" he inquired slowly.

"Dancin', I expect. Rather a picturesque ceremony. Ever seen a native ball?"

The other shook his head. "Ought to be rather interestin'," he said at last. "Make a fit subject for letter-writin' next mail—it's about time I sent 'em a decent epistle. Last one was four fines."

"Shall we just stroll across, then? The headman had often asked me to drop in. Get one of the boys to carry a lantern. Hi, boy! Mana teucan-ayer (where's the water-carrier)?"

The Chinese boy shouted something inarticulate from the kitchen in the rear, and a weird-looking, under-sized coolie, in a loose blue coat and khaki trousers rolled up above the knee, appeared hurriedly in answer to his call.

"Lampo, sana!" He jerked his thumb across the hills.

The creature hurried out, passing on his way to squash a huge spider, as big as a plum, with the flat of his grimy hand. He returned in a few moments with a hurricane lamp in one hand and a stout pole in the other.

The two men rose from their chairs, and Holliday poured out some whisky.

"Have a stenga," he said. "Say when!" And he tipped soda-water into each tumbler from a bottle with a glass ball stopper. The soda-water was a local preparation, and tasted rather of rubber.

"Ugh!" said Gordon, putting down his empty glass. "Pay us to invest in a seltzogene. Filthy tack this! However, mustn't grumble, I s'pose. Ought to think ourselves lucky we can get any at all—in this damn, God-forsaken wilderness!"

The two men strolled out into the night together; the water-carrier was waiting for them with the lamp a few paces ahead, and, skilfully manipulating the light so that a considerable portion of the path was always visible, trotted along a yard or so in their wake.

They climbed the hill, slowly descended into the valley below, and took a path which led between the flooded fields of padi, and eventually through a narrow strip of jungle beyond. They strode along in silence, each absorbed in his own thoughts and puffing at a well-used pipe.

The jungle is never still, and at night myriads of unseen beings join in a wonderful humming chorus, combining to produce a sound not unlike the music of the telegraph wires in a gale. Every now and again branches crack and fall to the ground, perhaps naturally, perhaps due to the stealthy movement of some giant ape. Stags utter their cough-like signals to their kind, unseen woodpeckers tap-tap-tap with monotonous persistence, and sudden nightly fears draw forth a chorus of shrieks from adjacent monkey colonies.

The two men trudging along, side by side, were not unused to these matters, and the teucan-ayer, who patiently manipulated the swinging lantern, knew them well. To the white races these sounds are due to a natural order of things, but to the darker-skinned, less matter-of-fact members of humanity these are the voices of great hidden spirits endowed with boundless powers for good or evil.

Gordon followed Holliday into the Murut village through a cloud of smoke which made the eyes smart and irritated the nostrils. Almost nude figures were dancing in the flickering light of the huge fires, waving aloft long poles with something round and dark on the end of each. The headman of the village came forward to meet them, and, after a short conversation in Malay with Holliday, led the way to a native hut, raised from the ground on many long poles. The headman clambered up a rickety ladder and the two white men followed, squeezing into a small hole in the wall which served as a door.

Two native women in black velvet coats, brightly coloured sarongs, and many huge silver ornaments, were sitting on the floor near the entrance. The headman said something in his own dialect, and one hurriedly left the hut, while the other—an older woman—disappeared into an inner room, reappearing eventually with an earthenware jar and two cups of Chinese origin.

"Sam-su!" whispered Holliday. "Don't drink it if you've never tasted it before."

The other nodded and said nothing.

There was a smelling oil lamp swinging from one of the beams which supported the roof of sago leaves, but the glass was so grimed and blackened that very little light could filter through.

The liquor was poured into the cups and the white men raised them to their lips. With a deft movement of his foot, Holliday sent a small, roughly carved stool flying across the room, and, as the headman stooped to secure it, emptied the liquor from his cup out of the adjacent doorway; Gordon followed suit. Holliday apologised roughly for his clumsiness, and they followed their host into an adjacent apartment. There was a window cut in one of the walls, and through this the dancing forms were clearly visible.

They squatted down on native mats, and soon afterwards the headman left them.

Gongs were thumping on all sides, and weird whistles and hoarse cries rent the air.

"All pretty tight, I should say," said Gordon suddenly.

"Sam-su's a pretty elevatin' liquor," replied the other drily. "See what they've got on those poles?"

The other strained his eyes, striving to pierce the gloom.

"Can't quite make out. Thought they were melons or pomoloes at first. By Gad! they look damn like human heads!"

"They are," said Holliday. He bent forward and blew some nicotine out of the stem of his pipe. "Human heads, my lad, preserved by judicious smoking over the fire. They trot 'em out on these nights as a sort of special treat."

The other said nothing for a moment—he was thinking.

"I should rather like one of these for a curio," he said at last.

Holliday grunted. "Damn queer taste you've got, I must say. Bi-la! I expect you'll grow out of it."

Gordon was not listening.

"I've got a wonderful specimen of a straight kris, with carved sarong and engraved blade; an opium pipe, a native bamboo axe, several rotan-woven hats, and a padi planting-stick; but I shan't call my collection anything like complete until I've managed to lay hands on one of those heads. They're typical of the country and its customs."

"It's a damn unhealthy country," said Holliday slowly, "and its customs are as low as the dirty races that inhabit it. Still, each to his taste. Lookin' at it from a purely commercial point of view, those heads are worth about a five-pound note, I'm told—to a collector at home. Still, that wouldn't induce me to risk my skin gettin' one."

He paused, tilted back his topi, and mopped his brow with a loud bandana handkerchief.

"I've lived out here," he continued, "for close on nine years, and I've always made it a rule not to interfere with native religions, prejudices, or superstitions. They think a great deal of this head-huntin' craze, and now it's being stamped out—more or less—they prize those grim relics they still possess all the more. As a plain matter-of-fact, if you were to pinch one to-night and try and clear with it, they'd not improbably knife you right away."

Gordon was filling his pipe deliberately, pressing the dark tobacco into the blackened bowl. He threw the pouch on to Holliday's knees.

"It would be a bit of sport, wouldn't it?" he said.

"It depends what you term 'sport,'" replied the other. "It'd be somethin' like lookin' at a hunt from the fox's point of view. Then there's another thing. You're newly out, and you'll probably laugh at the whole idea. You've never squatted on the ground in a way-back Kampon and listened to the old men spinnin' yarns. You don't know any of the native folk-lore; but I do. Behind all their tommy-rot and fetish there's somethin' real. Ask any native what'd happen to you if you stole a head. He'll tell you, as sure as there's a sun in the sky, that you'd be haunted."

Gordon was not laughing, as the other had anticipated. On the contrary, he was looking at him in silent wonderment. He had never known the older man to talk so long or so seriously before.

Outside the gongs boomed and throbbed, the natives leaped and shouted, the fires flashed and smoked.

"That's jolly int'resting," admitted Gordon suddenly. "But I mean to get a head before I leave. Surely you don't believe in ghosts and spooks?"

"Perhaps I do, and perhaps I don't," replied Holliday shortly. "But sometimes, when you're livin' alone with the jungle all round you, and no sort of society whatever, you begin to fancy things exist which common sense tells you can't be. Ah, well, you won't understand, and the time's gettin' on. This won't get us up at five in the morning, and I want to put the coolies on padjak work (piecework) weedin' the hills to-morrow."

He rose and stretched himself; Gordon followed suit, and they both passed into the outer room. The older of the two women was busy finishing off a small basket in rotan. Gordon stooped and examined the work. It was very neat, and the basket was made to carry over the shoulders like a haversack.

"B'rapa (how much)?" he asked, and showed a silver dollar.

The woman grinned, Holliday whistled, the exchange was made, and the two men clambered out of the hole and down the rickety steps, Gordon carrying the basket. The headman hurried up as the white-clad figures passed the fires. Everywhere they stepped aside to avoid recumbent natives, drunk with the deadly sam-su. A dozen semi-nude enthusiasts still continued the dance, but then steps were laboured, and their cries sounded queerly forced. The hari-besar was finished. The fires were burning low, all the gongs but two had ceased to play.

The chief left them at the entrance to the village, and Holliday voiced their thanks for the hospitality extended. The dwarfed teucan-ayer had appeared stealthily from nowhere in particular, and the lantern was ready to light them on their way back to the bungalow. It was dark beneath the overhanging trees, and the path was badly marked. Suddenly Gordon kicked something, stopped, and bent down.

Holliday went on a few paces and then noticed that the other was not following. He glanced back.

"What's up?" he cried.

Gordon was slipping something into his native-woven basket.

"Cocoa-nut," he replied shortly, but there was a queer, triumphant smile on his sunburnt face, and he carried the rotan basket as carefully as if its closely-woven texture hid a treasure as fabulous in value as the Koh-i-Noor.

Gordon ran a few paces to where the other had halted, and the lantern jerked on its way again. Suddenly Holliday started back, swore fiercely, and began beating about in all directions with his long malacca.

"Snake on the path," he said. "Ought to wear gaiters, I s'pose. Beastly things—snakes. Come on!"

Up the dark hill paths, between the waving branches of growing rubber, wound the little procession—the two white men and the little brown-skinned teucan-ayer with the swinging hurricane lamp.

The night was very still, save for the distant subdued throbbing of belated village gongs and the humming of insects, which never ceases in the East till the curtain of night is withdrawn. As they approached the bungalow a couple of fox-terriers ran out, barking, to meet them, and followed them joyously into the house. A tailless, ginger-coloured, diminutive cat was washing itself on a long chair on the verandah, scarcely pausing to look up as the two white men mounted the steps. A meal was waiting for them in the inner room under a white cloth, the outer surface of which was literally covered with insects of all descriptions—jumping, flying, and crawling. Gordon lifted it up and shook it over the rail of the verandah. Holliday sat down, and, pouring out a thimbleful or so of gin and a colouring of Angostura, helped a large tabloid of quinine down his parched throat.

As he put down his empty glass he suddenly caught sight of the native basket his companion had bought when leaving the village. Gordon was unlacing his boots somewhere out on the broad, open verandah, swearing loudly over an obstinate knot.

Holliday stretched out his hand and caught hold of the bottom end of the basket. It slipped from the chair on to which Gordon had thrown it, and something fell out and rolled away across the floor. One of the terriers ran under the table and sniffed at it suspiciously as Holliday stooped, felt for it with his hand, and picked it up.

He drew it from under the cloth into the lamplight, then started, and nearly dropped it again. It was not a cocoa-nut, as Gordon had said, but a human head—one of those hideous, shrivelled relics that had taken so prominent a part in the evening's entertainment.

Holliday sat staring at this grisly memento for some moments in silence, thinking. The problem was somewhat complex. He had scarcely allowed Gordon out of his sight, and yet he had somehow managed to attain his desire—the possession of a Borneo "head." His collection of native curios was almost complete.

So deep was he in thought that he did not hear the entry of Mena—his Dusun ngi (housekeeper). She wore a long sarong, displaying a fair amount of shoulder and neck, rather after the style of an ultra-modern evening dress, and was puffing idly at a fat hand-made cigarette.

For a native woman she was really beautiful, though a connoisseur might have quarrelled with the broadness of her nose, and perhaps some slight suggestion of thickness in her lips. She glided in from the open passage which led from the kitchen, her bare feet scarcely making a sound on the rough wooden floor, and was just about to slip past her master on to the verandah for a quiet siesta while the white men supped, when her sharp black eyes caught sight of the stolen head.

She stopped still, gasped, and uttered a shrill scream.

Holliday started up and dropped the hideous relic, which rolled away into a far corner; Gordon ran in from the verandah, and both men stood staring at the native woman inquiringly.

"Deri mana?" (where did you get it), she gasped, pointing with a trembling finger.

Holliday laughed, and jerked his thumb across the table towards his friend.

"Lien Tuan ada kasih," (the other assistant brought it), he said in crude Malay, such as all Borneo planters affect.

The girl's eyes opened wide in undisguised terror, her nostrils dilated.

"Take it back!" she commanded hoarsely. "Give it back at once—it is not safe to keep, Tuan. Kau sudah honto!" (you will be haunted).

Gordon laughed, shrugged his broad shoulders, strode across to where the grim head lay, and picked it up deliberately. The girl shuddered, shrank back, and disappeared on to the dark verandah. Gordon snapped his fingers and laughed again loudly.

"So much for native superstitions," he said. "This spends the night on my dressing-table, beside my Bajau kris!"

Holliday said nothing, but pulled out his pipe and started rubbing tobacco in the palm of his rough hand.

"I had rather you than me," he said at last.

Gordon shrugged his shoulders and turned on his heel.

"Well, I've got the damn thing, anyway, haven't I?" he cried defiantly.

The older man nodded.

"Yes," he said, "you've got it, but I wouldn't keep it long, if I were you."

Gordon looked back over his shoulder. "Good night!" he said, pausing at the door. "Good night, old man!" And Gordon had disappeared.

Holliday heard him drop the head on to the table and bawl out to the boy to fan out his kalambo (mosquito curtain) more thoroughly. He heard him throw his slippers into a corner, and eventually a thud and a creaking of springs announced that the younger man was in bed.

Holliday pushed his heavy brown moustache back from his lips and thoughtfully twirled the ends.

"Bi-la!" he murmured. "I daresay he's right, after all. Experience goes for little in these days, and youth must be served. Ah! would you?"

He drew the skin tight over his great brown wrist and neatly secured the tiny mosquito as it struck. He stretched his arms and yawned.

"To bed—to bed!" he muttered, and turned out the light.

Holliday moved suddenly in his sleep, stirred, stretched himself, then sat bolt upright in bed. The clock on the chair by his side was ticking away merrily, occasionally breaking out into a louder and more pronounced tickety-tack-tickety-tack, after the manner of all cheap timekeepers. A cricket was calling somewhere down in a far corner. There was no other sound except, perhaps, the rustling of the sago-leaf roof in a gentle breeze from the sea.

And yet—and yet Holliday *knew* something was wrong. The air, instead of being clear and cool, as is customary in Borneo in the hours that follow midnight, seemed thick and heavy, and he fancied he could detect the presence of some faint perfume.

On the other side of the wooden partition Gordon lay sleeping. Was it on his account he felt so anxious, so disturbed? He turned his eyes towards the intervening wall, hoping to gain a glimpse, perhaps, through some crack or crevice to reassure him, ease his fevered mind, and allow him to resume his sleep.

Suddenly he started. What was that? A voice—Gordon's?

"Oh, my God!"

The words were uttered as by one in mortal terror.

Holliday tried to rise, but somehow his limbs seemed paralysed, and he could not move. And then the darkness lifted suddenly, and, somehow or other, he knew that he could see, in spite of the wooden partition between, all that was passing in Gordon's bedroom.

He saw a figure lying on a bed beneath a thin mosquito curtain, and he knew that that figure was Gordon's. On a table beyond the bed stood a long, straight native weapon in its sheath, and beside it, on its side, lay the hideous head he had handled only a few hours before. The room appeared strangely lit, and the centre of this luminous haze seemed to be the "head."

Holliday, by some mysterious means rendered momentarily powerless, gazed as if fascinated at the grisly relic. Suddenly a cold sweat bathed his forehead and his hair rose on end. The head had shifted from its position and now stood upright on the table. As he watched, mute with horror, the head seemed to rise in the air till it hung, unsupported, about five feet from the floor. Then he became aware, rather than actually saw, that there was a shadowy suggestion of a body and two arms groping about, apparently aimlessly, in the queer half-light.

Then he saw the weapon on the table lifted from its position and whirled suddenly from its hand-carved sheath.

And then Gordon rose in bed and sat staring in terror at the apparition before him.

Holliday gasped. "A dream!" he muttered. "All a dream!" But then a mosquito that had somehow invaded the privacy of his curtained bed thrust its proboscis into his ankle—and he knew that he must be awake. Just there on the chair by the bed that infernal alarm clock tick-tacked away merrily—and far away, beyond the slopes of rubber, a stag was coughing.

The awful apparition stretched out a shadowy arm and drew back the curtains from Gordon's bed, and then Gordon made a swift movement, drew a revolver from beneath his pillow, and fired once—twice. The smoke cleared, but the apparition still hovered menacingly over the bed. A cry of helpless agony broke from Gordon's lips.

"Holliday! Help! Holliday! Oh, my God!"

But Holliday could not move—was powerless to speak.

Suddenly Gordon threw himself from his bed, and, turning twice to fire at his ghostly pursuer, fled on to the verandah, followed by the awful apparition, the light passing with it.

Holliday, helpless to aid him, saw his companion rushing madly from the verandah out into the darkness of the tropic night, and the shadowy form, with the sword, passed swiftly and silently after him.

An awful cry of agony, a deafening crash, and all was dark again.

Holliday hurried out on to the verandah. The dogs were whining queerly under the house. He called them each by name, but they did not come. He grazed his shin on an overturned chair. An overturned chair! His heart beat tumultuously, and he plunged into Gordon's room.

He held the lantern high above him.

"God in heaven!" he cried.

There was no one on the bed, and the mosquito curtains had been ripped away on either side!

He reeled and turned towards the table.

The wick, badly trimmed, burnt low for a moment, and then the flame flickered suddenly back to normal.

The circle of yellow light fell on to the wooden table. There, on its side, lay the hideous native head; by it, too, rested the Bajau kris, unsheathed and wet with blood! On the other side of the reeking weapon, just out of the circle of light, was something round and white, resting on what appeared to be a dark, irregular stain.

Holliday leaned forward and moved the light towards it.

"My God!" he screamed, "it's Gordon!"

And, lamp in hand, he crashed senseless to the floor.

IX

THE CURE OF KOOMANIS

"QUEER, ISN'T IT?" remarked the D.O. (District Officer) drily.

Openshaw held it gingerly between a finger and thumb. "And that," he mused aloud, "spells death."

"Instanter," added the D.O. "Death in ten seconds; and the peculiar thing to me is that when that little arrow has done its dreadful work—sudah habis—it is finished! *Par exemple*—a native will eat with impunity a monkey shot by a sumpitan."

Openshaw whistled. "And they puff it through that," he said, jerking his head towards a long, hollow shaft standing in the corner of the Rest House.

The D.O. nodded. "Ever seen a Borneo head? They collect 'em, y'know. Int'resting hobby, eh?"

Openshaw shuddered involuntarily as his companion balanced the hideous trophy in his hand.

"Smoke 'em in the fire till they're black, and the skin is preserved. Sort of memento of their palmy days. String 'em up in their houses and have a look through 'em occasionally, same as you might look up a bunch of old friends in some family photo-album. Choice idea."

"Well, I'm damned!"

"Superstitious lot too, these natives," continued the loquacious Porson. "Think these beastly specimens bring 'em no end of luck. Devil of a to-do if somebody pinches one—no end of trouble. I had a bit of a row over this beauty. However, here's makan."

A white-clad Chinaman, his long tow-chung tucked into a side pocket, announced that the evening meal awaited them in the room below. Openshaw followed his new friend down the wooden stairs. He had just arrived from England, and the steamer that had brought him from Singapore was still at anchor in the harbour. On the morrow he intended taking the train to the rubber estate on which he had contracted to assist. He was rather surprised no one had come down to meet him, but, in blissful ignorance of Oriental manners and customs, surmised that business was too pressing to enable the manager to get away.

As they sat smoking over their liqueurs after dinner Porson remarked suddenly:

"Talking about superstitions, there's one estate up the line the natives all swear blind is haunted. Awf'ly strange, y'know—only been started about a year and lost two managers already. The first was found smothered in a sago-swamp—wasn't a bad one, either. And the second—well, he disappeared altogether. Police search, y'know, armed patrols, inquiries, detectives, an' all that—never a ghost of a clue."

He bit his cigar in two and grinned. Openshaw whistled. The D.O. rose suddenly and yawned.

"Bi-la," he said. "Sihaya pergi tidor (I'm going to bed)."

They went up together. As they parted on the high verandah Openshaw turned suddenly.

"By the by," he asked casually, "what estate did you say that was?"

"Koomanis. Why? What's the matter?"

Openshaw was staring out into the night. "Good God!" he gasped. "Koomanis! That's where I've signed on!"

On the following morning they left the Rest House together—Openshaw having sent his luggage on ahead—and strolled towards the little station through a street of bright Chinese shops, drained by two deep, evil-smelling trenches on either side of the road. Swarms of dusky children played in the dust, and just round a corner a chorus of weird cries announced the presence of a market. On the station they parted with a warm handshake.

"Tabi, old man—best of luck!" cried the D.O. as the train moved away. "Perhaps it was only coincidence after all. Cheer up."

Openshaw agreed loudly, albeit with inward misgivings, and walked to his seat in the long, bumping carriage marked "Europeans Only." There were only two other occupants of the car—a doctor with a large red Chinese umbrella, and an elderly, bearded padre in flowing white gown with a bright red sash and a white topi. Neither looked up as Openshaw sat down, and he began to realise that one can feel very lonely in the East—even among one's kind.

"Kinabalu," remarked the doctor suddenly, pointing back with the stem of his pipe. "Don't often see it as clear as that."

He relapsed into silence, and the newcomer gazed in wonderment at the great guttering light rising through the haze of the early morning.

The long white train bumped along on a most pernicious set of metals—over swamp and between dark, overhanging banks. It jerked suddenly to a standstill by the barracks, and a tall Sikh in military uniform helped the Chinese guard with some barang (luggage), the padre got out, and the train moved on again.

"Koomanis!"

The guard's hoarse cry roused Openshaw from his reverie. He hurried out and checked each article of luggage as it was thrown with studied carelessness from the van. The long train jerked unwillingly on again, and Openshaw stood alone by the shining rails, amid a pile of barang, surveying the spot that was to be his home for three long, weary, baking years.

Through the palm trees to his right he could just catch a glimpse of a very blue sea; to his left rose a steep declivity ascended by means of a winding path; before and behind him the sleepered track, bordered by many trees. A hornbill flew suddenly high above him, shrieking hoarsely. This was the only sign of life. Openshaw shivered, and realised that nobody was there to meet him, to offer him a word of welcome. No sweating coolies ran down to take his barang. He swung suddenly round on his heel and, grasping his stick, strode swiftly up the steep hill-path.

Half-way up a sharp little fox-terrier darted towards him and then disappeared again, whining pitifully.

"Strange!" muttered Openshaw. He rather liked dogs. He stopped suddenly, mopped his brow, and glanced ahead.

Before him, raised from the ground on four stout posts, rose a neat, modern bungalow, atap-roofed (roofed with sago leaves), with a broad verandah approached by a short flight of steps.

He hurried forward, then stopped, staggered, and almost fell, for, mutilated, lying amid a pool of blood at the foot of the stairs, was a headless human form.

Openshaw's blood ran cold.

"My God!" he gasped. "It's a white!"

He stood for a moment transfixed with horror. A sound caused him to turn sharply. The little fox-terrier was just behind him, whining softly. He stooped and patted it, and the animal licked his hand. Each felt grateful for the other's company.

Openshaw pulled himself together, sprang over the corpse, and mounted the wooden steps. The bedroom door stood open, and the bed had been recently slept in. The manager, disturbed in his sleep by the barking of his dog, had leapt out of bed and been met—by what? Openshaw looked down at the dog—it had followed him into the bungalow.

"Perhaps you know, old boy," he said. "I wish to heaven you could speak."

Half an hour later Openshaw met the other assistant on the hill-path beyond the house.

"Hullo!" cried the other. "You the new man?"

Openshaw nodded. "My name's Openshaw," he said.

"And mine's Mason."

Their hands gripped.

"Boss up yet?" he inquired suddenly.

Openshaw looked him straight in the eyes. "He's dead!" he cried hoarsely.

Mason gasped, then sat down suddenly on a boulder and pulled out his pipe.

"Poor devil! I knew it would come. Poor old chap! How we've stuck it these last few months I don't know. Anyhow, it's finished now—sudah habis!—and the estate can go to the devil for all I care. We'll pay the coolies, settle up, and clear, eh?"

Openshaw did not answer at first—he was thinking. He saw in his mind's eye a drawing-room in a cosy little flat in town, a glowing fire casting deep shadows on the wall, and a beautiful girl, tall and graceful, with coils of wonderful raven hair. "Yes, Kenneth," he heard her say, "when you are a manager I will come out to you." The thought gave him courage. There were possibilities about this billet.

"It's no damn use at all stayin'!" Mason was saying, puffing at his blackened briar. "I draw all that's due to me and my fare home from the estate coffers. We'll take the next boat to Singapore—*Chow-fa,* isn't it?"

Openshaw drew himself up. "I don't blame you," he said slowly. "If I'd been in your shoes these last few months I'd do the same, but I haven't. I'm interested, I'm keen, and the place appeals to me. I'm sticking on here."

Mason laughed, turned on his heel, and strode back across the estate.

"I'll send some coolies over to bury him," he shouted back. "I'm going to pack—right now."

He walked a few paces and then looked back. "But you'll follow in a week," he said.

The body of the late manager was buried that day, and Mason left with all his worldly goods by the only train. He tried hard to persuade Openshaw to the very last to give up his resolve, but to no purpose.

A very lone man, inexperienced but firm, watched the rocking train till it vanished round the bend. He felt that he had cut himself off from the whole world. He turned away with a deep sigh—and then he smiled. The little fox-terrier was sitting mournfully a few yards away. It rose and trotted after him as he made his way back to the house. At least, he had one companion in his solitude.

In the hours that had elapsed between the discovery and Mason's departure many important things had been arranged. The only two rifles on the estate were now in the possession of stalwart Pathan watchmen, who were ordered to patrol the path round the house all night, coughing each time the manager's window was passed.

A Chinese cook had been brought from the other bungalow, and had consented to work all day, but stubbornly refused to sleep there at night. Mason had advised Openshaw to occupy the other house, but the newcomer had his own views, and stuck to his guns. Openshaw did not sleep that night.

The morning's train brought a pleasant surprise. A white-clad figure leapt out, almost before the engine had jerked to a standstill, and Porson—the loquacious D.O. from the Rest House at Api-Api—was soon gripping him by the hand. A black orderly followed him and stood at attention outside.

"Met Mason last night," he puffed. "Told me all the lurid details. Really here officially, y'know! My! but you've struck a lovely billet. What the devil do you mean by hanging on? Gad! that's a beast of a hill, though."

"I've a theory," said Openshaw slowly. "Have a drink? Boy!"

The new cook ran in.

"Dua gin slings, lakas (quickly)!" He had learnt that on the boat.

The boy returned in a few moments with two glasses of pink liquid on a tray.

"Well, my budding detective," remarked Porson suddenly, "and what's the nature of the theory?"

Openshaw smiled. "It hasn't matured sufficiently yet," he said, "but I think I'm on the right track."

Porson had a vast fund of information. He tramped the estate all day with his new friend, and the fox-terrier trotted tirelessly after them, occasionally darting into the jungle and evincing boundless delight in disturbing hosts of chattering monkeys.

They visited the Mandors (Chinese overseers) in charge of toiling bands of coolies, and Openshaw began to see the why and wherefore of things, and picked up no end of Malay.

"The Malay language, as used in Borneo," the D.O. explained, "consists of a conglomeration of Chinese and Malay words interspersed at judicious intervals with naughty cuss words in almost every tongue under the sun. If you're ever at a loss for a word, swear; they'll understand."

Openshaw smiled and made a mental note of this. To a practical mind rubber-planting is much like everything else—it stands to reason.

"I'm damn glad I met you," remarked Openshaw as they sat down to their evening meal.

"Got your watchmen out yet?" asked Porson, putting down his empty glass.

"Not yet. They're due out at eight."

"H'm! I should have 'em out a bit earlier if I were you. Doesn't do to take too many risks."

Openshaw thought. "No," he said at last, "I forgot it grew dark so soon."

They wandered out on to the verandah. Porson sank into a big "Borneo" chair. They smoked for a while in silence.

"Jove!" said Openshaw suddenly. "You do look comfortable. I'd like to take your photograph like that."

"Label it 'Overworked Government Official,'" grinned Porson, "and send it home."

Openshaw got up. "That's the very idea," he said and disappeared. He returned a few moments later with a camera and tripod in one hand and a saucer in the other.

"Flash powder," he explained, and dived behind a black cloth.

"Beautiful! Don't move." He thrust his cigar into the powder.

There was a short pause, a blinding flash, and then something brushed past Openshaw's sleeve and struck the wall behind him with a smart tap. He stooped down.

"Bug?" asked the D.O., rubbing his eyes.

Openshaw was holding something to the light. His face had turned an ashen grey. Then he drew his pistol smartly and fired deliberately twice into the darkness.

Two watchmen ran to the foot of the steps. Openshaw turned to the astonished D.O. "Tell them to go on duty at once," he said.

Porson obeyed, then turned inquiringly to his companion.

"A damn narrow squeak," said Openshaw in a queer, strained voice. He held a short, frail dart between a finger and thumb. "Our old friend the Sumpitan," he said.

The D.O. whistled. "I shall sleep well to-night," he murmured.

Porson left next day by train for Api-Api.

"Well, I've done my duty," he said, "and I shall report that the late manager died in the same mysterious way as his unfortunate predecessors. You say you'll not be requirin' police assistance just yet? Very well, I report that the new manager is taking every precaution, and—"

"—is confident of running the murderous marauder to earth baniak lakas (very quickly)."

They both laughed as the train pulled up. Porson's face suddenly became serious.

"You mean to stay?" he asked, regarding his companion earnestly.

Openshaw swallowed a lump in his throat and held the other's hand for quite a minute.

"Thanks, old man," he said huskily. "I must. By the by," he whispered suddenly, "don't forget to send me those dozen arrows. I want them badly."

And the train moved on.

The two stalwart Pathans patrolled the path round the bungalow early that night, and Openshaw developed the photograph. He held the curling film up to the ruby hght for a moment and gazed at it intently. Suddenly he gasped, and passed it into the fixing solution.

"Jove!" he said as he turned into bed. "What an extraordinary bit of luck!"

The morning's train brought a long cardboard cylinder, and Openshaw did not trouble to guess at its contents. He worked for an hour with a brace and fine bit, boring deep holes into the wooden sill of his bedroom window. Then he put on his coat and strolled out across the estate.

A few weeks later Porson received a short note by native messenger. He tore it open and anxiously scanned the contents.

> "Dear Porson—All well to date. If you are game for a little quiet amusement, come up to-night. What reward do you offer for the body of the highwayman? Best chin-chins,
>
> "OPENSHAW."

He saddled his pony and went.

Openshaw was out when he reached the bungalow. The D.O. ordered a drink, gave his pony in charge of a watchman, and waited patiently. About an hour later the manager strolled in, followed by the terrier. The two men exchanged hearty greetings, and the D.O. noted with satisfaction that Openshaw looked well and almost cheerful.

"I can promise you some excitement to-night," he said, and threw his mud-stained boots into a corner.

"Theory still going strong, then?"

"Rather! First-rate! We retire to the bathroom, which leads off from my bedroom, at 9.30 p.m. Soon after, I calculate, the fun should commence. Game?"

"Absolutely. Any news?"

"Cabled the directors since you left. Had a very satisfactory reply. They've been getting a bit uneasy, you know. The fact is, I'm Tuan Besar (manager) here for good if I can hold on. They're sending me two assistants—on the way now."

"Hearty congrats!" cried the other. "And, by Jove, you'll deserve it!"

"And there's another thing," mused Openshaw. "There's a girl over there waiting to come out to me." He waved his hand towards the calm blue sea below them.

Porson smiled. "So that accounts for it all," he said. "Old man, I wish you joy—loads of it!"

At dusk the two tall sentinels came on duty. Openshaw and the D.O. ate their evening meal in silence. Porson was too excited to eat much, but the manager's hunger was great. A day's hard work on a broad estate is an excellent appetiser.

"Come on," said Openshaw at last. "Got your pistol?"

The D.O. tapped his pocket. They strolled through the sleeping apartment and descended the two stairs on to the concrete floor of the bathroom beyond. Porson noticed that the unglazed window of the bedroom stood half open. A small oil-lamp was burning on a table, and through the mosquito curtains be suddenly caught sight of a still form asleep on the bed. "Who's that?" he gasped.

"A dummy," whispered Openshaw, and pulled the bathroom door to. There were two holes bored in the woodwork of the door.

"You can get a good view of everything that goes on in that room from here," said Openshaw.

The clock on the verandah coughed ten.

"The guard has gone off duty," he whispered. "Patience, *mon ami,* we are going to see something soon."

Hours seemed to pass as the two men waited in grim silence, each clutching a loaded revolver.

Suddenly there came a soft sound outside—just a rustle of something—and that was all. Perhaps it was only the breeze in the rubber trees, a falling leaf; perhaps—

Porson's hair seemed to rise on end. The window began to open—very slowly. He clutched involuntarily at Openshaw's arm. Through the aperture came the spear-tipped end of a bamboo tube. There were black fingers on the casement now.

Click!—something passed through the thin mosquito curtains and struck the wall beyond.

Click!—another something was sticking in the motionless form on the bed.

Then, as the cold sweat poured down Porson's face and neck, two black hands grasped the sill. His finger sought the trigger.

An awful pause, and then a terrible, inarticulate cry broke upon the stillness of the Eastern night. There was a heavy thud on the path without.

Openshaw flung open the door and plunged, pistol in hand, into the room. The D.O. followed.

"Sudah habis—it is finished," said the manager calmly, and Porson heard footsteps hurrying on the path outside.

Together they ran down the verandah steps and out into the night.

Under the bedroom window the two Pathans were bending over something dark and one of them carried a hurricane lamp. The two white men joined them, and the watchmen came swiftly to attention.

"Don't touch the window-sill!" cried Openshaw in Malay. He knew something of the language now.

The figure of a short, muscular Murut lay doubled up on the path, his broad features hideously contorted in the agony of death.

Openshaw bent down and picked up a bamboo tube, a short cylinder of wood bound with ratan, and an unsheathed parang. A watchman handed him a curved sheath, ornamented from end to end with tufts of human hair, alternately black and white.

"Take him away," ordered Openshaw. "And one of you can go to bed."

The two friends sat on the verandah smoking peacefully. The fox-terrier lay sleeping, curled up comfortably in a corner, and the twinkling of myriads of tiny lights below revealed the movements of a host of Dusun men and women busy spiking fish in the shallow water of the bay.

"Well, you're a marvel," remarked Porson suddenly. "Damned if I know what to make of you. And, by the by, what was the matter with the window-sill?"

Openshaw grinned. "The point of a poisoned arrow every two inches," he said drily. "Caught in his own trap—see?"

Porson made a queer sound with his tongue on the roof of his mouth. "And the theory?" he asked at length.

"It all dawned upon me when I remembered your learned lecture on arrows and head hunting; native wronged by a white; thirsting for white heads. Follow?"

Porson nodded thoughtfully.

"You remember my narrow escape that night? Well, after that I knew he was there, watching his opportunity. I carefully laid my trap, guarded diligently until to-night, then the watchmen, instructed by me, pretended to mutiny and slip off to bed. Well, you know the rest."

The D.O. puffed for a moment in silence. Then he said: "But supposing there are others?"

"There aren't," replied Openshaw drily, and, drawing a square of paper from his pocket, thumped it down on the table before the astonished D.O.

It was a photograph taken by flashlight. Porson held it close to the light. He recognised himself reclining lazily in the long Borneo chair, but, clearly visible in a corner, one hand grasping the edge of the verandah, his pursed-up lips to the sumpitan, was the face of the hideous native they had just left stretched on the path.

"I see," said the D.O. slowly. "What a wonderful stroke of luck!"

Openshaw laughed. "All serene, I think, officer," he said. "You can make out your official report in the morning. And there'll be a couple of cables—if you don't mind."

"I understand," said Porson, slapping his companion warmly on the back. "One to the directors and the other—to the girl."

X

LONELY VALLEY

I

THE BURLY SKIPPER of the steamer "Lohengrin," at anchor off Yokohama, looked across the little cabin at his Chinese Chin-chu (super-cargo), Soon-Chong.

"Chin," he growled, "I'm broke. They did me down in town last evenin' for something over twenty quid—a good bit of which I wanted to send home to the missus—and I'm damned if I know which way to turn for a little ready money. No, you're a man of brains—like the rest of your cunnin' race—and so I've just strolled down to look at you and hear what suggestions you've got to make. One thing's certain: I've got to secure a tidy sum of money—and that shortly. It's no damn use talkin' to me about gambling—my luck's dead out. You and I've sailed together without a single break these eleven years and more—and I reckon we understand one another a little."

The portly Chin-chu, in a wonderful shore-going garb, consisting of very wide black satin trousers and a white coat, across which stretched an enormous gold watch chain, smoked placidly, seated in a corner of the cabin by a small table littered with papers. He rarely spoke at all, never without careful consideration, and always in the most perfect English—without even the characteristic substitution of the letter "l" for "r."

"To make money," he remarked slowly, "you must buy low and sell high."

The skipper snorted and turned very red under his deep tan.

"I'm not a blasted idiot. Chin!" he spluttered. "What the devil do you take me for? I tell you I've got no money—so how in the name of goodness do you expect me to buy low?"

The Chinaman's face expressed nothing. He puffed once or twice at the plated pipe resting on the table, carefully brushed the miniature bowl, and put the whole contrivance gently on a shelf above him.

"I see," he said, after a few moment's silence. "You must obtain something for nothing—and sell it for a great deal."

The captain was scraping his briar with the blackened blade of an enormous jack-knife. He grunted amiably.

"That's much more in my line, if there is a little hard cash needed, no doubt you'd be delighted to oblige me; but, mind you, I'm never over keen on borrowin'. It's so darned hard to pay back, and once you get on that blasted task—you never finish. Can't think how you Chinamen stick those metal pipes. Lot of messin' about with baccy that looks more like fibre than the real article; four puffs at the most, through dirty water—and then it's all over."

He pressed some dreadful-looking ship's tobacco he had just sliced from an oblong block into the bowl of his pipe with a dirty thumb.

The placid Chin-chu smiled faintly.

"Each one to his taste, Captain," he replied. "As regards business: You are willing to leave everything entirely in my hands."

The skipper nodded, his bearded face hidden behind a huge hand, a lighted match, and a full pipe.

The Chinaman rose, took down a smart white topi from its hook, and paused with one hand on the handle of the door. The skipper looked at him hard.

"Got a notion," he asked abruptly.

"Yes. I think you'll have reason to thank me. I shall be back after it is dark. You will be on board, sir?"

The captain nodded.

His companion turned to a cupboard and drew out a long fawn mackintosh and a soft felt hat. These he rolled carefully and pressed into a neat flat basket with a leathern handle. He went out without another word, and rowed shorewards.

The skipper strolled back to his own cabin to lounge and read till evening. The "Lohengrin" was sailing at one the next morning for Hong Kong, there to pick up a large consignment of Chinese coolies for the Borneo Rubber Estates.

A pretty Japanese maiden stood at the open door of her father's shop. Every now and again she glanced down the long row of queer swinging signs, towards the quay, where the boats lay at anchor. Suddenly she started. Three shrill whistles came from somewhere round an adjacent corner. She looked behind her, and observing that her father was busy within, slipped into the sunlit street to greet the smartly-dressed Chinaman she had seen passing the afternoon before.

The Chin-chu smiled pleasantly.

"Your father will not like to hear of your speaking to me—a Chinaman," he said calmly in Japanese. "Meet me here after dark, and we will walk where you are not known."

She laughed merrily, pressed a dainty finger to her lips, and ran back to the shop. The placid Chinaman strode away.

It was dark when Soon-chong returned through the brightly-lit thoroughfares. He caught sight of the pretty Japanese girl standing in the shadows. He signed to her to walk on the opposite side of the road to himself until they were well away from her father's shop. Half-way between two lamps, set well apart, he crossed over and took her arm.

"You must not be out late," he said. "But I have a little dinner for two on board my ship. Would you like to join me for an hour?"

The girl hesitated. It was not quite the thing, she knew; but this well-dressed Chinese gentleman seemed so chivalrous and his manner was very persuasive.

"I shall be seen," she faltered.

"I have prepared for that," he said quietly. "No one shall see you come or go. I will escort you safely home. It will be better than the bright lights of a tea-house."

He led the way round a dark corner and opened the wicker basket he still carried. Soon two figures in male attire stole by less frequented paths to the quay and stepped into a waiting boat.

The Chin-chu helped her up the gangway and led the way to his cabin.

"It is very dark," she whispered fearfully. "Perhaps I ought never to have come. You will see me back soon?"

She stepped forward, and suddenly the door closed quietly after her. She turned to find she was alone. The awful truth then began to dawn upon her. She screamed aloud and beat upon the door with her dainty hands. The only answer was the creaking and clanking of the busy winches. She flung herself into the only chair and sobbed bitterly.

As the Chin-chu had said, no one had seen her come—and no one would see her return to the well-known street and her father's home.

On deck the burly skipper encountered the calm figure of his super-cargo.

"I have something in my cabin which will bring you three hundred Malay dollars in Borneo," said Soon-Chong. "I shall tell you nothing further till we sail."

"Good man!" remarked the skipper, and narrowly escaped joining a heavy case as it brushed by him and fell slowly, by a series of jerks, down an adjacent hatchway.

The "Lohengrin" sailed in the early hours of morning, and in due course reached Api-Api, via Hong Kong. It was there that Taverner, the D.O. from Lonely Valley struck a bargain with the skipper, drank a half-bottle of champagne with him, and returned to his solitude, way-back, with a beautiful young Japanese housekeeper. He knew nothing of her history, and the Chin-chu wove a wonderful romance, telling of a dying father's last instructions to him—that she should become an honoured member of a white man's household!

Taverner could not see a desolate home in Yokohama, distraught parents, and a fierce, earnest brother, vowing a most terrible revenge on his sister's abductor.

II

Lonely Valley was the popular name of the very unpopular magistracy of Tembakut, situated eighty odd miles from the coast town, amid the stunted jungle growths and fetid swamplands of the interior.

The winding Ketatan River ran tolerably near the huge combine bungalow and native court-house, where Taverner presided daily, wielding the weapons of crude justice—with occasional reference to his superior officers in far-off Api-Api. Yo-San, his beautiful new acquisition, rode in front of him on a sullen kerbau, led by a native guide, after the only railway had brought them barely half-way. She was very calm now and resigned. Orientals rarely display emotion, and she had already begun to look on matters in a more philosophic light. Besides, things might have been a great deal worse, and the Tuan Hakim (magistrate) was very kind.

Living together in that great solitude, there sprang up a wonderful feeling of regard between these two of East and West. Taverner, a student of languages, mastered a great deal of Japanese, and Yo-San, recovered from the first qualms of home sickness, eagerly assimilated the rudiments of the English language and a fair amount of Malay. He bought her beautiful clothes and ornaments for her shining black hair and although they ate differently and at different times, he liked to see her seated opposite him at his evening meal.

Sometimes, in the hours between tea and evening makan, when the sun was low in the heavens and the deep blue was fading swiftly from the sky, she would tell him queer stories culled from her never-ending repertoire of quaint folk-lore which interested him greatly; tales of strange monsters and powerful gods and spirits of good and evil. Till, at last, Yo-San became a necessary part of his lone existence, and life would have been impossible without her.

One evening, just before darkness fell, Taverner noticed a native woman passing the bungalow, carrying an immense burden. She was followed by a burly native, short and thick-set, who strolled lazily after her, occasionally quickening her movements by means of a wicked-looking switch. It was just sights such as these that made the Tuan Hakim's blood boil—the deep-rooted British objection to a systematic bully. He ran down the steps, attired only in his sarong and singlet, tore the burden from the woman's back, and, handing it to the sullen native, told him to carry it the rest of the way himself. He watched the couple out of sight—a look of deep gratitude in the woman's eyes rewarding him for his trouble. He strode back to the bungalow and bawling out for his ayer panus (hot water), promptly forgot the whole incident.

About a week later he happened to be in Api-Api on a question of dark rumours of native unrest in his neighbourhood. As he entered the Government House, Pierson, the D.O. at Parpar, slapped him warmly on the back.

"Come and have a stenga with me," he said. "I've got something here that'll interest you. Come and be introduced."

He followed his friend to a table in a corner of the concrete floor, where sat another man, attired in khaki, sipping a gin-sling.

"Mr. Taverner—Mr. Davidson," shouted Pierson. "Now, d'you know, I'd have taken you two men for brothers! You're short and Taverner here's pretty tall, but, by gad, your faces are identical!"

"Brothers in misfortune," laughed the man at the table, rising to shake hands, and they all three sat down again together.

Taverner learnt in conversation that his new acquaintance was an Australian, prospecting for copper in the interests of a small syndicate.

"Look after yourself!" he cried, as Davidson left by the train next day. "If you're up my way there's always open house, y'know, but I don't guarantee the natives in my neighbourhood. There's a lot of war palaver goin' the round."

The prospector laughed easily and waved as the train moved off.

"Smart chap, that," remarked Pierson, as the two strolled back to the Rest House.

"Yes," agreed the other. "He'll do well if he's careful. Looks the sort of man that won't let grass grow under his feet. Phew! it's getting beastly warm. What say to a sling?"

"By the by," said Pierson later in the day, "there's a huge 'sweep' on the Derby being arranged in Singapore. First prize is about £20,000 I'm told; tickets fifty dollars—are you game?"

"Rather," assented Taverner, banging his empty glass on the table to attract the boy's attention. "Who's agent here?"

"Wallace, of Hudson and Co. Shall I get you a share?"

The D.O. from Lonely Valley felt in an upper pocket and produced a bundle of notes.

"Here's fifty. Get me a ticket," he said. "Might as well go the whole hog. I suppose it's tolerably safe?"

"Safe as houses!"

"Well, get them to send the bally bit of paper to Yong-See, my agent here. He'll lock it up in his safe till I'm next in town. I've a lot to do, and I'm back home first thing tomorrow. Likely I shan't see you again. Bye-bye."

He rammed on his topi and went up to interview the Commissioner of Police.

A long, lean, white-faced man stood at the door of his bungalow, twirling the ends of his thin black moustache. His head was bare, for it was evening and the sun was sinking behind the house.

Around him grew many-hued tropical flowering plants, and a neat sandy path wound its way from the luxurious bungalow down towards the wooden clock tower by the railway. Annesley-Tarne, Commissioner of Police, was thinking deeply.

"I wonder where the devil he got her from," he was muttering to himself. "There's scarcely a single Jap woman in this country I don't know of, but this new acquisition of his is a cursed mystery."

He paced up and down the broad verandah many times, still absorbed in the same theme.

"They tell me," he meditated, "that she's the prettiest woman on the West Coast. I must really look into this. No wonder there are rumours of risings near Lonely Valley. I don't expect he leaves himself much time for his duties! Boy—! Ah, there you are, you lazy skunk! Pack my barang. I go to Tembakut to-morrow. Tahu. (understand)?"

The white-clad boy disappeared, and the dark commissioner continued his monotonous walk to and fro.

He lit a cigarette and threw the match-end over the rail.

"Don't know what these juniors are coming to!" he asserted suddenly, and went in to superintend the packing.

III

Two days later Taverner was not a little surprised to see the slim form of his superior ascending the verandah steps. The commissioner stretched out a slender hand.

"I have given my escort instructions to house themselves with your men," he announced. "I shall be staying the night, of course. I presume you have a respectable bed, and that the mosquito curtain has a minimum amount of holes?"

"You can have my bed," said Taverner, "and I'll guarantee the kalambo (mosquito curtain). As for myself, there's always a camp-bed in reserve. We don't exactly live in luxury back here, you know!"

"I was rather under the impression you did," drawled the elegant commissioner, stretching himself out on the most comfortable chair within reach. "There are rumours—just vague whispers, you know, of a most beautiful partner in your exile—a Japanese lady, I believe. Someone remarked on her beauty—I forget exactly who it was, but I can vouch for his good taste. He seemed agreeably impressed."

Taverner felt and looked uncomfortable.

"Oh, Yo-San," he replied offhandedly. "I've sent her away to the kitchen—pro tem."

"I should like to see her," said the commissioner.

Taverner shrugged his broad shoulders and called: "Yo-San! mari-sini (come here)!"

And Yo-San came.

Annesley-Tarne was not easily surprised. He had carefully studied and copied Oriental manners and customs, and his features rarely reflected his inward thoughts. But when little Yo-San came slowly through the verandah doorway, in answer to her master's call, he started back in amazement.

"Baniak chantek (very beautiful)," he murmured. Then turning to Taverner. "Where did you get her?"

"Bought her," said the D.O. shortly, and his jaw closed tightly, but there was a queer light in his blue eyes the commissioner did not like.

Annesley-Tarne said no more, but turned to contemplate the view, and Yo-San seized the opportunity and stole softly away to the back. She felt instinctively that the man who had looked her up and down with that cool piercing stare was dangerous.

As he gazed over the rail of the roughly-built verandah, the commissioner made a great resolve—that, by means fair or foul, he would have this beautiful Japanese woman for his own!

He turned the matter carefully over in his mind that afternoon, while his host was busy trying a native case in the adjacent court-house. His first notion had been to demand her of the D.O. at the price he had paid for her, but he now perceived that this would scarcely be advisable. His second plan seemed the sounder. He would use his powers of persuasion.

When Yo-San ventured on to the verandah, under the impression her master's guest was sleeping, Annesley-Tarne sat suddenly up in his chair and smiled graciously. He was rather annoyed to observe that the lady was far from impressed. As a matter of fact, she shrank from him.

"I wish to speak to you," he said in Malay, and signed to her to sit down on a chair by his side. The girl tremblingly assented.

"Now, I want you to listen to me very carefully," continued the commissioner, smoothing his black hair with both hands. "You are not to say a word of this to the other Tuan. Tahu?"

The girl nodded, but said nothing.

"Well, I wish you to leave this bungalow and come home with me to Api-Api. You will be an important person there—the commissioner's ngi (housekeeper); whereas, here"—he waved a slim hand eloquently—"you are nothing. In Api-Api you will have bright shops. I will buy you beautiful trinkets from Singapore. Everything of the best I will give you—anything you care to demand will be yours. You will come with me to-morrow?"

The girl rose from her seat and drew herself up.

In the sudden overflow of her indignation, somehow, all sense of fear was dispelled. Her dark eyes blazed like live coals, her nostrils dilated.

"Tuan," she panted, "you have spoken—and I have been forced to listen. You have told me to say nothing to the Tuan Hakim; I have promised—and I shall not speak. But, understand, great Tuan, I am his and he is mine. I would not change my place here for all the jewels in the Mikado's palace. While the Tuan Hakim lives, I stay with him. Where he goes, I go."

With a sudden movement of intense passion, Yo-San drew a tiny fan from her broad blue sash and struck the commissioner with great force across the face.

He uttered a cry of pain, swore violently and felt instinctively with one hand to see if blood were drawn. He sprang to his feet with an oath, but Yo-San had vanished. He stepped forward to follow her, and in the doorway came face to face with Taverner.

"Where are you going?" asked the young man abruptly.

The commissioner spluttered.

"You have a nasty scratch on your face from somewhere," said the D.O. calmly.

"It's nothing," muttered Annesley-Tarne. "A loose end of cane in that confounded chair of yours."

"Are you sure it wasn't a woman's fan?" asked Taverner, folding his great brown arms, and regarding his superior coldly.

The commissioner tried to meet the other's gaze, and failed.

"I want to talk to you," said the D.O. suddenly. "I want you to understand, once and for all that, commissioner or no commissioner, the man who meddles in my household affairs stands a good chance of getting his neck wrung!"

Annesley-Tarne, during the whole of his career, had never felt so ridiculously small. He made an effort, swallowed an awkward lump in his throat, and fixing both eyes on a certain cocoa-nut palm a little distance off, attempted to assume an air of dignity.

"I don't think you are quite aware of the importance of my position," he began. He wished to goodness the younger man would take his eyes off his face.

"I was, unfortunately for you perhaps, an involuntary eye-witness of all that occurred," said Taverner. "I am quite aware of the significance of the position you hold officially, but I fail entirely to recognise your right to take advantage of my absence to endeavour to lure away from me my only companion. I am now going to ask you to give your word of honour that while you are under my roof you will have nothing to do with my personal property."

"I make no promises. Why upon my soul—!"

"You either promise what I ask or you go back to Api-Api immediately, the same way as you came." Taverner's eyes blazed.

The commissioner swore violently, seized his topi and stick, and shouted violently for his boy.

"My God, Taverner!" he snarled, as he strode down the stairs, "I'll see that you pay for this."

Taverner, leaning over the verandah rail, watched him depart in silence.

Taverner went about his duties like one in a trance, expecting every moment to receive his "order of the boot" from headquarters—for gross insubordination. However, days lengthened into weeks and weeks into months, and still the D.O. held his post at Tembakut, and presided over the petty quarrels of the dwellers in and around Lonely Valley.

Somewhere close at hand the storm clouds of native unrest were rising ominously. Almost every week warning messages would be brought to the court-house by some friendly native; whispers of sharpening parangs, of immense stores being collected of poisoned darts, of a thirst for heads, of wild threats to push the usurping white races into the sea across which they had come to wrest the land from its rightful owners. And still Taverner stayed on and worked hard, and Yo-San sat by his side on the verandah at the end of the day and whispered fantastic imaginative tales of far-off Japan.

He never spoke to her of Annesley-Tarne. He knew just how she felt with regard to him, and trusted her implicitly. And then, one day, the stormcloud burst.

Early one sweltering afternoon a Dusun, covered in blood, staggered up to the door of the bungalow and sank exhausted on to the stairs. Taverner ran down and lifted him up. He called for water and poured it between the native's parched lips.

"Deri mana (whence come you)?" he asked, as soon as the man's eyes opened.

"Deru si-blas-sana, Tuan (from right over there, sir). The Muruts are in revolt and are taking heads. A white man—I know not whom—has fallen already. It is war, Tuan Hakim, war—"

He choked suddenly and rolled over awkwardly. Two native police ran up with bandages and water in a pail, but the friendly Dusun was already far beyond human aid.

Taverner went into the house, examined his store of ammunition, and then sat down to write. Half an hour later a k'rani clerk was speeding towards the nearest railway station, astride the D.O.'s pony, to telephone headquarters, while a native runner was on his way with the official despatch for the commissioner at Api-Api.

IV

Annesley-Tarne had not forgotten his district officer in Lonely Valley, nor had the vision of his beautiful Japanese ngi faded from his mind. His recent rebuff but served to add an extra keenness to his mad desire, and every minute of his official life he strove to plan the total ruin of his enemy. Never would that awful ride on the back of a clumsy water-buffalo in the heat of a tropic day fade from his memory! Then he grew patient. An opportunity would come, sooner or later, he assured himself, and then he would strike, and there would be no quarter given. Once Taverner was got rid of, Yo-San, powerless to resist, could not fail to be his.

One afternoon, as he lounged in the shade of his great bungalow, the telephone bell rang furiously. A coloured clerk in his private office answered it. The commissioner strained his ears to hear what was said. At first the conversation seemed disconnected, then the import of the message began to dawn on him. The Muruts near Lonely Valley were up! It was a call from Taverner, his enemy. A demand for reinforcements and instructions. Annesley-Tarne rubbed his hands together and laughed aloud. He strolled to the telephone and snatched the receiver from the native clerk.

An excited k'rani was speaking at the other end. "Who is that?" demanded the commissioner.

"K'rani clerk Tembakut," came the faint reply.

"What d'you want?"

"Muruts are rising. Reinforcements required, sir, immediately. The Tuan Hakim awaits instructions."

"How many men has he?"

"Eight only, sir."

"Tell him to leave half in charge of the courthouse, to take the remainder, advance to Berbinta, and report on the actual condition of affairs."

He slammed down the receiver and strolled out on to the verandah, tapping a fat cigar on the stiff cuff of his white shirt.

"Well, well, Taverner, mon ami!" he remarked to himself, "you will never come back, you know!"

He lit the cigarette and idly contemplated the faint blue rings as they mounted heavenwards.

Taverner heard the commissioner's message in grim silence. The k'rani clerk saluted and descended the steep flight of wooden steps to the path. So this was what Annesley-Tarne had meant when he told him he would make him pay. It was a splendid move, Taverner told himself bitterly. His superior officer had him 'twixt Scylla and Charybdis. If he refused to go he would be dishonoured. If he went it would mean certain death. Annesley-Tarne knew the temper of the surrounding tribes as well as he, and already he had heard that an unknown white head had fallen.

The young D.O. sat on the verandah steps that night with Yo-San by his side. A gentle breeze shook the ataps above him and whistled softly in the lalang just below. Bull-frogs were croaking in the swamps and myriads of hidden insects hummed in the bushes, on the walls, and in the heavy air.

"Yo-San," said Taverner presently, "to-morrow I shall leave you, and perhaps I may never come back. Here is a bundle of notes, about $1,000. I want you to take them and sew them into your kimono. If I am killed and the Muruts advance on the bungalow, the k'rani will take you to the railway and see you on to the train for Api-Api. When you get there go to my agent Yong-See; he will look after you and book your passage back to Yokohama. He will tell you where to go in Hong Kong. I have written to him to-day. We have had a pretty decent time together while it lasted, but all good things must come to an end sometime, I s'pose."

He looked out into the darkness and did not see the tears stealing down his companion's cheeks.

On the following morning, leaving half his men on duty at the bungalow, he rode away with the remaining handful of native police. Yo-San waved to him from the high verandah, and he shook his malacca in the air once or twice. Dear old Lonely Valley! He would never see it again? And Annesley-Tarne was waiting in Api-Api, waiting for the welcome news that he had fallen.

Yo-San watched until the tiny band had crossed the padi-fields, and the vast jungle had swallowed them up, then she threw herself into a long cane chair and sobbed as though her heart would break. He had been so good to her—so unlike other men of his race—and his dollars, sewn in her clothing, pressed even now against her sad heart. His last thoughts before his departure had been for her comfort and safety.

A week passed and no news came. The native corporal had sent all the Government papers down to the coast town, as Taverner had instructed. Daily the k'rani rode to the railway and telephoned to Api-Api for instructions, and every time the answer came, "hold on."

One evening as Yo-San sat in the long chair on the broad verandah, she heard a sudden patter of feet on the path below. Then came the challenge of the native sentry and a hoarse Malay reply.

She hurried down the steps, anxious for news of her master. An almost nude Dusun stood below, streaming with perspiration and breathing hard, one hand pressed to his side. On the ground in front of him was a basket, covered with a bloodstained cloth of native texture.

"The Tuan Hakim," he gasped, "is dead. All his men sudah kasih mati (are killed). See here!"

He lifted the basket and drew off the cloth. A human head lay within and its skin was white.

Yo-San uttered a scream of horror and started back. Then she took the basket gently in one hand and held it up to the bright light from the sentry's lantern.

"Where did you get it?" she cried.

"I heard the noise of fighting, Nono, and the sound of pistol shots and snapang (rifles). I hid in the bush till the danger was past. The head of the Tuan Hakim I found behind a tree where it had fallen. I placed it in a basket and brought it here that the other white Tuan might know."

Yo-San ran up the steps and entered her room. She found a bundle of dollar notes in a drawer and threw them to the messenger. The head in the wicker basket she covered reverently and handed to the waiting corporal.

"The Tuan Hakim is dead," she said in a queer, strained voice. "I ride to-morrow to the railway. Look at his features well that you may report his death to the Tuan Commissioner. Then bury his head here—in Lonely Valley."

She crept into her room and closed the door fast. All the long night she lay staring at the stars outside. To her it seemed that the end of all things had come.

Early next morning she departed for Api-Api, accompanied by the faithful k'rani. The clerk phoned the news of the D.O.'s death to the commissioner from the station, and carelessly mentioned that Yo-San was leaving for the town.

"Very good," said Annesley-Tarne. "I will send reinforcements to-morrow. If the natives advance, hold on till help arrives."

He hung up the receiver and went back to his evening makan.

"Everything has turned out very nicely," he said to himself, flicking an impudent insect from his plate. "Taverner will trouble me no more, and Yo-San—well, I'll see that she's met when the train comes in to-morrow."

He went to bed that night, all his doubts set at rest. He did not dream; on the contrary, he slept remarkably well, and woke next morning refreshed. In ten hours or so the train would be due at Api-Api, bringing with it the late D.O.'s beautiful ngi.

"I have not forgotten that afternoon at Tem-bakut yet," he thought. "We must curb that spirit of rebellion, my pretty one. It may serve for the housekeeper of a common D.O., but not for a commissioner's ngi!"

V

When Taverner was scarcely two days journey from the court-house his party fell into a cleverly planned ambush. From the trees above them there suddenly descended a shower of poisoned darts—the deadly Sumpitans were at work—and his handful of men fell, writhing in agony, before scarcely a shot could be fired. The D.O.'s pony took fright and bolted with him, eventually throwing him from its back into a tangled mass of prickly undergrowth. His left arm was badly sprained, and, lying in agony where he had fallen, he saw the stealthy forms of the murderous natives speeding in the track of his maddened steed.

He remembered nothing more till on recovering consciousness he found himself on the floor of a native hut, and knew that for some reason or other his life had been spared—for a time at least. As he lay on his back wondering why his arms and legs were not bound, a figure darkened the entrance. Taverner gasped. Where had he seen that woman before? Then he remembered a sultry evening months back in Lonely Valley when he had made an unwilling native carry his wife's barang.

"Jove!" he told himself, "what a stroke of good luck."

"The Tuan is awake," said the woman softly.

"Where are the natives fighting now?" he inquired anxiously, thinking of Yo-San and the court-house at Tembakut.

"They have gone back si-blas-sana," replied the woman. "They are fearful at what they have done and dread the white man's vengeance."

Taverner sat up and gazed around him. The walls of the hut were of dried sago leaves and bamboo and the roof was of the same material. The woman gave him some milk in a cocoa-nut shell and he drank it eagerly.

"How did you find me?" he asked presently.

"My husband fell when they killed the little Tuan who came with his servants seeking precious metals. When the Tuan Hakim came, the Muruts hid in the trees and all the mata-mata (policemen) were killed. They followed the white Tuan's horse till they found it, but the Tuan Hakim was not on its back. Thinking they had slain him also, and seeing that the other tribes did not rise as well, the Muruts fled away, and I stayed behind here, because I am old and my husband is dead. As I crossed the jungle path I saw a white topi in the grass. I looked closer, and there I saw the Tuan who was kind to me many months back. I brought you here, Tuan, five days ago, but you have much panus-panus (fever), and I feared you would not live."

Taverner thanked her in Malay and contemplated his swollen wrist.

"I must go back to Tembakut," he said. "They will think me dead. And the little Tuan who came for copper—you say he is dead, too?"

"Yah, Tuan, he and all his servants."

"Poor devil!" murmured the D.O. "Smart chap, too! Poor beggar! I told him the natives were treacherous. I wonder what they are thinking in Lonely Valley?"

"Were all my men killed?" he asked suddenly.

"All, Tuan."

Taverner felt in his pocket and produced a wad of sodden notes. He marvelled secretly at the woman's devotion and honesty.

"Here," he said, "I do not know where you will go or what you will do, but money is always useful, and without it one starves."

The woman took the money from him without a word, and thrust it in her sarong.

Taverner suddenly caught sight of his topi in a corner of the hut. He rose to his feet unsteadily and marked time with each leg in turn to get the stiffness out of his joints, holding on to the insect-infested wall. Then he reached for his helmet, knocked it several times to clear it of cockroaches, and put it on. The woman fetched him his Malacca and his belt, from which hung the holster that contained his revolver. He bent his head to avoid knocking it on the low roof, crawled through the tiny doorway, and descended the rickety ladder to the ground. The woman accompanied him to the path and indicated the way towards Tembakut. He had hardly gone a hundred yards when she ran after him.

"Here is some fruit!" she said, holding out a bundle done up in a coloured cloth. "The Tuan Hakim already has milk in his flask."

Taverner thanked her, and started once more on his weary journey. He was weak from fever, and his left hand rested helplessly in a side pocket of his coat, but he stepped manfully forward, walking in the shade of the trees until the sun sank in the west and darkness began to fall.

Towards evening, two days later, a haggard form staggered from the jungle on to the open ground of the vast padi-field, and saw the well-known courthouse half a mile ahead of him.

"Thank God!" he cried, sinking exhausted on to the grass. "Home again; a comfortable bed and a good meal, and dear little Yo-San to greet me. My word, how I long for a pipe of good baccy!"

He sat for a moment chewing a coarse blade of grass, and then sprang to his feet and trudged on again. His topi was battered, his khaki torn and stained, his boots bursting out at the side. He almost ran the last hundred yards.

The sentry on duty by the steps, dozing over his rifle, started suddenly up, uttered a wild cry, dropped his gun, and fled.

Taverner called after him sternly, but he disappeared into the guard-house panic-stricken.

"Thinks I'm a ghost, I s'pose," said Taverner, laughing aloud, and then strode up the steps to the verandah.

"Now, I wonder where that little girl is," he murmured. "Hi! Yo-San! Yo-San, mari-sini!"

He waited a moment, and then searched all the rooms in turn.

"Gone!" he cried in anazement. "Her barang's gone, too! What's it all mean? I told her to wait till I was killed and the Muruts advanced. Who could have told her of the massacre?

The woman said my men were all struck down by those awful Sumpitans."

He hurried back on to the verandah and called again.

"Hi! K'rani, sini (here)."

The scared black face of the native clerk appeared suddenly at the bottom of the stairs.

"Here," said Taverner. "Come here, you idiot!"

The k'rani mounted the stairs reluctantly.

As he reached the verandah Taverner nearly sent him back again with a sharp thump on the chest with his heavy fist.

"Now, perhaps you'll realise I'm alive!" he said.

"But, Tuan," gasped the unfortunate clerk. "The head! A native has brought us your head—in a basket—last night!"

"My head, you hoonooh!"

Taverner started. "Heavens!" he cried. "Then they brought Davidson's head here, and Yo-San thought it was mine, and so she has fled to Api-Api, and is there, perhaps, by now!"

The k'rani nodded. "I have told the Tuan commissioner you were dead," he said.

"Yes?" asked Taverner.

"And he promised reinforcements. He asked after the Mem Yo-San."

Taverner started forward and seized him by the wrist. "And you told him?" he cried.

"Yah, Tuan, I told him she would go to Api-Api to-day."

"You blasted fool," shrieked the D.O., pushing the unfortunate clerk from him with such force that he rolled headlong down the stairs to the path below.

"Is my other pony here still, you blockhead?" he shouted, as the k'rani staggered to his feet, rubbing his head ruefully.

"Yah, Tuan, it is still here."

"Then find it and saddle it, and bring it round here in half an hour. Send me a boy, too, at once, I want some food."

He ran into his bedroom and searched till he found a complete set of clean garments. In a quarter of an hour he had secured a sufficient amount of boiling water from the kitchen to permit him to indulge in a refreshing bath and a shave. He dressed hastily, found a decent topi, and swallowed the scrap meal his cook had managed to get together.

When darkness fell he rode out alone along the familiar path towards the railway, some sixteen miles away. As he neared the line three hours later he drew from his holster a large five-chambered revolver and examined it carefully.

"Annesley-Tarne," he whispered hoarsely, "you sent me to my death in order that you might steal my Yo-San from me. If you have taken her, I swear by all that's holy I'll shoot you in cold blood, even if I hang for it!"

As the lights of the little cluster of Chinese shops grew more distinct, Taverner suddenly cocked his head on one side and listened.

"A goods train!" he cried. "Pray heaven it's bound for the town!"

He spurred on his steaming mount, and galloping up to the tiny station, flung the reins to the Chinese railway official.

"Stop that goods train for me," he cried, "at all costs. I must get to Api-Api to-night."

VI

Annesley-Tarne was not the kind of man to do things by halves. He quite appreciated the fact that his appearance at the station would create a scene when he confronted Yo-San. On thinking matters carefully over, he decided that Taverner's agents would be instructed to look out for her, for he believed the girl to have no personal friends in the town. He called, therefore, on Messrs. Yong-See that morning, and was admitted immediately to the inner office, where the head of the business sat busily writing in Chinese, with a queerly constructed bamboo brush.

The Chinaman rose and bowed deferentially.

"Good morning, sir. Any big orders for me this morning?"

He looked down at his long, tapering finger nails, and then rubbed his hands together in anticipation of fresh business. He was well aware that the Commissioner of Police dealt with his equally prosperous rival across the way.

"You are the late Mr. Taverner's agents, I believe?" said the commissioner solemnly.

"That is so, sir. His affairs have always been in our hands."

"Well, he once expressed a wish to me that if anything should happen to him, I would do all I could for his woman. She has herself left me word to the effect that she is coming here by this afternoon's train and that you are arranging to meet her. Well, I would like to do all I can to carry out poor Taverner's wishes, so I think it would be best for you to have the girl escorted to my bungalow, where my boy will have a room waiting for her till the next vessel sails for Hong Kong."

The Chinaman looked up sharply.

"Mr. Taverner wrote to me personally before he left for the interior," he said. "He did not mention anything of this in his letter."

The commissioner tapped his foot impatiently on the bare floor.

"That may very well be," he said, "but I am determined to carry out his verbal wish expressed to me when I was last at Tembakut, and I shall look to you to see that the woman is brought to my bungalow this evening."

He turned on his heel and strode out into the sunlit street.

The Chinaman stood staring after him for some moments, a queer look on his almost expressionless face.

"It doesn't sound quite right," he said to himself. "It's strange he didn't mention the matter in his letter to me, he is usually so concise. Still, Taverner is dead, and the Commissioner of Police is not one for a poor tradesman like myself to argue with."

He went back into his office and took up his pen again. Then he rang a small copper bell which stood at his elbow near a pile of bills. A younger Chinaman hurried in.

"When you meet the late Mr. Taverner's ngi," said the manager, "you must take her to the house of the Tuan Commissioner of Police."

He commenced to write again, and the assistant went quietly out, closing the door after him.

"I should not be at all surprised to learn," murmured Mr. Yong-See to himself "that the noble commissioner had notions of appropriating the young lady for himself."

The tall Commissioner of Police visited a tiny jeweller's shop and picked out some of the best examples of native silver work in stock.

He glanced at his gold hunter as he left the jeweller's. It was nearly time for midday makan. The train would be in somewhere between five and eight, and there was a possibility of its being a couple of hours later. Railways wink at scheduled times in the byways of the East. Still, one thing was pretty certain, Yo-San would be safely in his bungalow before midnight. He strode through the main street, with its evil-smelling trenches, whistling gaily. For the first time for many weary months he had actually something to look forward to! Returning to his bungalow on the hill, he made minute preparations for Yo-San's reception. He had inquiries made as to Japanese articles of diet, and when the desired information was obtained, sent out his boy with orders to lay in a good stock.

During the intense heat of the early afternoon he lounged on the verandah, smoked and read. And so the day gradually wore on towards the time when his desire would be at last attained.

A sudden commotion below caused him to look up suddenly from his book. Natives were running from all directions towards the seashore. Coolies jostled shop proprietors and British officials pushed heedless coloured beings from their path.

"I wonder what's the excitement," he murmured drowsily.

"I wish to goodness the damn'd people wouldn't disturb my afternoon's rest. Hope it's not a native row. Boy!—Booy!"

"Yah, Tuan." The servant hurried on to the verandah.

"Find out for me what all that blasted noise is about, at once."

The boy hurried through the house, ran out at the back entrance, and descended the steep path to the street. He returned in a few moments and stood by the commissioner's chair till he deigned to raise his eyes from the book he was reading.

"Well, what is it?"

"A Japanese warship at anchor, Tuan," replied the boy. "The people are running to the shore to look at it."

"Japanese warship? Damned inconvenient time to look in, I must say. Have they landed any men yet?"

"No, sir, not yet. They will wait till the cool of the evening, I think."

"H'm! Expect they will," grunted the commissioner. "That will do."

The boy went out, and Annesley-Tarne returned to his book.

When the sun was sinking over the sea a landing party of Japanese blue-jackets came ashore and roamed about the town, followed by a crowd of laughing and chattering natives and Chinese boys.

They swarmed into the shops in the main street and bought cheap finery and highly-coloured clothes. They entered the gambling den at the corner and before they again reached the streets many coins had changed hands.

A group of these yellow-skinned sailors left the main body and wandered idly towards the railway station, attracted by the whistle of an approaching locomotive.

The train drew up and there emerged from the four long carriages members of almost every Oriental race—Chinese men and women, a Japanese shopkeeper, Malays, Bajau, and Dusun tribesmen. From the "Europeans only" compartment there stepped five or six white-clad Englishmen, planters and Government officials.

As the little group of Japanese sailors gazed laughingly at the busy scene, one of them suddenly started back, the smile vanishing from his broad face.

A beautiful Japanese girl had alighted on the platform and was talking to a couple of Chinamen in white coats. Her face was sad and her eyes inflamed as if from recent weeping, and she looked anxiously about her as she walked away with the two young men.

The Japanese sailor slipped suddenly behind the station building. His companions, warmed with liquor, did not notice his absence, and moved on their way back to the brightly-lit shops without him.

"Found!" cried the sailor, in his native tongue. "My little Yo-San!"

The darkness had now fallen, and under its cover he crept after the three forms as they mounted the hill towards Annesley-Tarne's beautiful bungalow. He watched from behind a bush, until the two Chinamen returned without her, then stole from tree to tree till the wall of the house rose up before him. He drew himself up till he could see into an inner room.

"Patience," he whispered, and creeping under the raised floor, began sharpening an ugly-looking blade on the leathern sole of his shoe.

VII

Taverner climbed on to the last truck of the goods train as it slowed down, and thanked his stars that the compartment he had struck was comparatively clean. He made himself as comfortable as he could under the circumstances and, lighting his pipe, prepared to while away, as best he could, the jolting, tiresome journey to the town. He was tired and ill, and his left arm still worried him as the train jerked him from side to side. Ever and anon his fingers closed lovingly over the butt of his shining revolver, and he would glance anxiously over the side of the truck in hopes of catching the faint glimmer in the sky of the lighted shops of Api-Api. At last his pipe went out, his head fell on to his chest, and he sank into a deep sleep.

He dreamed that he was back in Lonely Valley and it was evening. He heard the ataps rustling and the crickets from the walls.

Yo-San was sitting at the foot of his long chair fanning him gently and whispering a quaint tale of old Japan. He stretched out his arms to embrace her, and then the train jolted suddenly to a standstill.

He sprang to his feet, rubbing his eyes, and looked over the side. The engine driver and his fireman were walking to and fro by the side of the line, stooping down every now and then in the darkness.

"What's the matter?" cried Taverner.

"Run short of fuel," came the reply, in Malay. Taverner swore, and jumping from the truck, ran towards the two men.

"How far are we from the town?" he cried impatiently.

"About seven miles, Tuan."

"And how long before you will be able to start again?"

"Tida tahu (don't know). Perhaps one hour, perhaps two."

Taverner seized his stick and strode furiously along the line in the direction of Api-Api. He looked at his watch as he passed the engine. It was nearly eleven o'clock. Perhaps even now he was too late? The thought maddened him. He broke into a sharp trot, but soon slackened down into his habitual stride. He had not a great deal of strength left in him. Two miles further on he came to a small station. An idea suddenly occurred to him. Perhaps there was a trolley? These were scarcely used on the line now, owing to a series of accidents that had recently occurred. Still, in a case of emergency, one might be found.

He discovered the stationmaster in bed, and dragging him into the open, demanded the immediate services of six strong coolies and a trolley. The Chinaman demurred, but a few dollar notes and a whisper of "important Government business" overcame his scruples, and in less than half an hour Taverner was again well on his way to Api-Api, seated on an open truck, propelled by perspiring coolies.

The clock in the tall wooden tower was just striking midnight when he leaped from the trolley, tipped the natives, and strode towards the bungalow of the Commissioner of Police. He did not heed the commotion which still prevailed in the main streets of the little town. There was only one thought in his fevered brain—the desire for revenge. He was tempted to enquire after Yo-San at the shop of his agents, but something whispered within him that it would not be wise to show himself in the streets, and he felt certain, somehow, that the luxurious bungalow above him sheltered his beautiful ngi.

He crept through the bushes as silently as a passing shadow. There was still a light in the verandah, and from the kitchen at the back came a sound of ribald laughter.

"They would not make that noise if he were here," he murmured. "Annesley-Tarne is still at the club. Perhaps there is some special dinner on. I forget." He passed a weary hand over his burning forehead.

"I wonder where he has hidden Yo-San?" he whispered presently. "Perhaps I can find her before the brute comes back?"

He stole into the shadow of the house and tried to peer in at an open window. Suddenly he heard a sound of footsteps on the path and a familiar music-hall tune being whistled. The Commissioner of Police was returning from the club. Taverner could just catch a glimpse of the tall form of his enemy as he mounted the verandah steps. "Been drinking pretty heavily," he muttered, and loosened his revolver in its case. He waited a few minutes, and then drew himself up.

"Hark! What was that? Voices in the room above! Annesley-Tarne was talking loudly, and he thought he heard a woman moaning faintly. He strained his ears.

"My God!" he whispered, "it is Yo-San!"

He snatched his revolver from his pocket and hurried on tip-toe towards the broad verandah. Suddenly he became aware of a darkly-clad, short, thick-set figure a few paces ahead of him. In the light of the moon, as the unknown form turned the corner, he caught the flash of steel. Who could it be? he wondered. A native thief—a common housebreaker, perhaps? Strange that he should choose the house of a Commissioner of Police. He started back. The man was climbing the verandah, unconscious of his presence, and he wore the uniform of a sailor! Tavemer swore fiercely between his teeth. Who this marauder was he neither knew or cared, but it was just his infernal luck that he should choose the very night he wanted, of all nights, for himself and Annesley-Tarne. Just they two! That was all, excepting, of course, Yo-San!

He sprang for the verandah as the other man disappeared within, and followed. He resolved that he would not be robbed of his revenge. Perhaps, after all, the commissioner would be aroused and follow the other man on to the verandah, and then Taverner would meet him face to face. The sailor had entered a room.

There was a cry of rage, a startled scream and, in a second, Tavemer was at the doorway, peering in.

He saw a bed, native mats, much handsome furniture, and a huge clock, with a swinging pendulum, ticking on the wall. A standard oil lamp burned in one corner.

Annesley-Tarne stood, half-dressed, in the centre of the broad apartment, his hand closed on the slender wrist of the sobbing Yo-San. Confronting them both, his teeth clenched, his brown hand clasping a shipping knife, stood the other man, and Taverner now saw that he was Japanese. Soon he began to talk very quickly in his native tongue, and Taverner understood.

"Yo-San," he cried, "I have looked for you all the world over, ever since they stole you away. I swore to our father I would avenge your disgrace, and to-night my chance has come."

Annesley-Tarne threw the girl from him to the floor, and rushing across the room felt for the handle of the drawer in which his pistol lay. But the sailor was too quick for him. The keen blade rose and fell, and the tall Commissioner staggered back, coughing blood.

The young sailor turned to his sister, and held her tenderly in his arms for a moment.

Had Taverner known what was about to follow he would have rushed in and stayed the murderous hand. But he misunderstood, hesitated, and was too late. In a flash the keen blade rose and fell twice, and brother and sister rolled to the ground, locked together in one last embrace.

Taverner reeled into the room and stood gazing at the beautiful still form on the floor.

"Yo-San," he cried, "my beautiful Yo-San!"

He bent down and kissed the rich black hair. Then he stole softly away and descended the hill to the town. He was glad that the boys in the kitchen had not been roused by the sounds of the struggle. His revolver was back in its holster now. His work had fallen to the lot of another. Perhaps, after all, it was just as well. He straightened himself up and brushed the leaves from his clothes. Almost in a dream he entered the courtyard of the rest house and, knocking up the startled cook, demanded a room for the night.

As he blew out the lamp the scene in the commissioner's bungalow came back to him in all its vividness.

He threw himself on to the bed, and heedless of the open mosquito curtains, sobbed as he had never sobbed before.

VIII

Entering the dining-room next morning at breakfast time, Taverner ran into Pierson, the D.O. from Parpar.

"Great Jupiter!" he cried, "it's Taverner! We heard you were chopped up long ago, old man! Where, in the name of Heaven, have you sprung from?"

Taverner smiled faintly.

"I was saved by a native woman," he said. "It was Davidson, the little Australian prospector, who was killed, and the people at Tembakut mistook his head for mine!"

Pierson whistled.

"Jove! now, isn't that weird! I told you your faces were as like as two blessed peas! I say, though, have you heard the news? It's pretty awful, I can tell you, and a damn narrow shave you must have had. Annesley-Tarne seems to have collared your woman just at the critical moment when a Japanese relative came in search of her. Anyhow, the boys found him this morning, the girl, and a Japanese sailor from the warship out there, all dead on the floor together!"

Taverner sank into a chair and turned very white. The other man called for spirits.

"Of course you're upset, old chap," he said. "I don't wonder at it. You and your little girl were good pals."

Taverner drank some brandy and drew himself up.

"I'm unnerved," he said slowly. "Yes, I was fond of Yo-San, and I'd have given my soul to have saved her from him. He was always hanging round after her. Well, he's got his deserts!"

Pierson was thinking.

"You never heard where she came from?" he asked at last.

"Not the least notion. I bought her from a skipper of a steamer, and she was very young."

"Does it occur to you that if the commissioner hadn't stolen her at that very time, you might have got your quietus instead?"

Taverner made a queer sound with his tongue on the roof of his mouth.

"By Jove! I never thought of that."

"Taverner, old man, you've had a rotten time," said Pierson presently. "You ought really to take the next boat home."

Taverner shrugged his shoulders and laughed bitterly. "So I would," he said, "if I could afford it. Borneo's hell for me now, and I'm tired of it all. Think of Lonely Valley without her!"

He strolled to the window and looked out.

"Say," he called out suddenly, "did you ever hear the result of that 'sweep?' "

"I'd forgotten that," said Pierson. "I saw the list yesterday—it was only wired over last thing. Oh, here it is. The winning horse was Dimitri. Your ticket was sent to Yong-See."

Taverner made a pencil note on his cuff. "Bet it's a blank," he said.

After breakfast he strolled out alone. "Just going to the agent's," he cried, "and then up to report myself to the deputy. So long."

He startled the assistant in Yong-See's store by his unexpected entry, and the owner himself nearly fell down with amazement.

"Still flourishing, you see!" Taverner cried, and sat down on a pile of biscuit tins. "I want to run through one or two papers," he went on, "before I return to Tembakut. Things are quieting down again up there, y'know."

The Chinaman fumbled with the keys of his safe and then handed Taverner a bundle of envelopes tied together with green tape.

"I think everything is there," he said.

A tiny pink card fluttered from one of the envelopes and fell on to the bare floor.

Taverner turned it carelessly over with his foot, then started back in mute astonishment.

The card bore the following inscription:

SINGAPORE IMPERIAL LOTTERY.
DERBY, 19—.
"DIMITRI."

XI

THE TERMS OF THE CONTRACT

I

TOWARDS Manah-Manah, where someone had whispered there was gold for the asking, three men rode through jungle and swamp on as many huge, lumbering water-buffaloes.

They had started from the coast five days before with three natives leading their beasts; there was barely another day to go—and Godfrey Olsen had turned, secretly and suddenly, bored with the whole concern.

It was a sort of last hope for these three, and on it they had staked their few remaining dollars. Armitage had been a Government clerk in the F.M.S., Trent a fourth engineer on a passenger vessel, and Olsen many things, for all of which he was eminently unsuited. They had run across each other in the Continental at Singapore. Trent had wanted to fight somebody, and had hit on Armitage—Olsen had been slung out with them for some reason or other that he never very clearly understood. Anyhow, they had struck up a friendship—and then somebody told them about the gold.

They had heard tales of mineral wealth before, but somehow this story seemed to ring truer than most—and adventure was the keynote of existence with all of them.

A possible fortune a day ahead—and Olsen was fed up! He was chafed and sore through sitting astride his enormous kerbau, he was bitten from head to foot, unshaven, heavy-eyed, and weary.

Here was the secret of all of his many failures—he lacked grit. His spirit had sunk so low that no amount of cheering would wake it up again, and he began to ponder within his tired brain for some excuse to fall out of the expedition.

"Native hut ahead!" shouted Trent over his shoulder.

Armitage grunted to signify that he had heard. Olsen said nothing, but raised himself slightly and craned his neck. He moistened his parched lips with his tongue, and presently felt for his pipe and pouch.

"There will be no gold when we get there," he told himself. "There never is. If I drop out tonight I shall save myself a couple of days more torture—that's all. Lord Almighty, I'm sore all over!"

He swore savagely and thrust the tobacco into the bowl, muttering to himself all the while.

"Eh?" asked Armitage, looking back.

"Nothing, old man. I was humming a tune."

"Humming—eh? I'm glad that's how you feel! Here, sling us that pouch when you've done with it. I've come down to dust, and my main supply's wrapped up out of reach. Christopher, but this is an awful way of travelling!"

"It might be worse," laughed the ex-engineer. He had grit enough for two.

"It might be a darned sight better!" growled Olsen. "Here, catch!"

He threw it badly, and it fell into the undergrowth. His native found it and handed it to Armitage. Olsen looked up and saw the hut Trent had shouted back about.

It stood in a little clearing away from the path, raised high above the ground, on many long poles, and a rickety bamboo ladder led up to a ridiculously tiny aperture which served as a door.

A muscular native came round from the back of the hut, carrying a rough axe and the branch he had been chopping, and stood staring at the newcomers. One of the guides shouted to him in Malay, but the man only waved his hand which held the axe, and uttered a queer sound in his throat.

The first two buffaloes were level with the hut, Olsen's native had halted twenty yards behind the others, and was drawing a thorn from his foot, during that minute Olsen had seen something he had failed to notice before.

At the back of the house a coarse hemp line was stretched to a sapling ten feet away, and on this line hung two brightly-coloured sarongs—one red and white, the other a brilliant green. He knew enough about sarongs to know that they were good, too good for the man with the axe.

The native was pulling at his kerbau, uttering guttural cries of encouragement. Olsen bellowed to him to stop, indicating that his pipe had gone out and that he could not light it while the beast was moving.

He looked again at the sarongs and then at the hut. He was becoming interested. To whom did the bright cloths belong? Did those four ramshackle walls actually conceal the owner?

He held his breath. He had seen a piece of matting drawn aside to reveal a window in the wall, and a hand, hung with many bangles, rest for a moment on the wooden ledge.

It was a small hand—not that of a woman who toiled—and some of the bangles were of yellow metal; he fancied it was gold!

He raised his hand to his topi rather awkwardly, and the hand waved and disappeared. He looked towards the others—they had dismounted and were talking to the owner of the hut. His own native was polishing the ring through the kerbau's nose with the sleeve of a tattered bajau.

Olsen deliberately kissed his hand, and the matting fell back into place. He waited for a moment, staring at the window. Presently the hand reappeared, and something fell on to the trampled grass beneath the house.

Olsen slipped painfully from his buffalo and strolled, apparently unconcernedly, towards the hut. He puffed laboriously at his pipe, thrust his hands into the pockets of his riding-breeches, and peered at the ground.

"Lost something?" Trent was coming towards him, mopping his brow with his handkerchief.

"It's all right, old man. I see it now. It is only a bit of root—I thought at first it was a snake!" He laughed loudly and stooped down.

Trent stopped and wiped the rim of his sun-helmet. When he looked up Olsen was getting on to his beast again.

"Come on, boys," bawled Armitage. "We're wasting no end of time as it is. The blithering idiot's deaf and dumb!"

Trent ran to find his kerbau; Olsen was looking at something held in the palm of his hand. It was a ring, too small to fit any of his fingers, beautifully wrought in gold. It was formed to represent a dragon, the tail passing through the jaws and looped several times round the neck.

He slipped it into his pocket and waved as his kerbau started once more on its way.

II

That night Olsen complained of fever, and on the next day was unable to sit upright on his buffalo. There was nothing else for it—he had to be left behind. The other two, leaving instructions with his native, rode on towards their goal without him.

"Hard lines," said Armitage, looking back to where the smoke still rose from their last night's encampment.

"Pity," agreed Trent. "Only a bare day to go, too."

Armitage looked hard at his companion's back. "Look here, Trent, Olsen mustn't lose by this. If we strike lucky we'll play the game."

"Of course—if we do."

Olsen felt distinctly grateful when he saw them disappear beyond the trees. An hour later he sat suddenly up and demanded breakfast. The boy looked surprised.

"The Tuan is better?" he asked.

"The Tuan is hungry."

He threw a riding boot with no little degree of accuracy. The native dodged and ran to obey. A little later they started their ride back.

Towards midday they drew near to the lonely hut in the little clearing.

Olsen fell limply along the buffalo's back, and presently they halted by the bamboo ladder. The guide shouted, and

Olsen heard the sound of someone moving about within the house. Matting moved aside, and the native they had seen the day before appeared at the door.

The black guide pointed to the drooping form of his master.

"Fever!" he shouted. "The white Tuan is ill."

The man at the door stared at him for a moment, then suddenly his features contorted and the muscles of his face twitched. He waved his hand furiously in the direction of the path, then disappeared, and the matting fell back into place.

Olsen sat bolt upright and swore. For some reason or other the native wanted no one in the house.

Trickery had failed—he must use other methods. He slipped to the ground, and, as he did so, the matting moved again, and, with unexpected swiftness the native sprang from the house and stood before him, a bamboo tube in his hand.

He raised the tube to his mouth.

"Tuan!" screamed the guide wildly, "The sumpitan!" He ducked behind the kerbau.

Olsen turned white. The sumpitan—the poisoned arrow that kills instantly!

He had no time to take shelter—the hideous weapon was levelled at him. A sudden wild desire to preserve his own life at any cost rose within him, spurring him to instant action. He clutched at his belt and, as he did so, dodged instinctively.

Something whizzed by his head, almost grazing his ear. He drew his revolver and shot the native where he stood.

At the sound of the report, the kerbau threw up its great snout and plunged into the forest, the guide after it. In the palm trees a thousand monkeys shrieked and gibbered.

Presently they were silent, and Olsen found himself standing alone, the smoking weapon still in his hand, the dead man lying crumpled awkwardly on the ground before him.

It was the first life he had ever taken—and he felt afraid. The sudden hush seemed to accentuate the serious nature of his crime.

It had been in self-defence, but he knew he had brought the quarrel on by endeavouring to find his way by trickery into her house.

He looked up and saw her standing before him at the foot of the ladder.

So noiselessly had she descended that he had not heard the bamboo creak. He stood gazing at her, her strange beauty rendering him momentarily speechless. She was so unlike anything he had ever seen before, he could not think to what race she could possibly belong. She was darker than women of the white races, yet lighter than any dark woman he had yet seen. Her hair was black, her features were fine, her brows well-marked, her eyes dark and lustrous. She wore the green sarong he had seen the day before, secured above her breast by a magnificent gold brooch, with a necklace like palm leaves of gold, golden anklets, and many bangles of white and yellow metal.

Presently she spoke in a Malay tongue, but with a clear, rich accent in place of the usual guttural.

"Bury him in the forest," she said. She spoke calmly, as if the death of this man were nothing.

He found his tongue. "Who are you?" he demanded. "What in the name of everything are you doing here? Who was this man? Was he deaf and dumb?"

"I ask you no questions," she replied proudly. "I shall expect none in return. Enough that I am of royal blood, and henceforward your slave. Take the body into the jungle—there is a spade behind the hut."

III

When Olsen returned, hot and perspiring, his hands grimed and torn, she was still standing where he had left her.

"I am hungry!" he cried. "May I come in?" He tried to appear at ease, but her great dark eyes troubled him.

He made a step towards the ladder, but she stopped him with a movement of one hand.

"Listen, while you are with me I will be your slave, but there must be no end save death. If you return to your own country, I go with you. These are my terms, white man. If you like them not—go. If you accept them—here is my house, and yours."

She turned and disappeared beyond the matting which sealed the door.

Olsen, his topi tilted back from his forehead, stood looking after her in amazement. He had come out for adventure—and had found something far more strange than he had ever bargained for.

He hesitated, bit his moustache, then went up into the house.

IV

Ten days later Olsen heard a sound in the clearing, and, looking out, saw Armitage standing at the foot of the ladder.

"Good Lord! It's you! Where's Trent?"

"He's way-back, looking after the claims. Why didn't you follow?" He stood with his arms akimbo, looking up at the little door.

"Why! Because my boy killed the blighter that was here and eloped with everything, including the kerbau. What was I to do? I tried to do the Sherlock business and follow the trail, but I lost it after a few miles. I managed to find my way back here—and here I am." He lied easily.

"Phew!" ejaculated Armitage, "So you've been through things, too, have you? When I get back to the coast I'll give information against your native. Man alive, we've found enough gold to fill a battleship. It's everywhere—for the picking up. I reckon we can get it back to the coast by buffalo—enough to convince people, anyhow. Then we'll have all the proper business gone into and get the right to cut a road to the nearest railway. Jove, we'll have our own railway before long."

He stopped abruptly, and executed a weird war-dance round the clearing.

Olsen's heart sank. Then the improbable had happened—they had found yellow metal—and he was out of it. His inherent laziness had wrought his ruin. He had been but a day off from a fortune—and had turned back.

"You lucky devils!" he cried bitterly, as soon as the other came within range.

Armitage stopped. "Lucky?—here, what's up? We're all in this, aren't we? Lord, man, you don't think we're sharps, do you? Why, we've marked you out a third of everything, and I'm just off to the coast to break the news to the Government Johnnies down there. Come down, you giddy anchorite, and join in my expressions of glee."

Olsen crawled down the ladder. He could scarcely believe his ears. He gripped the other's hands, both of them, and held them tight.

"Here," said Armitage presently, "we'll start right away. Bring any provender you happen to have in that rabbit-hutch, and come right now. Two can do business better than one in these cases, and you're a better hand than I am at pitching a yarn. You can't get to Trent without a mount, anyway. He's not expecting you. He's half-afraid some wild beast has devoured you. I've left him with all the ammunition in case he runs into trouble. Come on."

"I can't," said Olsen.

He was thinking of her. She was away in the jungle getting fruit. He hoped she would not return before his friend had gone. He did not want the others to know about her.

"Can't? Why, you're raving. Take a dose of quinine, old chap!" He laughed, and began dragging Olsen to where the native stood with the buffalo.

Olsen looked back at the little door and the rough matting, hesitated, then laughed—a dry, humourless cackle.

"All right. I'm coming, of course. I must have been just drunk at seeing you again and hearing all the news."

He turned and went back into the hut.

He must not go without leaving some message. He drew out a tattered pocket-book, and wrote as well as he could in Malay characters:

"Godfrey Olsen, Continental Hotel, Singapore. Will come back. Business."

As he rode behind Armitage a lump rose suddenly in his throat, and he looked back over his shoulder, half-expecting to see her running after him along the ill-marked path. He had promised never to leave her while he lived. Still, business was business, and Fate was Fate, and there seemed no other way out of it. One thing was certain—he would go back. But he never did, for when they reached the coast-town Armitage received news of a fortune and bought Olsen out. Besides, Olsen had met Marjorie Dering!

V

"Godfrey," cried Mrs. Olsen, "there is a parcel here for you."

He came in from the hall into the luxuriously furnished drawing-room. She was sitting by a little inlaid Moorish table, looking delightfully fresh in her morning frock.

Olsen bent over her and kissed her.

"A parcel for me?"

She nodded. "It came while you were dressing, and it looked so interesting that I opened it. You don't mind, do you? I thought perhaps it was a wedding present, come late. It's from the East, too, but there's no writing inside—just this."

She held up a long ivory handle, shaped like an arm, with three claws at one end.

He whistled softly and took it gently from her.

"It looks like a Chinese back-scratcher," he said laughingly. "Are you sure there was no writing?"

"None whatever. I wonder who could have sent it."

"Someone who knows your fondness for curios, I expect."

He handed it back to her and stooped to pick the wrapper from a basket at her feet.

She held the curio by the thin end, and surveyed it thoughtfully.

"A Chinese back-scratcher!" she said. "I wonder if that's what it is? It certainly looks something like one."

She saw his sun-burnt neck placed temptingly before her, and, laughing merrily, stroked it playfully with her new toy. At that moment he started to his feet, the wrapper between his fingers.

He uttered a cry, and put his hand to his neck.

"I'm so sorry!" she exclaimed. "Have I scratched you?"

He did not answer, but remained in the same position, staring fixedly at her, a strange light in his eyes.

"Godfrey, dearest, what's the matter? Don't look like that!"

Suddenly she saw that his eyes were glazing. His lips moved, but no sound came from them. He rolled suddenly over and lay on the floor.

She screamed, and sprang to her feet, both hands to her head, horror-stricken.

"He's dead!" she screamed. "Dead! The thing was poisoned!"

She clutched feverishly at the torn wrapper and turned it over in her hand.

There was no writing beyond the original address and another written across it in red ink.

It had been forwarded to her husband from the Hotel Continental, Singapore!

XII

HARI BESAR

WAY BACK UP the Ketatan River a crocodile slid suddenly into the muddy water, but Zariman heeded it not as he lay hidden in the coarse undergrowth and watched. Around him were the varied greens of the jungle; beneath him was the warm brown of the earth; before him, intermingled with huge, spreading cocoa-palms, rose many queer-shaped, ramshackle huts, mounted on long bamboo poles, for all the world like a cluster of musty fungi.

The day was drawing to a close, and just over the ridge, which seemed so near, the sun—a fiery ball—was sinking into the deep-blue sea.

Zariman lay so still and silent that a roosa (deer) came softly through the trees and fed within a yard of him. Zariman could have killed it with his sharp parang, but to-day he did not want to kill. He was waiting patiently for the night. And at last darkness fell, the shrieking of myriads of insects marking its advent. Fires crackled merrily in the Kampon, and high up on a rubber-planted slope a Chinese lantern revealed the progress of some solitary traveller.

From a hut near by the rhythmic booming of gongs broke the stillness of the tropic night, and then, more beautiful to his ear than any music, a woman's voice began a song so weird and plaintive that Zariman's heart throbbed in time.

He rose to his feet, and uttered a shrill cry. The singing ceased abruptly, and there was a pause. Then a shadowy form in the darkness, a cry of joy, and a soft, warm body lay panting in his arms.

"Nadil!" he whispered.

"Zariman!" and nothing more.

"Nadil," he ventured presently, "I will ask your father tomorrow."

She shook her head disconsolately, and fidgeted nervously with her necklace of silver.

"It will be useless," she said. "He will not listen, and the price is too high for you, Zariman."

He started, and the blissful vision he had treasured faded suddenly away.

"The price! Nadil, what is the price?"

She looked down at the ground and turned over the sandy soil with her bare toes. Then she slowly raised her eyes to his and spoke.

"Zariman, you have always told me that you loved me—that you would do anything for me. You are a man, Zariman, brave and strong, and they tell me you have taken heads. Listen! A white Tuan came down to the Kampon last night, riding through the flooded padi-fields on a kerbau (water-buffalo)—and my father would sell me to him—"

"The price, Nadil? Tell me the price!"

"As the white Tuan left my father I crept through the lalang and listened. Two hundred dollars and a kerbau is the price!"

"And the white Tuan, Nadil?"

She buried her brown head on his breast and her slender frame shook with sobs.

"He comes for me in two days, Zariman. He will carry me away si-blas-sana (right over there). Oh, buy me! Buy me before he comes! I cannot be his ngi (housekeeper)!"

Zariman's face darkened as he held his beloved tightly to him, and he remembered his sharp-edged parang at his side.

Suddenly there came a crackling of leaves and a snapping of twigs, and a tall, lithe figure leaped from the bushes and stood menacingly before them, a flaming brand in one hand. His dress and build revealed him to be a Sikh, who, many years before, had intermarried with a woman of Dusun race, and now reared his sapi (cows) and grew his padi, living in their midst.

Nadu uttered a cry of terror as her father seized her arm and tore her roughly from her lover's embrace.

"So it is you," he cried, "who leads my daughter from her home at night, you hoonoon?"

"I came here but to ask her of you," replied the young man sullenly.

The tall Sikh laughed an ugly laugh, displaying in the glow of the firelight a perfect set of white teeth.

"You? You spawn! So you would desire the most beautiful woman in Borneo for your bride? How, think you, can you pay the price?"

The young man drew himself up to his full height.

"I am a Dusun," he replied boldly, "and not a foreigner, and I have taken heads in war! I will buy your daughter from you."

"And your price?"

"One hundred dollars!"

The Sikh spat fiercely.

"You would insult her before the eyes of her father? One hundred dollars for the most beautiful woman on this island! Begone! Go, play with your heads! I have no business with such as you!"

"And *your* price?" demanded the young man, not heeding his fury.

The Sikh looked at him queerly.

"Since you must know," he replied slowly, "two hundred dollars and a kerbau is my price for her—but you must find it quickly, for there comes another to whom dollars are as water!"

He laughed scornfully, and, turning on his heel, hurried with his daughter towards the village.

Zariman watched till the darkness hid them from his sight, then flung himself at full length on the ground and buried his brown head in his arms. His flat, conical hat of woven ratan fell and rolled away, but he did not trouble to seek it. A sensation of utter misery had seized him, and life seemed very blank and useless now. The price the Sikh had demanded was far beyond his means, even could he wait until the harvest of his padi—and in two days! He swore fiercely and spat into the darkness. Wüd thoughts crossed his fevered brain. Steal Nadil? No? That would be impossible, for he would have to leave the small possessions on which his livelihood depended and fly with her, penniless, to the beyond; and he doubted not that her father would guard her well until the white man came—and paid.

For hours he lay on the damp ground, and faint mists were beginning to rise when he fell into a light sleep. Suddenly he became aware that he was not alone. He started to his feet, rubbing his tired eyes. Nadil was by his side. She laid a warning finger on his lips.

"Hush!" she whispered. "I have scarcely a moment. See, I am trusting you, Zariman! What will you do if the white Tuan takes me away?"

Zariman drew his sharp parang and severed a stout branch above him at a blow.

"I shall have a white head then!" he cried hoarsely, and Nadil kissed him suddenly and fled.

All the long, dreary, tropic day Zariman toiled and thought. Seated on his primitive plough, he churned up his acre of padi-land, ever and anon halting his stubborn kerbau with a tuneless "Ta-han!" and the breeze in the jungle, the rustling of the lalang, all seemed to whisper in the same sad strain—Nadil was lost to him for ever!

In the evening he tethered his weary beast outside his lonely atap-roofed hut and wandered aimlessly along the new railway line which led to Pinarut.

"Tabi!" came a voice from the darkness, and a stout Dusun woman in velvet coat and highly-coloured sarong passed him, leading a tiny child.

"Tabi!" he replied, his lips forming the word of greeting mechanically.

Instinctively he remembered the missing planks in the rough bridge, and then the bright lights of the Chinese shops broke upon his unhappy thoughts. There, on his right, was a gambling den, in which a surging mass of coolies and others were playing fan-tan and kindred games of chance, and drinking the intoxicating sumsu. Why should he not drown his thoughts, too? He drew himself together and strode in at the open door.

Fifty loud greetings fell upon his ears, and he answered them in kind. He called for drink, quaffed it quickly, ordered another, and was soon eagerly watching the fall of the tiny black and red dice.

He drank deeply again, and the Chinaman at the table, a queer, attenuated figure, raked in his coins.

Suddenly he started. There was a roar of voices in his ears, loud native curses and Chinese oaths, and, as he rubbed his leaden eyes, he caught the flash of knives and saw a heavy brass dice-box fly through the air and strike the lean proprietor on the temple. A table was hurled to the ground, splintering beneath a heavy weight; there was a mad stampede for the open, and, amid a crash of broken glass and a roar of flames, the great oil lamp had been torn from the hook where it swung and dashed to the floor.

Zariman sprang for the door, and, wisdom prompting him, fled madly across the line, and dived into the jungle beyond; nor did he pause until, from a clearing on a hill, he saw the roof of the gaming den fall in amid a shower of sparks, carrying with it the major portion of the adjoining dwellings.

It was then that Zariman realised he was carrying something in his hands.

It was an oblong wooden box, with a frail metal handle, such as all Chinamen use. How it had come into his hands he did not remember.

Sitting under a big tree which topped the hill, he tried the lid—it was locked. He drew his parang and forced the lock.

The box flew open and papers fell out on every side—bundles of papers. Zariman's heart leaped. Notes! Dollar notes! Fifty-dollar notes! Hundreds of Borneo paper dollars! Wealth untold—and whose, if not his own? The Chinaman whose hoard he now held in his shaking hands was dead beneath the ruins of his smouldering den. But for Zariman this treasure would have perished too!

He sprang to his feet and leaped thrice into the air. His head was clear now—his mind made up. Nadil should yet be his!

Then he sat down again and thought—and remembered. If he went to her father now with so much money trouble would certainly ensue, for her father loved him not, and it was known to all the world that Zariman was poor. No; he must lay his plans carefully, and strike swiftly and soon, even as he had promised, to the falling of a white head—the head of a Tuan Besar of a mighty race of people, who came in great engine-kapal across the seas, and lived on the lands they had stolen.

Footsteps! He closed the box swiftly and slipped it behind him.

"Tabi!" came a clear, ringing voice.

It was the Tuan Besar on his way back to his bungalow. A spirit within told Zariman that this was his time—his opportunity. He drew his parang.

"Hari Besar to-morrow!" called the white man suddenly.

Zariman started. He had forgotten! To-morrow was a feast day when all the world drank and was merry. A sudden gleam of hope flashed across his mind—a vision of a bloodless victory.

"Tabi! Tabi, Tuan!"

The white man was gone into the darkness, his hurricane lamp swinging beside him; the sharp parang slipped noiselessly back into its sheath, and Zariman, his precious box under his arm, stole softly home to sleep and dream of all the eventful morrow might bring.

Nadil came, with downcast eyes, to the Ketatan River for water. It was scarcely light, but all the village was astir, and myriads of tiny nude forms trotted aimlessly between the long poles which supported the clustered houses. Hens scratched busily in the dust, a cock crowed lustily, and three or four sapi (cows) browsed on the luscious herbage by the riverside. From the lalang by the bank a shrill cry came suddenly, a cry so familiar that her trembling heart beat tumultuously.

"Nadil," came a soft whisper, "to-night there will be a boat down in the rushes by the jack-fruit-tree. At what hour comes the Tuan?"

"When eight strikes," she murmured, stooping down to the stream.

"At the fall of darkness, then, I shall come. If you are not down by the tree I shall seek you, Nadil. Do not fear, I shall come in time."

A rustling in the lalang and Zariman was gone. Nadil shouldered her gourd and made her way back to her father's house, her step lighter than it had been for many days.

The sun shone relentlessly down and loud beat the Dusun drums—with monotonous persistence they throbbed all day. Dance followed dance, and Dusun youths, almost naked, seated astride their buffaloes, urged them madly through the muddy water of the padi-fields. Sumsu flowed freely, and scarcely a male inhabitant of the little Kampon remained sober. For this was the Hari Besar, the feast-day, the day of rest from toil, the day of excess.

Somewhere down in the jungle a sturdy brown form smoked and waited patiently, hearing the sounds of merriment from afar. Sometimes his limbs ached for the dance, his throat yearned for the burning liquor; but then a vision of Nadil rose before him, and the desire was dispelled. And the day drew on and on.

Far away, across the hills, a tall, white-clad figure, mounted on a sturdy pony, was starting on his way, followed by a group of coolies with a pikul (hammock), to buy a "wife."

Throb, throb, throb came the sound of the beaten gongs, loud rang the discordant shouts of the revelling Dusuns. Darkness fell suddenly over hill and valley, forest and swamp, and the jungle stirred and woke.

Zariman drew his big canoe from the lalang, thrust it noiselessly into the muddy waters and waited.

What was that? A scream? A cry of fear? Nadil! He drew his parang and sprang ashore. A dark figure staggered towards him and fell, gasping, into his arms. A second form was reeling close upon her heels—it was the tall Sikh, her father.

Zariman let the girl sink gently to the ground and turned to meet his adversary. A spluttering of drunken oaths in some tongue unknown to Zariman, a flash of steel on steel, and the tall Sikh slipped and fell. Zariman knew he was not wounded, but drunk. He placed his foot on his neck and laughed.

"See here, 'father,' " he cried mockingly, "I buy your daughter now. Sana (over there) you will find my padi-land and my kerbau. Take it—she is worth it."

He lifted his foot, but the other did not attempt to rise. Zariman, seizing his precious burden, fled softly with her to the waiting canoe. He paddled swiftly to midstream, and soon the dark waters were rushing silently by. There was a commotion at the other end of the village, where a tall, white-clad figure was calling for the Sikh in broken Malay. A man staggered into the firelight, and the white man clutched his wrist in a vice-like grip.

"The girl! Where is the girl?"

The Sikh eyed him dully.

The white man shook him until his teeth rattled.

"The girl—you kiti! Where is the girl?"

"Gone!" the Sikh cried hoarsely. "Stolen!" and relapsed into a stupid silence.

The white man flung him to the ground and kicked him as he lay there inert. Then he turned and strode furiously away.

Dawn broke upon the hills, and the deep jungle and a long oblong box, and upon a boat which sped rapidly between densely-wooded banks, and upon a sturdy brown man and a girl, who, radiantly happy, dipped her dark hands into the rippling waters as they bubbled by.

THE BLACK SPIDER

THE FURY of the storm had died down. But the *Batilcoa* still dipped and rolled to the tune of an enraged sea-god whose anger was gradually diminishing. There was a suggestion of dampness in the corridors and a constant rattling and shifting of heavy weights overhead that was eloquent of the thoroughness with which the original labour of screwing, lashing, and stowing had been undone.

Of the two hundred or so first-class passengers only two could muster sufficient courage to face breakfast in the saloon. One was a thin, dapper Englishman with a good-humoured, weather-beaten countenance. The other was a tall, slim girl.

The man—whose age might have been anything between forty and fifty—sat at a small table at the starboard side, his table-napkin across his knees, studying the menu. He glanced up presently and caught the girl in the act of looking at him.

Two forlorn people in a forest of white tables! It seemed absurd.

"Why don't you come across here, Miss Seldon? I hate eating alone."

Bianca Seldon flushed and smiled.

"So do I. My companion—Mrs. Parrett, you know—is completely knocked out. I'd rather you came over here, if you don't mind, Doctor. I don't think one notices the movement so much nearer the middle, do you?"

Andrew Langley crossed over.

"It was a wild night," he said. "Did you sleep?"

She shook her head.

"Not much." A sudden thought made her smile. "I suppose one oughtn't to laugh. But it really is too funny. Poor

Mrs. Parrett was supposed to look after me—and I've been doing nothing but look after her ever since we left Southampton."

"Not a good sailor?"

"By no means. She was ill in the train before we embarked. Dr. Langley, I suppose that really was a storm last night?"

He raised his brows.

"I should imagine so. What did you think it was?"

"A really bad one, I mean?"

Langley rubbed a spot on his chin that his razor had somehow missed.

"The worst I ever remember—and I've done a few trips. Why?"

"I'm glad to hear you say that, because the second officer spoke of it as a *squall*."

Her companion laughed.

"One of the first duties of an officer on a passenger ship is to keep up the courage of the passengers. As a matter of fact, he's not the only one aboard who's heartily glad we pulled through with as few casualties as we did."

Bianca's dark eyes opened wide.

"Casualties! You mean people were injured?"

Langley looked at his hands.

"Er—yes. Just one or two, you know."

"But not passengers?"

"Good heavens, no. Lascars, principally. It's these risks that inspire people to take up the sea as a profession. By the way, I shouldn't say anything to Mrs. Parrett. It might frighten her. What are you eating?"

"Anything!"

The doctor found a pair of glasses in his top pocket, rubbed them carefully, and perched them on the bridge of his nose.

"You mean that?"

"Why, certainly. I'm not feeling the least bit ill, if that's what you think, only I do like to have my meals on as firm a floor as possible. The purser tells me you're from Borneo. Perhaps you've met my brother?"

Langley started.

"Not Barry Seldon?"

"That's right. He manages an estate near Mirabalu. I'm going to join him there."

The man leaned back in his chair, staring at her incredulously.

"Barry Seldon! Of course! You couldn't be anybody else's sister."

"Couldn't I?"

"Not very well. You're extraordinarily like him, you know. Can't think why it didn't occur to me before. I imagine it's because he's known all over the island as Barry and nobody thinks of him as Seldon at all. So you're going to Mirabalu? We shall be quite near neighbours."

Bianca's eyes sparkled.

"Now isn't that just too delightful! Mrs. Parrett's going on to Foochow and I shall have to find my way from Singapore without her. I wonder if you're willing to undertake a fearful responsibility?"

Langley was engaged in smothering his grape-fruit with castor sugar.

" 'Fearful responsibility?' Just what do you mean?"

"Taking charge of me from Singapore to Mirabalu."

The doctor relinquished his spoon and sat up.

"I shall be delighted, of course."

"Then that's settled. What an idiot Barry was not to tell me you were coming by this boat. It would have saved such a lot of trouble."

"Barry didn't know. I was due back a month ago, but managed to get my leave extended." He surveyed her doubtfully. "I don't know that you're going to be altogether satisfied with this arrangement. I have no small talk and my dancing is execrable."

"You can tell me about Mirabalu," suggested Bianca hopefully.

"In about half-a-dozen sentences. Mirabalu is a wilderness populated by half-baked niggers and Chinese coolies, with about seven white men to look after them. There's not another white woman for fifteen miles."

The girl laughed. "What a charming description! If it's really as bad as you try to make out, why does anybody live there at all?"

"That is a question which invariably crops up at about the fourth whiskey. The queer thing is that nobody's ever been able to answer it. Whenever a chap goes on leave he takes a fond and final farewell of his friends, murmurs something vague about influence and a comfortable job at home—and drifts back to the same old area as soon as ever his time is up."

Bianca frowned.

"Then it can't be such a desperately bad place after all," she declared. "Would you like to live in England?"

The doctor shuddered.

"Not on your life. D'you know, Miss Seldon, I believe there were only nine days in the entire seven months when it didn't rain."

"There you are," cried Bianca triumphantly; "you men are all the same. You drink more than is good for you, develop liver trouble, and distort your outlook on life. Really and truly, I expect Mirabalu is a delightful spot, with glorious views and any amount of amusement to be had if one only takes the trouble to look for it."

Langley smiled.

"You'll find out soon enough."

"I suppose I shall. Anyhow, I've fully made up my mind to enjoy myself."

"You'll be bitten to death." said the doctor.

"I don't care. Barry says you get over that."

"You'll be eternally pestered by a mob of disorderly young ruffians each with a proposal of marriage in his mind."

"I shall like that."

"And you'll be very unwise if you accept any of 'em, because your brother's bungalow is the very best in the neighbourhood; the only one, in fact, with glass windows." He chuckled to himself and moved to one side to allow the steward to take his plate. "You'll like Mirabalu, the life, the views, everything. Presently you'll be bored to extinction—and then you'll like it so much that you won't want to leave it at all. Mirabalu's an acquired taste, but once acquired it sticks to you like a leech until—"

"I see," said Bianca thoughtfully, "but you didn't want to let me down too lightly at first. I suppose that's the line you take in your profession. You swoop down upon your unfortunate patient, send him to bed, terrify him with an endless list of probable complications, until the poor wretch feels so utterly grateful to you for saving him from such terrors that he cheerfully sends an enormous cheque by return mail!"

The purser's steward, entering suddenly, stared around the saloon until his eye fell upon Langley. He came across to the table.

"Excuse me, sir, but Dr. Murphy sends his compliments and would like to see you in the cabin."

The doctor glanced up sharply.

"Oh—what's the trouble?"

"I don't know exactly, sir. I think he's got his hands pretty full."

"Wants help, eh?"

"That's my opinion, sir."

Bianca, who had been trying to see out of a porthole, touched Langley's arm.

"I believe we've stopped," she declared.

"Been stopped this half-hour, Miss," said the steward. "Our wireless carried away in the storm last night and we haven't been able to pick up calls. They've just brought aboard a fellow who was tied to some boards. The chief steward thinks he's Japanese, possibly washed overboard from the ship we passed yesterday afternoon. He was fully dressed, with a small box strapped to his waist. I saw him when they got him up."

"Is he still alive?" interposed the doctor.

"I believe so, sir; he's in a bad way. Must have been in the water for hours."

"Very well. I'll come along now. You'll excuse me, Miss Seldon, won't you?"

"Why, of course. Isn't there some way in which I could help?"

Langley shook his head.

"There are plenty of stewardesses," he reminded her; "besides, you may have to look after your friend."

"No," said Bianca; "they won't let me. Do send for me if you're short-handed."

"We're short-handed right enough," put in the steward. "All the staff that aren't sick themselves are up to their eyes in it. There's hardly a bit of china left in the kitchens—and how we're going to serve dinner to-night I don't know."

"We'll be in Colombo to-morrow," said the doctor grimly, "and nobody's likely to want much dinner before then! Let's see—which way do we go?"

As he made his way down the corridor at the steward's heels, it occurred to him that Bianca Seldon was going to be something in the nature of a disturbing influence in Mirabalu. For one thing, she displayed an enormous amount of character for a girl of her age, and, for another, she was a great deal too good-looking. For all his morbid description of the place where he lived and worked, he knew Mirabalu as a colony that was essentially masculine—masculine in its outlook, its amusements, and its excesses.

There was not a more amiable group of men to be found anywhere, and why Barry Seldon had been such an unmitigated ass as to bring his sister out there, Langley didn't know. He wasn't in the least sorry for Bianca, for she could look after herself and was bound in any case to have a tolerably good time—but he was mortally sorry for Mirabalu. For some reason or other he was feeling depressed that morning and was prone to regard Bianca in Mirabalu, and a bottle of fire-water in a camp of Indians, as one and the same thing. They had been perfectly all right up to now. But—when she arrived—

He found the ship's doctor in his shirt-sleeves. He was a fat, broad-featured man with a Belfast accent, and dark lines under his eyes which betrayed that he had been up all night.

"I hate to trouble you again, Doctor—" he began; but Langley cut him short.

"Trouble be damned, Murphy! If you had had the nerve to attempt to carry on without me I should have been mortally offended. What do you want me to do?"

"Have you had breakfast?"

"I've had enough to carry me along, thanks. I don't mind betting you haven't had a bite yourself!"

"Right—but I'm going to now. I wish you'd take that poor devil of a Jap off my hands for a bit. The steward here will show you where he is. I tell you, Doctor, I never want another night like this. I've had eight more fresh cases through my hands since you turned in and I don't think one of 'em will live."

Langley dropped a hand lightly on Murphy's shoulder.

"Get some food into you and try and close your eyes for a spell."

A patch of green water obscured the port-hole and receded again, revealing a stretch of blue sky.

"We're getting into clear weather again," said Murphy.

"That's something to be thankful for. Well, cheerio! I'll be getting along to see my man."

He found his patient in a spare second-class cabin. A man in a white coat rose as he came in.

"Did Dr. Murphy put you here?" Langley asked.

"Yes, sir."

The man moved aside so as to allow Langley to come close to the berth.

"How is he?"

"Pretty queer, sir. He's in a high fever now, and keeps talking, first in Japanese and then in English."

The doctor bent down.

"It'd be a pity to let him slip through our fingers—after all he's gone through." He glanced at a chart fixed to the wall by a couple of pins. "You've been up all night, too, I suppose?"

"Yes, sir."

"Anybody about who can relieve you?"

"No, sir. Dr. Murphy told me I'd have to hang on for a bit longer."

"Ah! Well, we'll see what we can do."

He drew a card from a silver case and bit the end of his pencil thoughtfully. He wrote something and handed it to the man.

"Take this along to the dispenser."

"Anything else, sir?"

"Yes. I want you to go to the first-class saloon and find Miss Seldon. If she's not there, the purser will tell you where she is. Ask her if she'd mind coming to see me here as soon as possible. You can turn in after that. I shall want you back at one o'clock."

"Very good, sir." At the door he paused and looked back. "Er—I suppose Dr. Murphy will understand? You see, he told me—"

Langley took him by both shoulders and pushed him out of the room.

"I'll make it all right with Dr. Murphy," he assured him and went back to his patient.

The Japanese was moving restlessly and a crimson spot burned at each cheek-bone. He seemed to be gabbling something that Langley could not catch, clutching all the while at the white coverlet with fingers like yellow claws. Suddenly he sat bolt upright, a gaunt fragile figure in a borrowed pyjama-coat that was four sizes too large.

"The box," he said in English, staring before him with glazed eyes, "—they must not take that! They will forget to feed it . . . the thing will die. I want it to grow . . ."

The doctor forced him gently back and covered him.

"Your box is here all right," he muttered, rather for something to say than having the least hope he would be understood.

The man struggled feebly for a few minutes, then relapsed into the vague, restless state in which Langley had found him.

There was a box in the corner, a square box of painted wood with a double row of perforations round the top. It measured approximately a foot square.

Langley picked it up and, holding it to the light, tried to see in. He was about to put it down when he became aware that something was moving about inside.

He whistled softly to himself.

"Good Lord! This then, whatever it is, is alive too."

He set the box on the closed top of the washing cabinet and stood looking at it, his hands deep in his trouser pockets. He had the usual scruples concerning prying into other people's property, but he was equally prepared to set such scruples aside when it was a question of an animal requiring sustenance. He could not make up his mind as to the nature of the beast. The movements had been queer—similar in some respects to those of a bird. And yet, he did not think it was a bird. He brought his head closer. There was a peculiar, unpleasant odour about the box that both puzzled him, and—was very nauseating.

He glanced at his patient through the mirror, then withdrew a kind of skewer with a polished knob that appeared to secure the drawer. It had occurred to him that this drawer might contain a supply of the particular type of food that the creature required. But to his amazement he found nothing but minute metal cylinders, securely corked and labelled in Japanese characters, and a hypodermic syringe!

He closed it again and replaced the fastening.

He remained for some seconds, gazing at his own reflection in the glass, then deliberately withdrew a second rod and threw open the lid.

He dropped the skewer and sprang back a yard, nearly falling over the foot of the bunk. At the same moment, the door behind him opened softly.

Queer, hairy claws appeared over the edge of the box, waving suspiciously. The box tilted, then fell on its side and there emerged—an enormous spider, its body as big as his two fists. The thing was black and, hardened as he was to jungle phenomena, Langley thought he had never seen anything quite so loathsome in his life. A second later it had disappeared and then he saw it racing up the white-painted wall with a glistening strand waving behind it that might have been a rope. It sought refuge in a corner of the ceiling.

He heard Bianca's little gasping cry behind him.

"Dr. Langley, what is it? Oh, isn't it horrible!"

He backed towards her, his eye still riveted on the monster.

"It's a spider," he said calmly. "Our friend here brought it on board with him in that box. I'm afraid I let it out, and our problem of the moment is how to get it back again. Don't stay here if you're frightened."

He reached over and pressed the bell.

"I am frightened," said Bianca; "but I'm going to stay."

"Splendid! Well, keep as far away as you can. It may start roving in search of food—and some of these things have poisonous bites."

"But I've never heard of a spider as big as that."

"Nor have I. As a general rule I prefer them about an inch long. The Japanese gentleman on the bed, however, isn't satisfied yet. He wants it to grow!"

The girl stared at the yellow face with its two crimson spots.

"Do you mean to say he keeps that thing as a pet?"

Langley nodded.

"He's been babbling about it a good deal in his delirium. He seems to have it on his mind."

"I'm not in the least surprised," said Bianca.

A steward knocked on the door in response to the doctor's summons.

"Don't come in," said Langley. "Find me the biggest jar you can—one with a large opening—and bring it here at once."

Ten minutes later the knock came again and Langley put his head round the door.

"That's not large enough," she heard him say. Then: "That's better. I think we might manage with that."

She saw him cross the floor, armed with a large receptacle that might have been used for salt. He placed a camp-stool on the floor, under where the spider was crouching, and mounted it gingerly.

A feeling of nausea swept over her and she shut her eyes.

Minutes passed and suddenly she realised that he was bending over the washing cabinet, doing something with a towel.

"Get me a piece of string, Miss Seldon, if you don't mind. I've got him inside."

She returned presently and watched him pass the cord several times round the mouth of the jar. He swore softly to himself as the knot slipped. The second time, she bit her lip, then went over to him and put her finger on the cord, to hold it for him.

He dumped the imprisoned insect in the cupboard and shut the door.

"Thanks awfully. You didn't like doing that, eh, Miss Seldon?"

"No, I didn't. I hated it. But I like to make myself do the things I hate. It wasn't really very difficult, once I'd assured my weaker self that the creature was safely inside and couldn't possibly hurt me. It was nothing to what you did."

"No," smiled Langley. "But I'm a—a doctor—and have to do a whole lot of unpleasant things."

"You were going to say 'a man,'" she challenged him. "I don't see why you didn't. Why do men hate referring to themselves as men? Women aren't ashamed of their sex."

"That's possibly because they've nothing to be ashamed of."

She moved forward impulsively.

"I'm glad you consented to look after me. I know I'm in good hands. I think you're a *super-man.*"

They met that evening at dinner.

The band was playing and there were perhaps a score of people scattered among the tables.

"Tired?" asked Langley.

"Not in the least, thank you. I think our patient is better already, don't you?"

The doctor pursed his lips.

"He has a grip on life that is positively uncanny," he said. "We're going to pull him through, you know. I understand the spider has found a new keeper?"

"Yes. Hales—and isn't he a most peculiar looking man?" commented the girl, with a shudder. "I'm told he pushes lumps of meat under the towel and the brute stands up on its hind legs and asks for more. Do you believe that?"

"No," said Langley firmly, "—I don't. But the fact that it eats meat doesn't altogether surprise me. There are such things as bird-catching spiders, you know. We've discovered our friend's name, by the by. It's Kamaga."

"That's interesting. I hate to have to refer to a human being as 'him' or 'it.' Spelt with a K?"

Langley nodded.

"Spelt with a K. Has he disclosed anything more about the spider?"

"Oh, yes—whole strings of it. It's perfectly weird at times. You'd think he knew you were there and was propounding his theories. He talked this afternoon about Japanese gardens and the infinite pains taken to dwarf things. Then he spoke of himself. It's awfully difficult to get a connected story, because he has a disconcerting habit of reverting suddenly to his own language. At least, I suppose it's his own."

"What did you gather?"

She held her head on one side and screwed up her eyes.

"Oh, that he's a sort of scientist. He aims at increasing the size of things—everything. That's his main theme. He hammers away at that for hours."

The doctor looked up from the wine-list.

"Increasing the size of things, eh? You don't suppose he was responsible for the exaggerated growth of that confounded insect?"

She uttered a little cry.

"You mean that he—"

"I mean that a creature like that would command a high price at a zoo or a freak show. I don't believe a spider of that size exists under normal conditions. There was a drawer under the box which contained drugs, and a syringe. God! I wonder if he's doping that thing with something he's discovered?" He shuddered. "Let's forget about it and have some dinner."

"It didn't look very dopey," insisted Bianca. "It went up the wall like a streak of lightning."

"You saw that?"

"Of course, I was at the door. Don't you remember?"

"I do," said Langley. "But I'd like to forget it. If I really thought there were insects like that in the tropics, I'd never place any confidence in a mosquito-net again!"

"Bigger and bigger and bigger,' he keeps saying," pursued the girl, with evident relish. "If he really goes on as he's started, it ought to add a new zest to big-game hunting."

"We'll drop it," said the doctor coldly, "—if you don't mind."

They were on the point of disembarking at Singapore when Kamaga joined them at the taffrail. He had borrowed a suit of clothes that almost fitted, and presented the appearance of a sleek, good-looking boy.

"Good-bye, Miss Seldon," he said. "I shall never forget what you have done for me."

Bianca crimsoned and clung tightly to the doctor's arm.

"Really, Mr. Kamaga, I had little or nothing to do with your case. If you wish to thank anybody, you should thank Dr. Langley. It was he who pulled you through."

Langley turned.

"Oh, it's you, Kamaga. Glad to see you're better. You're lucky to be here at all. You've the finest constitution of any man I've ever come across. Come along, Miss Seldon. I'm going to take you to the hotel—without further delay."

They moved a few paces nearer the head of the gangway, and still Kamaga followed.

"I am coming to Borneo very soon," he enlightened Bianca. "I shall be seeing you again."

"Oh, yes, Mr. Kamaga? Er—good-bye."

"Good-bye," said Kamaga, a shade of wistfulness in his voice.

She lost sight of him in the crowd, but felt somehow that he was staring after her until the rickshaw had whirled them out of sight—into the atmosphere of Singapore's dust and intense heat.

"Infernal cheek!" said Langley. "What did I tell you?"

"I don't suppose he meant any harm," returned Bianca.

"Harm!" snorted the doctor. "He means nothing but harm. Cultivates spiders as big as footballs, and means no harm? Damn him!"

The girl was drinking in the sights and Kamaga was already a back number in her memory.

"I don't see that it's anything to get huffy about. It's a hundred to one we shan't see him again. Aren't those black kiddies just sweet! I'd like to take one home with me."

"You wouldn't," declared the doctor. "They're like lambs; they grow up! I can imagine nothing more unpleasant than a sheep about the house!"

Dr. Andrew Langley was dining with Stewart—magistrate at Mirabalu—on a high veranda with an oil-lamp above and a pall of blackness all round.

It was ten months since he had left the *Batilcoa* at Singapore, and he was beginning to forget that he had ever had a vacation at all.

Langley rested both elbows on the rail and peered into the darkness.

He nipped the end from a cigar, lit it carefully, and threw the match into the night.

"Barry can be mighty hot-tempered at times," he remarked suddenly.

Stewart was pouring out liquor from a long earthenware bottle with a Dutch label.

"I know," he replied, without looking up. "It takes a good deal to rouse him, but when he's really thoroughly incensed—then look out! But what made you say that?"

"Something that occurred on his estate the other day. Jimmy, has anyone complained to you lately about Barry Seldon?"

The magistrate shook his head. He was a long, lean man with straight, clean-cut features, and eyes that were particularly blue.

"Don't think so. Has he been knocking his coolies about or something?"

The doctor emptied his glass.

"Not exactly. He kicked a stranger off the plantation last Thursday—kicked him pretty thoroughly, as a matter of fact. The fellow went away swearing blue murder. I thought you'd have heard of it by now."

Stewart grinned.

"Oh? What sort of stranger?"

"A yellow skinned blighter of some education who met Bianca on the boat coming out—and tried to renew the acquaintance. Barry warned him once before."

The D.O. came slowly forward, his face flushed, his fists clenched at his sides.

"I don't think I quite understand you, Doc. A Chinaman—and Bianca!"

Langley glanced from the end of his cigar to his friend.

"There's nothing to get excited about. The fellow was washed past us in a storm and one of our boats picked him up. He was unconscious, of course, and Bianca volunteered to nurse him until one of the staff could be spared to take her place. We hoped to have seen the last of him at Singapore—

but, unfortunately he rolled up here three months ago. He's Japanese."

Stewart started.

"Not Kamaga?"

"Yes. That's his name. You know him?"

"By sight only. He's taken over a few odd acres that were not the remotest use to anybody and put up some ghastly looking buildings. I was away when he came, but Brown saw him. Nobody raised any objection to his being there—so we let him stop." He clenched his teeth. "Some of these chaps have the cheek of the devil! If I hear the suspicion of a complaint against him, I'll have him deported."

The doctor nodded sympathetically.

"My sole regret is that I was the person who was instrumental in saving his wretched life. If you've got a couple of decent packs of cards in the house, I'll play you *Canfield,* for pennies."

It was close on midnight when a man rode furiously into the clearing that surrounded the bungalow and called to the magistrate from the saddle.

"Stewart!—Are you up there?"

The D.O. looked over.

"Hullo, Wright! You look hot. Come up and have a *peg*. The doc's here."

The newcomer slung his reins to an orderly and came up the steps, three at a time.

"I can't stop a minute," he panted. "Miss Seldon's up there alone."

He grabbed at the glass Stewart held out to him and drained it at a gulp. It was at that moment the magistrate noticed that Wright was white to the lips.

"Alone? Where's Barry?"

The planter caught at Stewart's arm.

"God—it's awful! We were up there—the three of us. The others had gone, and Miss Seldon had just come out in her dressing-gown to persuade Barry to go to bed. She was frightened at something, I think, and didn't want to admit it before me. I had picked up my hat and was making for the dining-room door when a ghastly thing happened—Something black squeezed its way through the open window and dropped to the floor in front of us."

He paused for breath.

"Well?" ejaculated the D. O. impatiently. "What was it?"

Wright stared wildly, and swallowed hard.

"You'll think I'm mad, or drunk or something. It was a thing like a spider, only a million times bigger than any I've ever seen."

The doctor glanced up sharply.

"It was black, you say? About how big?"

Wright stared vaguely around the veranda as if seeking some object with which to comparé it.

"It was tremendous. The body must have been nearly a yard long. For a matter of seconds we all stood there, paralysed. Then I pushed Miss Seldon behind me and Barry pulled open the drawer in which he kept his pistol. The next thing I knew, the brute had sprung upon Barry and bitten him . . ."

"Bitten him?"

The magistrate's face wore a puzzled expression.

"Yes! It all happened so quickly. He staggered backwards with an ugly, gaping wound in his neck. The entire drawer came away with his hand and somehow or other I managed to get hold of that automatic.

"I fired at the thing, of course, and I suppose I hit it. Anyhow, one of my shots found the lamp-glass and blew it to atoms. That was when the creature was crossing the table, and I aimed a bit too high. The lamp flared up and smoked like blazes, and through the fog that descended upon the room like a pall, I caught sight of a shadowy horror clawing itself out by the way it had come.

"When I had adjusted the wick, and got back to Barry—*he was dead!"*

Stewart took him by both shoulders and shook him violently.

"Dead! Are you quite sure?"

"As certain as I stand here. The thing's bite had poisoned him. I got Miss Seldon to her bed, sent in the black girl who looks after her, and dispatched a runner to the doctor's place. Then I reconnoitred the ground all round the house, but could find nothing. I had another look at Miss Seldon, found Barry's pony—and came across."

Dr. Langley reached for his hat.

"The *black spider!*" he muttered, staring straight before him.

A moment later all three men were in the clearing.

They reached the veranda together.

Stewart threw open the dining-room door and went in, the doctor following at his heels.

A cloth had been hastily thrown over the body. Langley removed it.

"Well?" asked the magistrate presently, a lump in his throat.

"Dead," said the doctor and put back the covering. He rose to his feet and glanced round the room. "I must see Bianca."

Suddenly Wright—who was in the doorway—raised a warning finger.

"Keep quiet a minute. What was that?"

Above the chirping of the crickets, the ceaseless hum of insect creation, there floated to their ears the sound of a woman screaming.

Stewart clutched Langley's arm.

"Bianca!"

The other faced him squarely.

"Rubbish," he insisted. "It's more likely some native girl in the Kampon, on the other side. The sound came from a good way off."

He crossed the floor, and, gaining the passage, knocked loudly on the door. There was no response. He tapped again. The others, listening in silence, heard the handle turn.

"Jimmy! Wright! Come here, both of you!"

The room was in darkness and the doctor was striking matches, feverishly looking for the lamp.

"Stop just where you are for a moment!"

A light flickered and presently the apartment was dimly illuminated. They saw an empty bed, an overturned chair, and the figure of a black woman lying in the middle of the floor.

The doctor turned her over.

"She's had a deuce of a knock from behind, but she's still breathing. We must send somebody to her." He looked up. "Are you fellows armed?"

Stewart tapped his pocket significantly. He was unusually pale and beads of perspiration stood out on his forehead.

"Then it was Bianca we heard! That spider has been back again." He turned fiercely on the planter. "You ought never to have left the place."

Wright spread out his hands, babbling incoherently.

"I? What on earth was I to do? I had to find you! I had nobody to send . . . I hit the thing, I tell you . . . how was I to know . . . ?"

"The spider has not been back," said Langley calmly.

"But man alive!" shouted the D.O., "Bianca's gone. Don't you understand that? She was taken from here."

"I know, but not by the black spider. The spider's master is the perpetrator of this fresh outrage."

Both men stared at him incredulously.

"The spider's master! What in the name of heaven—"

"I haven't time to explain it all to you now. We've got to find our mounts and ride like the devil. Wright, you'd better round up the estate watchmen and a couple of dozen reliable coolies and bring them across after us. Then send for Stewart's men. I want you fellows to be prepared to fire the scrub. Do you understand?"

The planter nodded grimly.

"I'll fix that all right. Where are they to *go?*"

"To Kamaga's place. I want them to surround it and await instructions."

The magistrate's fingers were moving nervously and his forehead was deeply furrowed.

"Kamaga's place! What on earth has that blighter to do with black spiders?"

"Everything," said Langley. "He breeds 'em. Poor old Barry has been the victim of one of his ghastly experiments. No, I'm not mad, old man. I know what I'm talking about. Come on."

They rode into the night, taking an easterly direction through the rubber trees.

A pale moon bathed the hillside in yellow light. A fresh breeze from the sea rustled the leafy branches overhead and from the strip of jungle at the foot of the slope a hornbill shrieked.

"A whole regiment to tackle one Jap," shouted Stewart suddenly.

"I'm not afraid of Kamaga," returned the doctor. "If he was all we had to contend with I shouldn't worry."

They galloped down a steep incline and on to the flat land again. The doctor ducked to avoid a branch and swung himself to the ground.

"There's a fence of some sort here. I noticed it when I came past last week."

The magistrate, joining him, flashed an electric torch on a high wall of painted stakes, set closely together.

"He didn't mean anybody to get in here!"

"Or out!" added Langley, as he moved off to the right.

"There's a light up there," said the D.O., peering through.

"And a gate here. It's padlocked on the inside. We shall have to break it down."

They had found a stake and were wrenching off pilings when Stewart turned and looked back.

His eyes had long grown accustomed to the darkness of this lone glade where even the moon's rays scarcely penetrated.

What he saw there behind him froze the blood in his veins. He dropped to his knees, pulling his companion after him, as a black horror—crawling painfully on five of its eight legs—crept from the trees and scaled the fence barely ten feet from them. They heard it drop on the other side.

"God!" exclaimed Stewart. "It's incredible!"

Langley had picked up the pole again.

"It's interesting to know that spiders have a homing instinct," he muttered. "Kamaga must have taken it there in some way—and let it loose. We can get through here."

They clambered through on foot, leaving their mounts tethered by the trees.

There was a broad, moss-covered track on the far side. Negotiating this, they made for a solitary light that showed ahead, then slowed down to a brisk walking pace as the first belt of outbuildings emerged from the shadows.

Stewart went first up the crazy ladder and pushed the door wide open. There was a strip of matting across the floor, a Japanese stool and a piece of low furniture, like a desk without legs.

As the Englishmen entered, Kamaga—clad in a white kimono that was guiltless of embroidery—came softly though a curtained aperture and stood before them.

Langley had him covered.

"The game's up, Kamaga," he jerked out. "Put up your hands. Do you hear me?"

The Japanese raised his arms slowly.

"Good evening, gentlemen," he said quietly. "You have doubtless good reason for breaking your way into my home. I shall be interested to learn your motive."

"Kamaga," interposed the doctor, "I saved your life on the *Batilcoa*. We want you to tell us where you have taken Miss Seldon."

Stewart's finger, hooked round the trigger of his automatic, restrained itself with difficulty.

Kamaga blinked.

"The lady has disappeared?"

The magistrate's anger boiled over.

"I can't stand this! Keep this blackguard here, Doc. I'm going to search this place!"

"Be careful."

"Oh, I'll look out for myself."

He plunged through the curtains.

Langley opened his case with one hand, struck a vesta on his shoe and lit a cigarette.

"It's no use beating about the bush, Kamaga," he told his prisoner. "I know everything."

The man's face betrayed no sign of emotion.

"Indeed?"

"I am referring to the black spider. You spoke of it in your delirium. You wanted it to grow—and grow—and grow. We know now, Kamaga, that it *has grown.* Keep your hands above your head, you yellow devil!"

A cry came from within.

"Doctor!"

"Hullo?"

"Bring Kamaga here. Make him walk in front of you and don't take your eyes off him for a second."

Langley pointed to the curtains.

"Get a move on," he said curtly. Kamaga obeyed.

He was on the point of passing through when the doctor caught the curtains up and ripped the material from the rod that held it suspended. He was taking no chances.

He found himself in a long, narrow apartment stocked with appliances and glass jars. Stewart had his back to them, gazing down a broad passage-way to a room beyond, the door of which stood open. There was an oil lamp in a bracket and its light was sufficient to reveal to the doctor's horrified gaze a menagerie of the most revolting specimens that it had ever been his fortune to encounter.

He saw tier upon tier of little square cages, each numbered and ticketed and containing specimens of insects of every sort and description, greatly magnified. A blue fly, as big as his hand—a centipede like a serpent, that kept up a ceaseless race to the roof of its prison, only to drop to the floor and begin again—a moth, with closed wings which, when opened, must have covered a couple of feet from tip to tip—giant ants—beetles—gnats . . .

At the far side of the room beyond, there was a bed, completely screened by mosquito-curtains, hung from a wooden ring fixed to the ceiling.

"I want Kamaga to tell me who is sleeping in that bed," said the magistrate.

The Japanese did not reply.

"Why don't you go and see for yourself?" asked Langley.

For answer, the D.O. stepped aside, revealing the form of a second enormous spider—a quarter of the size of the one that had poisoned Barry—crouching on the inner side of the opening, a metal collar round its middle and a long chain stretching from it to a staple in the wall.

"Shove Kamaga in here," suggested Stewart. "It may help him to find his tongue."

He caught one of the uplifted arms and began pulling the Japanese towards the doorway. On the very threshold Kamaga gave an unearthly scream.

"Oh, no! It will kill me! I am not ready . . ."

His gaze shot to the ceiling and, following it, the magistrate saw an enormous metal syringe hanging in a sort of cradle over a zinc tank.

"We don't want you to be ready, Kamaga," he said.

"Mr. Seldon wasn't ready when you let your vile creation loose on him. Come on, my friend. In you go!"

The man had struggled to his knees and hung limply, like a sack.

"Stop," he screamed. "I will tell you. I will tell you everything. The English lady is in there. She is tied, but I have not harmed her. No closer . . . oh, no closer . . . it can reach . . ."

Stewart threw him back towards the doctor and hooked down the syringe. He gave it an experimental pump up and down, then dipped its nozzle in the fluid in the tank and drew out the handle until it appeared to be full.

"What's that?" demanded Langley suspiciously.

"Don't know," said the other. "Dope for the spider I fancy. Isn't it, Kamaga?"

Kamaga inclined his head.

He squirted a steady shower of drops at the brute's head.

Presently, as he watched it anxiously, the flaps drooped and did not come up again—the legs drew gradually closer to the body, and, before the doctor could intervene, the magistrate had passed it on his way to the bed.

Langley's eyes were turned from the Japanese for the fraction of a second, but in that short space Kamaga found time to act . . . A cloth, snatched from the top of a case—fell over the doctor's head, completely enveloping him. He threw it off to find the tank overturned, flooding the passage with a sickly, sweet-smelling fluid. Every cage was open, and Kamaga was disappearing through the farthest doorway.

The doctor was left amid a host of crawling, buzzing, fluttering horrors, with Stewart—unconscious of anything except that he held Bianca in his arms—coming towards him.

"It's all right, Doc. I've got her."

Langley brought his boot down heavily on something and yelled at the top of his voice.

"Is there a way out through that room?"

"No, it's a *cul-de-sac.*"

"Then run for it, for all you're worth. Kamaga's slipped me and his entire menagerie's loose!"

By a miracle they got through. Langley declared afterwards that they owed their escape in this instance to the fumes of the chemical Kamaga had overturned to prevent them from employing it.

They were in the open again, with the door of the house shut securely behind them.

"We must go warily," said the doctor. "I've an idea at the back of my head that we haven't finished with Kamaga."

Bianca blinked up at Stewart and smiled faintly.

"May I try and walk, please?"

"You feel all right now?"

"Oh, yes, I think so. I'm stiff, of course, but that's all." She rubbed her eyes. "What a horrible nightmare! It seems to have been going on for years. I can't imagine how you found me. Did you hear my scream or did the doctor guess?"

"Both," said Langley. "Try and walk a few steps. That's splendid. Now try again. Keep moving your legs as if you were marking time." He pointed suddenly towards the huts. "Look, Jimmy! There he goes. He's making for the path."

"I can't see anything. Who was it?"

"Kamaga! He's thrown open the doors. Heaven knows what's hidden behind them. Bianca, we've got to run for it. You'd better hang on to both of us. If you find yourself falling, yell out—and we'll carry you."

They had gone twenty yards when Bianca screamed.

"Look! Look! Can't you see them, in that patch of moonlight? Spiders! Spiders! Hundreds of them!"

Both men glanced back. The entire place seemed alive with them. Stewart swept the girl from her feet and they raced headlong for the gate.

Kamaga was out of pistol-shot, but they appeared to be gaining on him, his white kimono clearly visible among the trees. Suddenly he halted, stared round him in bewilderment, and began coming back towards them.

A voice from the direction of the fence indicated clearly why he had turned.

"Stewart! are you up there? Stewart!"

The magistrate paused and bellowed back.

"We're coming now. Tell them to fire the forest. Look out for Miss Seldon. I'm sending her on ahead." He released the girl again. "Bianca," he told her, "the gate is immediately in front of you and Wright's waiting for you down there. I want you to go there—alone. Are you afraid?"

She looked straight up at him.

"I am afraid, Jimmy," she whispered—"but I'm going."

He found time for a single sentence more.

"I'm glad it was I who found you—and not the others. I'll tell you why—some day."

"I'm glad it was you, Jimmy," she said—and was gone.

"She's a wonderful little woman, Jimmy. What are we going to do now?"

The magistrate started moving off at a brisk pace through the trees.

"Try and secure Kamaga—dead or alive—before the fire gets a good hold. Can you see which way he's taken?"

"Yes. He's over there to the left. We'd better split up and endeavour to corner him."

It was ten minutes before Stewart had his quarry in range, and he fired wide to make him aware of the fact. Langley appeared on the other side.

The Japanese faced them placidly, a knife balanced on the tips of his fingers. He allowed them to approach within a few feet of him, then touched the naked blade with his lips.

"You will allow me the privilege of an honourable death, gentlemen?"

"Honourable be damned!" said Stewart.

Langley touched his sleeve.

"He means *hari-kari*. Better let him do it. It'll save a lot of trouble."

And then a peculiar thing happened.

A black mass dropped suddenly from the tree above them, smothering Kamaga with its enormous bulk.

Both men started backward.

"The *black spider!*" gasped the D.O.

They fled down the slope, with Kamaga's unearthly cry ringing in their ears and a belt of flame threatening to encircle them—and not once did they look back.

RAMBLE HOUSE's
HARRY STEPHEN KEELER WEBWORK MYSTERIES
(RH) indicates the title is available ONLY in the RAMBLE HOUSE edition

The Ace of Spades Murder
The Affair of the Bottled Deuce (RH)
The Amazing Web
The Barking Clock
Behind That Mask
The Book with the Orange Leaves
The Bottle with the Green Wax Seal
The Box from Japan
The Case of the Canny Killer
The Case of the Crazy Corpse (RH)
The Case of the Flying Hands (RH)
The Case of the Ivory Arrow
The Case of the Jeweled Ragpicker
The Case of the Lavender Gripsack
The Case of the Mysterious Moll
The Case of the 16 Beans
The Case of the Transparent Nude (RH)
The Case of the Transposed Legs
The Case of the Two-Headed Idiot (RH)
The Case of the Two Strange Ladies
The Circus Stealers (RH)
Cleopatra's Tears
A Copy of Beowulf (RH)
The Crimson Cube (RH)
The Face of the Man From Saturn
Find the Clock
The Five Silver Buddhas
The 4th King
The Gallows Waits, My Lord! (RH)
The Green Jade Hand
Finger! Finger!
Hangman's Nights (RH)
I, Chameleon (RH)
I Killed Lincoln at 10:13! (RH)
The Iron Ring
The Man Who Changed His Skin (RH)
The Man with the Crimson Box
The Man with the Magic Eardrums
The Man with the Wooden Spectacles
The Marceau Case
The Matilda Hunter Murder
The Monocled Monster
The Murder of London Lew
The Murdered Mathematician
The Mysterious Card (RH)
The Mysterious Ivory Ball of Wong Shing Li (RH)
The Mystery of the Fiddling Cracksman
The Peacock Fan
The Photo of Lady X (RH)
The Portrait of Jirjohn Cobb
Report on Vanessa Hewstone (RH)
Riddle of the Travelling Skull
Riddle of the Wooden Parrakeet (RH)
The Scarlet Mummy (RH)
The Search for X-Y-Z
The Sharkskin Book
Sing Sing Nights
The Six From Nowhere (RH)
The Skull of the Waltzing Clown
The Spectacles of Mr. Cagliostro
Stand By—London Calling!
The Steeltown Strangler
The Stolen Gravestone (RH)
Strange Journey (RH)
The Strange Will
The Straw Hat Murders (RH)
The Street of 1000 Eyes (RH)
Thieves' Nights
Three Novellos (RH)
The Tiger Snake
The Trap (RH)
Vagabond Nights (Defrauded Yeggman)
Vagabond Nights 2 (10 Hours)
The Vanishing Gold Truck
The Voice of the Seven Sparrows
The Washington Square Enigma
When Thief Meets Thief
The White Circle (RH)
The Wonderful Scheme of Mr. Christopher Thorne
X. Jones—of Scotland Yard
Y. Cheung, Business Detective

Keeler Related Works

A To Izzard: A Harry Stephen Keeler Companion by Fender Tucker — Articles and stories about Harry, by Harry, and in his style. Included is a compleat bibliography.

Wild About Harry: Reviews of Keeler Novels — Edited by Richard Polt & Fender Tucker — 22 reviews of works by Harry Stephen Keeler from *Keeler News*. A perfect introduction to the author.

The Keeler Keyhole Collection: Annotated newsletter rants from Harry Stephen Keeler, edited by Francis M. Nevins. Over 400 pages of incredibly personal Keeleriana.

Fakealoo — Pastiches of the style of Harry Stephen Keeler by selected demented members of the HSK Society. Updated every year with the new winner.

Strands of the Web: Short Stories of Harry Stephen Keeler — 29 stories, just about all that Keeler wrote, are edited and introduced by Fred Cleaver.

RAMBLE HOUSE's LOON SANCTUARY

A Clear Path to Cross — Sharon Knowles short mystery stories by Ed Lynskey.
A Jimmy Starr Omnibus — Three 40s novels by Jimmy Starr.
A Niche in Time and Other Stories — Classic SF by William F. Temple.
A Roland Daniel Double: The Signal and The Return of Wu Fang — Classic thrillers from the 30s.

A Shot Rang Out — Three decades of reviews and articles by today's Anthony Boucher, Jon Breen. An essential book for any mystery lover's library.
A Smell of Smoke — A 1951 English countryside thriller by Miles Burton.
A Snark Selection — Lewis Carroll's *The Hunting of the Snark* with two Snarkian chapters by Harry Stephen Keeler — Illustrated by Gavin L. O'Keefe.
A Young Man's Heart — A forgotten early classic by Cornell Woolrich.
Alexander Laing Novels — *The Motives of Nicholas Holtz* and *Dr. Scarlett*, stories of medical mayhem and intrigue from the 30s.
An Angel in the Street — Modern hardboiled noir by Peter Genovese.
Automaton — Brilliant treatise on robotics: 1928-style! By H. Stafford Hatfield.
Away From the Here and Now — Clare Winger Harris stories, collected by Richard A. Lupoff
Beast or Man? — A 1930 novel of racism and horror by Sean M'Guire. Introduced by John Pelan.
Black Hogan Strikes Again — Australia's Peter Renwick pens a tale of the 30s outback.
Black River Falls — Suspense from the master, Ed Gorman.
Blondy's Boy Friend — A snappy 1930 story by Philip Wylie, writing as Leatrice Homesley.
Blood in a Snap — The *Finnegan's Wake* of the 21st century, by Jim Weiler.
Blood Moon — The first of the Robert Payne series by Ed Gorman.
Bogart '48 — Hollywood action with Bogie by John Stanley and Kenn Davis
Calling Lou Largo! — Two Lou Largo novels by William Ard.
Cornucopia of Crime — Francis M. Nevins assembled this huge collection of his writings about crime literature and the people who write it. Essential for any serious mystery library.
Corpse Without Flesh — Strange novel of forensics by George Bruce
Crimson Clown Novels — By Johnston McCulley, author of the Zorro novels, *The Crimson Clown* and *The Crimson Clown Again*.
Dago Red — 22 tales of dark suspense by Bill Pronzini.
Dark Sanctuary — Weird Menace story by H. B. Gregory
David Hume Novels — *Corpses Never Argue, Cemetery First Stop, Make Way for the Mourners, Eternity Here I Come*. 1930s British hardboiled fiction with an attitude.
Dead Man Talks Too Much — Hollywood boozer by Weed Dickenson.
Death Leaves No Card — One of the most unusual murdered-in-the-tub mysteries you'll ever read. By Miles Burton.
Death March of the Dancing Dolls and Other Stories — Volume Three in the Day Keene in the Detective Pulps series. Introduced by Bill Crider.
Deep Space and other Stories — A collection of SF gems by Richard A. Lupoff.
Detective Duff Unravels It — Episodic mysteries by Harvey O'Higgins.
Diabolic Candelabra — Classic 30s mystery by E.R. Punshon.
Dime Novels: Ramble House's 10-Cent Books — *Knife in the Dark* by Robert Leslie Bellem, *Hot Lead* and *Song of Death* by Ed Earl Repp, *A Hashish House in New York* by H.H. Kane, and five more.
Don Diablo: Book of a Lost Film — Two-volume treatment of a western by Paul Landres, with diagrams. Intro by Francis M. Nevins.
Dope and Swastikas — Two strange novels from 1922 by Edmund Snell
Dope Tales #1 — Two dope-riddled classics; *Dope Runners* by Gerald Grantham and *Death Takes the Joystick* by Phillip Condé.
Dope Tales #2 — Two more narco-classics; *The Invisible Hand* by Rex Dark and *The Smokers of Hashish* by Norman Berrow.
Dope Tales #3 — Two enchanting novels of opium by the master, Sax Rohmer. *Dope* and *The Yellow Claw*.
Double Hot — Two 60s softcore sex novels by Morris Hershman.
Dr. Odin — Douglas Newton's 1933 racial potboiler comes back to life.
Evangelical Cockroach — Jack Woodford writes about writing.
Evidence in Blue — 1938 mystery by E. Charles Vivian.
Fatal Accident — Murder by automobile, a 1936 mystery by Cecil M. Wills.
Fighting Mad — Todd Robbins' 1922 novel about boxing and life
Finger-prints Never Lie — A 1939 classic detective novel by John G. Brandon.
Freaks and Fantasies — Eerie tales by Tod Robbins, collaborator of Tod Browning on the film FREAKS.

Gadsby — A lipogram (a novel without the letter E). Ernest Vincent Wright's last work, published in 1939 right before his death.

Gelett Burgess Novels — *The Master of Mysteries, The White Cat, Two O'Clock Courage, Ladies in Boxes, Find the Woman, The Heart Line, The Picaroons* and *Lady Mechante*. Recently added is A Gelett Burgess Sampler, edited by Alfred Jan. All are introduced by Richard A. Lupoff.

Geronimo — S. M. Barrett's 1905 autobiography of a noble American.

Hake Talbot Novels — *Rim of the Pit, The Hangman's Handyman*. Classic locked room mysteries, with mapback covers by Gavin O'Keefe.

Hands Out of Hell and Other Stories — John H. Knox's eerie hallucinations

Hell is a City — William Ard's masterpiece.

Hollywood Dreams — A novel of Tinsel Town and the Depression by Richard O'Brien.

Hostesses in Hell and Other Stories — Russell Gray's most graphic stories

House of the Restless Dead — Strange and ominous tales by Hugh B. Cave

I Stole $16,000,000 — A true story by cracksman Herbert E. Wilson.

Inclination to Murder — 1966 thriller by New Zealand's Harriet Hunter.

Invaders from the Dark — Classic werewolf tale from Greye La Spina.

J. Poindexter, Colored — Classic satirical black novel by Irvin S. Cobb.

Jack Mann Novels — Strange murder in the English countryside. *Gees' First Case, Nightmare Farm, Grey Shapes, The Ninth Life, The Glass Too Many, Her Ways Are Death, The Kleinert Case* and *Maker of Shadows*.

Jake Hardy — A lusty western tale from Wesley Tallant.

Jim Harmon Double Novels — *Vixen Hollow/Celluloid Scandal, The Man Who Made Maniacs/Silent Siren, Ape Rape/Wanton Witch, Sex Burns Like Fire/Twist Session, Sudden Lust/Passion Strip, Sin Unlimited/Harlot Master, Twilight Girls/Sex Institution*. Written in the early 60s and never reprinted until now.

Joel Townsley Rogers Novels and Short Stories — By the author of *The Red Right Hand: Once In a Red Moon, Lady With the Dice, The Stopped Clock, Never Leave My Bed*. Also two short story collections: *Night of Horror* and *Killing Time*.

John Carstairs, Space Detective — Arboreal Sci-fi by Frank Belknap Long

Joseph Shallit Novels — *The Case of the Billion Dollar Body, Lady Don't Die on My Doorstep, Kiss the Killer, Yell Bloody Murder, Take Your Last Look*. One of America's best 50's authors and a favorite of author Bill Pronzini.

Keller Memento — 45 short stories of the amazing and weird by Dr. David Keller.

Killer's Caress — Cary Moran's 1936 hardboiled thriller.

Lady of the Yellow Death and Other Stories — More stories by Wyatt Blassingame.

League of the Grateful Dead and Other Stories — Volume One in the Day Keene in the Detective Pulps series.

Library of Death — Ghastly tale by Ronald S. L. Harding, introduced by John Pelan

Malcolm Jameson Novels and Short Stories — *Astonishing! Astounding!, Tarnished Bomb, The Alien Envoy and Other Stories* and *The Chariots of San Fernando and Other Stories*. All introduced and edited by John Pelan or Richard A. Lupoff.

Man Out of Hell and Other Stories — Volume II of the John H. Knox weird pulps collection.

Marblehead: A Novel of H.P. Lovecraft — A long-lost masterpiece from Richard A. Lupoff. This is the "director's cut", the long version that has never been published before.

Master of Souls — Mark Hansom's 1937 shocker is introduced by weirdologist John Pelan.

Max Afford Novels — *Owl of Darkness, Death's Mannikins, Blood on His Hands, The Dead Are Blind, The Sheep and the Wolves, Sinners in Paradise* and *Two Locked Room Mysteries and a Ripping Yarn* by one of Australia's finest mystery novelists.

Money Brawl — Two books about the writing business by Jack Woodford and H. Bedford-Jones. Introduced by Richard A. Lupoff.

More Secret Adventures of Sherlock Holmes — Gary Lovisi's second collection of tales about the unknown sides of the great detective.

Muddled Mind: Complete Works of Ed Wood, Jr. — David Hayes and Hayden Davis deconstruct the life and works of the mad, but canny, genius.

Murder among the Nudists — A mystery from 1934 by Peter Hunt, featuring a naked Detective-Inspector going undercover in a nudist colony.

Murder in Black and White — 1931 classic tennis whodunit by Evelyn Elder.

Murder in Shawnee — Two novels of the Alleghenies by John Douglas: *Shawnee Alley Fire* and *Haunts*.
Murder in Silk — A 1937 Yellow Peril novel of the silk trade by Ralph Trevor.
My Deadly Angel — 1955 Cold War drama by John Chelton.
My First Time: The One Experience You Never Forget — Michael Birchwood — 64 true first-person narratives of how they lost it.
Mysterious Martin, the Master of Murder — Two versions of a strange 1912 novel by Tod Robbins about a man who writes books that can kill.
Norman Berrow Novels — *The Bishop's Sword, Ghost House, Don't Go Out After Dark, Claws of the Cougar, The Smokers of Hashish, The Secret Dancer, Don't Jump Mr. Boland!, The Footprints of Satan, Fingers for Ransom, The Three Tiers of Fantasy, The Spaniard's Thumb, The Eleventh Plague, Words Have Wings, One Thrilling Night, The Lady's in Danger, It Howls at Night, The Terror in the Fog, Oil Under the Window, Murder in the Melody, The Singing Room*. This is the complete Norman Berrow library of locked-room mysteries, several of which are masterpieces.
Old Faithful and Other Stories — SF classic tales by Raymond Z. Gallun
Old Times' Sake — Short stories by James Reasoner from Mike Shayne Magazine.
One Dreadful Night — A classic mystery by Ronald S. L. Harding
Pair O' Jacks — A mystery novel and a diatribe about publishing by Jack Woodford
Perfect .38 — Two early Timothy Dane novels by William Ard. More to come.
Prince Pax — Devilish intrigue by George Sylvester Viereck and Philip Eldridge
Prose Bowl — Futuristic satire of a world where hack writing has replaced football as our national obsession, by Bill Pronzini and Barry N. Malzberg.
Red Light — The history of legal prostitution in Shreveport Louisiana by Eric Brock. Includes wonderful photos of the houses and the ladies.
Researching American-Made Toy Soldiers — A 276-page collection of a lifetime of articles by toy soldier expert Richard O'Brien.
Reunion in Hell — Volume One of the John H. Knox series of weird stories from the pulps. Introduced by horror expert John Pelan.
Ripped from the Headlines! — The Jack the Ripper story as told in the newspaper articles in the *New York* and *London Times*.
Robert Randisi Novels — *No Exit to Brooklyn* and *The Dead of Brooklyn*. The first two Nick Delvecchio novels.
Rough Cut & New, Improved Murder — Ed Gorman's first two novels.
R.R. Ryan Novels — Freak Museum and The Subjugated Beast, two horror classics.
Ruled By Radio — 1925 futuristic novel by Robert L. Hadfield & Frank E. Farncombe.
Rupert Penny Novels — *Policeman's Holiday, Policeman's Evidence, Lucky Policeman, Policeman in Armour, Sealed Room Murder, Sweet Poison, The Talkative Policeman, She had to Have Gas* and *Cut and Run* (by Martin Tanner.) Rupert Penny is the pseudonym of Australian Charles Thornett, a master of the locked room, impossible crime plot.
Sacred Locomotive Flies — Richard A. Lupoff's psychedelic SF story.
Sam — Early gay novel by Lonnie Coleman.
Sand's Game — Spectacular hard-boiled noir from Ennis Willie, edited by Lynn Myers and Stephen Mertz, with contributions from Max Allan Collins, Bill Crider, Wayne Dundee, Bill Pronzini, Gary Lovisi and James Reasoner.
Sand's War — More violent fiction from the typewriter of Ennis Willie
Satan's Den Exposed — True crime in Truth or Consequences New Mexico — Award-winning journalism by the *Desert Journal*.
Satans of Saturn — Novellas from the pulps by Otis Adelbert Kline and E. H. Price
Satan's Sin House and Other Stories — Horrific gore by Wayne Rogers
Secrets of a Teenage Superhero — Graphic lit by Jonathan Sweet
Sex Slave — Potboiler of lust in the days of Cleopatra by Dion Leclerq, 1966.
Shadows' Edge — Two early novels by Wade Wright: *Shadows Don't Bleed* and *The Sharp Edge*.
Sideslip — 1968 SF masterpiece by Ted White and Dave Van Arnam.
Slammer Days — Two full-length prison memoirs: *Men into Beasts* (1952) by George Sylvester Viereck and *Home Away From Home* (1962) by Jack Woodford.
Slippery Staircase — 1930s whodunit from E.C.R. Lorac
Sorcerer's Chessmen — John Pelan introduces this 1939 classic by Mark Hansom.
Star Griffin — Michael Kurland's 1987 masterpiece of SF drollery is back.
Stakeout on Millennium Drive — Award-winning Indianapolis Noir by Ian Woollen.

Strands of the Web: Short Stories of Harry Stephen Keeler — Edited and Introduced by Fred Cleaver.

Summer Camp for Corpses and Other Stories — Weird Menace tales from Arthur Leo Zagat; introduced by John Pelan.

Suzy — A collection of comic strips by Richard O'Brien and Bob Vojtko from 1970.

Tales of the Macabre and Ordinary — Modern twisted horror by Chris Mikul, author of the *Bizarrism* series.

Tenebrae — Ernest G. Henham's 1898 horror tale brought back.

The Amorous Intrigues & Adventures of Aaron Burr — by Anonymous. Hot historical action about the man who almost became Emperor of Mexico.

The Anthony Boucher Chronicles — edited by Francis M. Nevins. Book reviews by Anthony Boucher written for the *San Francisco Chronicle*, 1942 – 1947. Essential and fascinating reading by the best book reviewer there ever was.

The Barclay Catalogs — Two essential books about toy soldier collecting by Richard O'Brien

The Basil Wells Omnibus — A collection of Wells' stories by Richard A. Lupoff.

The Beautiful Dead and Other Stories — Dreadful tales from Donald Dale

The Best of 10-Story Book — edited by Chris Mikul, over 35 stories from the literary magazine Harry Stephen Keeler edited.

The Black Dark Murders — Vintage 50s college murder yarn by Milt Ozaki, writing as Robert O. Saber.

The Book of Time — The classic novel by H.G. Wells is joined by sequels by Wells himself and three stories by Richard A. Lupoff. Illustrated by Gavin L. O'Keefe.

The Case in the Clinic — One of E.C.R. Lorac's finest.

The Case of the Bearded Bride — #4 in the Day Keene in the Detective Pulps series

The Case of the Little Green Men — Mack Reynolds wrote this love song to sci-fi fans back in 1951 and it's now back in print.

The Case of the Withered Hand — 1936 potboiler by John G. Brandon.

The Charlie Chaplin Murder Mystery — A 2004 tribute by noted film scholar, Wes D. Gehring.

The Chinese Jar Mystery — Murder in the manor by John Stephen Strange, 1934.

The Compleat Calhoun — All of Fender Tucker's works: Includes *Totah Six-Pack, Weed, Women and Song* and *Tales from the Tower,* plus a CD of all of his songs.

The Compleat Ova Hamlet — Parodies of SF authors by Richard A. Lupoff. This is a brand new edition with more stories and more illustrations by Trina Robbins.

The Contested Earth and Other SF Stories — A never-before published space opera and seven short stories by Jim Harmon.

The Crimson Query — A 1929 thriller from Arlton Eadie. A perfect way to get introduced.

The Curse of Cantire — Classic 1939 novel of a family curse by Walter S. Masterman.

The Devil and the C.I.D. — Odd diabolic mystery by E.C.R. Lorac

The Devil Drives — An odd prison and lost treasure novel from 1932 by Virgil Markham.

The Devil's Mistress — A 1915 Scottish gothic tale by J. W. Brodie-Innes, a member of Aleister Crowley's Golden Dawn.

The Devil's Nightclub and Other Stories — John Pelan introduces some gruesome tales by Nat Schachner.

The Disentanglers — Episodic intrigue at the turn of last century by Andrew Lang

The Dumpling — Political murder from 1907 by Coulson Kernahan.

The End of It All and Other Stories — Ed Gorman selected his favorite short stories for this huge collection.

The Fangs of Suet Pudding — A 1944 novel of the German invasion by Adams Farr

The Ghost of Gaston Revere — From 1935, a novel of life and beyond by Mark Hansom, introduced by John Pelan.

The Girl in the Dark — A thriller from Roland Daniel

The Gold Star Line — Seaboard adventure from L.T. Reade and Robert Eustace.

The Golden Dagger — 1951 Scotland Yard yarn by E. R. Punshon.

The Great Orme Terror — Horror stories by Garnett Radcliffe from the pulps

The Hairbreadth Escapes of Major Mendax — Francis Blake Crofton's 1889 boys' book.

The House That Time Forgot and Other Stories — Insane pulpitude by Robert F. Young

The House of the Vampire — 1907 poetic thriller by George S. Viereck.
The Illustrious Corpse — Murder hijinx from Tiffany Thayer
The Incredible Adventures of Rowland Hern — Intriguing 1928 impossible crimes by Nicholas Olde.
The Julius Caesar Murder Case — A classic 1935 re-telling of the assassination by Wallace Irwin that's much more fun than the Shakespeare version.
The Koky Comics — A collection of all of the 1978-1981 Sunday and daily comic strips by Richard O'Brien and Mort Gerberg, in two volumes.
The Lady of the Terraces — 1925 missing race adventure by E. Charles Vivian.
The Lord of Terror — 1925 mystery with master-criminal, Fantômas.
The Melamare Mystery — A classic 1929 Arsene Lupin mystery by Maurice Leblanc
The Man Who Was Secrett — Epic SF stories from John Brunner
The Man Without a Planet — Science fiction tales by Richard Wilson
The N. R. De Mexico Novels — Robert Bragg, the real N.R. de Mexico, presents *Marijuana Girl, Madman on a Drum, Private Chauffeur* in one volume.
The Night Remembers — A 1991 Jack Walsh mystery from Ed Gorman.
The One After Snelling — Kickass modern noir from Richard O'Brien.
The Organ Reader — A huge compilation of just about everything published in the 1971-1972 radical bay-area newspaper, *THE ORGAN*. A coffee table book that points out the shallowness of the coffee table mindset.
The Poker Club — Three in one! Ed Gorman's ground-breaking novel, the short story it was based upon, and the screenplay of the film made from it.
The Private Journal & Diary of John H. Surratt — The memoirs of the man who conspired to assassinate President Lincoln.
The Secret Adventures of Sherlock Holmes — Three Sherlockian pastiches by the Brooklyn author/publisher, Gary Lovisi.
The Shadow on the House — Mark Hansom's 1934 masterpiece of horror is introduced by John Pelan.
The Sign of the Scorpion — A 1935 Edmund Snell tale of oriental evil.
The Singular Problem of the Stygian House-Boat — Two classic tales by John Kendrick Bangs about the denizens of Hades.
The Smiling Corpse — Philip Wylie and Bernard Bergman's odd 1935 novel.
The Spider: Satan's Murder Machines — A thesis about Iron Man
The Stench of Death: An Odoriferous Omnibus by Jack Moskovitz — Two complete novels and two novellas from 60's sleaze author, Jack Moskovitz.
The Story Writer and Other Stories — Classic SF from Richard Wilson
The Strange Case of the Antlered Man — 1935 dementia from Edwy Searles Brooks
The Strange Thirteen — Richard B. Gamon's odd stories about Raj India.
The Technique of the Mystery Story — Carolyn Wells' tips about writing.
The Threat of Nostalgia — A collection of his most obscure stories by Jon Breen
The Time Armada — Fox B. Holden's 1953 SF gem.
The Tongueless Horror and Other Stories — Volume One of the series of short stories from the weird pulps by Wyatt Blassingame.
The Tracer of Lost Persons — From 1906, an episodic novel that became a hit radio series in the 30s. Introduced by Richard A. Lupoff.
The Trail of the Cloven Hoof — Diabolical horror from 1935 by Arlton Eadie. Introduced by John Pelan.
The Triune Man — Mindscrambling science fiction from Richard A. Lupoff.
The Unholy Goddess and Other Stories — Wyatt Blassingame's first DTP compilation
The Universal Holmes — Richard A. Lupoff's 2007 collection of five Holmesian pastiches and a recipe for giant rat stew.
The Werewolf vs the Vampire Woman — Hard to believe ultraviolence by either Arthur M. Scarm or Arthur M. Scram.
The Whistling Ancestors — A 1936 classic of weirdness by Richard E. Goddard and introduced by John Pelan.
The White Owl — A vintage thriller from Edmund Snell
The White Peril in the Far East — Sidney Lewis Gulick's 1905 indictment of the West and assurance that Japan would never attack the U.S.
The Wizard of Berner's Abbey — A 1935 horror gem written by Mark Hansom and introduced by John Pelan.
The Wonderful Wizard of Oz — by L. Frank Baum and illustrated by Gavin L. O'Keefe.
Through the Looking Glass — Lewis Carroll wrote it; Gavin L. O'Keefe illustrated it.

Time Line — Ramble House artist Gavin O'Keefe selects his most evocative art inspired by the twisted literature he reads and designs.

Tiresias — Psychotic modern horror novel by Jonathan M. Sweet.

Totah Six-Pack — Fender Tucker's six tales about Farmington in one sleek volume.

Trail of the Spirit Warrior — Roger Haley's historical saga of life in the Indian Territories.

Two Kinds of Bad — Two 50s novels by William Ard about Danny Fontaine

Two Suns of Morcali and Other Stories — Evelyn E. Smith's SF tour-de-force

Ultra-Boiled — 23 gut-wrenching tales by our Man in Brooklyn, Gary Lovisi.

Up Front From Behind — A 2011 satire of Wall Street by James B. Kobak.

Victims & Villains — Intriguing Sherlockiana from Derham Groves.

Wade Wright Novels — *Echo of Fear, Death At Nostalgia Street, It Leads to Murder* and *Shadows' Edge*, a double book featuring *Shadows Don't Bleed* and *The Sharp Edge*.

Walter S. Masterman Novels — *The Green Toad, The Flying Beast, The Yellow Mistletoe, The Wrong Verdict, The Perjured Alibi, The Border Line, The Bloodhounds Bay* and *The Curse of Cantire*. Masterman wrote horror and mystery, some introduced by John Pelan.

We Are the Dead and Other Stories — Volume Two in the Day Keene in the Detective Pulps series, introduced by Ed Gorman. When done, there may be as many as 11 in the series.

Welsh Rarebit Tales — Charming stories from 1902 by Harle Oren Cummins

West Texas War and Other Western Stories — by Gary Lovisi.

Whip Dodge: Man Hunter — Wesley Tallant's saga of a bounty hunter of the old West.

Win, Place and Die! — The first new mystery by Milt Ozaki in decades. The ultimate novel of 70s Reno.

You'll Die Laughing — Bruce Elliott's 1945 novel of murder at a practical joker's English countryside manor.

RAMBLE HOUSE
Fender Tucker, Prop.   Gavin L. O'Keefe, Graphics
www.ramblehouse.com   fender@ramblehouse.com
228-826-1783   10329 Sheephead Drive, Vancleave MS 39565

Printed in Poland
by Amazon Fulfillment
Poland Sp. z o.o., Wrocław